LONG ISLAND

A Novel

COLM TÓIBÍN

SCRIBNER
New York London Toronto Sydney New Delhi

Scribner
An Imprint of Simon & Schuster, LLC
1230 Avenue of the Americas
New York, NY 10020

First Scribner hardcover edition May 2024

SCRIBNER and design are trademarks of Simon & Schuster, LLC

Simon & Schuster: Celebrating 100 Years of Publishing in 2024

For information about special discounts for bulk purchases,
please contact Simon & Schuster Special Sales at 1-866-506-1949
or business@simonandschuster.com.

The Simon & Schuster Speakers Bureau can bring authors to
your live event. For more information or to book an event,
contact the Simon & Schuster Speakers Bureau at 1-866-248-3049
or visit our website a www.simonspeakers.com.

Interior design by Kyle Kabel

Manufactured in the United States of America

3   5   7   9   10   8   6   4   2

Library of Congress Control Number: 2023046729

ISBN 978-1-4767-8511-0
ISBN 978-1-4767-8513-4 (ebook)

for Cormac Kinsella

PART ONE

I

"That Irishman has been here again," Francesca said, sitting down at the kitchen table. "He has come to every house, but it's you he's looking for. I told him you would be home soon."

"What does he want?" Eilis asked.

"I did everything to make him tell me, but he wouldn't. He asked for you by name."

"He knows my name?"

Francesca's smile had an insinuating edge. Eilis appreciated her mother-in-law's intelligence, and also her sly sense of humor.

"Another man is the last thing I need," Eilis said.

"Who are you talking to?" Francesca replied.

They both laughed, as Francesca stood up to go. From the window, Eilis watched her walk carefully across the damp grass to her own house.

Soon, Larry would be in from school and then Rosella from after-school study and then she would hear Tony parking his car outside.

This would be a perfect time for a cigarette. But, having found Larry smoking, she had made a bargain with him that she would give up completely if he promised not to smoke again. She still had a packet upstairs.

When the doorbell rang, Eilis stood up lazily, presuming that it was one of Larry's cousins calling for him to come and play.

3

However, from the hallway, she made out the silhouette of a grown man through the frosted glass of the door. Until he called out her name, it did not occur to her that this was the man Francesca had mentioned. She opened the door.

"You are Eilis Fiorello?"

The accent was Irish, with a trace, she thought, of Donegal, like a teacher she had had in school. Also, the way the man stood there, as though waiting to be challenged, reminded her of home.

"I am," she said.

"I have been looking for you."

His tone was almost aggressive. She wondered if Tony's business could owe him money.

"So I hear."

"You are the wife of the plumber?"

Since the question sounded rude, she saw no reason to reply.

"He is good at his job, your husband. I'd say he's in great demand."

The man stopped for a second, looking behind him to check no one was listening.

"He fixed everything in our house," he went on, pointing a finger at her. "He even did a bit more than was in the estimate. Indeed, he came back regularly when he knew that the woman of the house would be there and I would not. And his plumbing is so good that she is to have a baby in August."

He stood back and smiled broadly at her expression of disbelief.

"That's right. That's why I'm here. And I can tell you for a fact that I am not the father. It had nothing to do with me. But I am married to the woman who is having this baby and if anyone thinks I am keeping an Italian plumber's brat in my house and have my own children believe that it came into the world as decently as they did, they can have another think."

He pointed a finger at her again.

"So as soon as this little bastard is born, I am transporting it here. And if you are not at home, then I will hand it to that other

4

woman. And if there's no one at all in any of the houses you people own, I'll leave it right here on your doorstep."

He walked towards her and lowered his voice.

"And you can tell your husband from me that if I ever see his face anywhere, I'll come after him with an iron bar that I keep handy. Now, have I made myself clear?"

Eilis wanted to ask him what part of Ireland he was from as a way of ignoring what he had said, but he had already turned away. She tried to think of something else to say that might engage him.

"Have I made myself clear?" he asked again as he reached his car.

When she did not reply, he made as though to approach the house once more.

"I'll be seeing you in August, or it could be late July and that's the last time I'll see you, Eilis."

"How do you know my name?" she asked.

"That husband of yours is a great talker. That's how I know your name. He told my wife all about you."

If he had been Italian or plain American, she would not have been sure how to judge whether he was making a threat he had no intention of carrying out. He was, she thought, a man who liked the sound of his own voice. But she recognized something in him, a stubbornness, perhaps even a sort of sincerity.

She had known men like this in Ireland. Should one of them discover that their wife had been unfaithful and was pregnant as a result, they would not have the baby in the house.

At home, however, no man would be able to take a newborn baby and deliver it to another household. He would be seen by someone. A priest or a doctor or a Guard would make him take the baby back. But here, in this quiet cul-de-sac, the man could leave a baby on her doorstep without anyone noticing him. He really could do that. And the way he spoke, the set of his jaw, the determination in his gaze, convinced her that he meant what he was saying.

Once he had driven away, she went back into the living room and sat down. She closed her eyes.

Somewhere, not far away, there was a woman pregnant with Tony's child. Eilis did not know why she presumed that the woman was Irish too. Perhaps her visitor would be more likely to order an Irishwoman around. Anyone else might stand up to him, or leave him. Suddenly, the image of this woman alone with a baby coming to look for support from Tony frightened her even more than the image of a baby being left on her doorstep. But then that second image too, when she let herself picture it in cold detail, made her feel sick. What if the baby was crying? Would she pick it up? If she did, what would she do then?

As she stood up and moved to another chair, the man, so recently in front of her, real and vivid and imposing, seemed like someone she had read about or seen on television. It simply wasn't possible that the house could be perfectly quiet one moment and then have this visitor arriving in the next.

If she told someone about it, then she might know how to feel, what she should do. In one flash, an image of her elder sister, Rose, dead now more than twenty years, came into her mind. All through her childhood, in even the smallest crisis, she could appeal to Rose, who would take control. She had never confided in her mother, who was, in any case, in Ireland with no telephone in her house. Her two sisters-in-law, Lena and Clara, were both from Italian families and close to each other but not to Eilis.

In the hallway, she looked at the telephone on its stand. If there was one number she could call, one friend to whom she could recount the scene that had just been enacted at her front door! It wasn't that the man, whatever his name was, would become more real if she described him to someone. She had no doubt that he was real.

She picked up the receiver as if she were about to dial a number. She listened to the dial tone. She put the receiver down and lifted it again. There must be some number she could call. She held the receiver to her ear as she realized that there was not.

Did Tony know this man was going to appear? She tried to think about his behavior over the previous weeks, but there was nothing out of the ordinary that she could think of.

Eilis went upstairs, looking around her own bedroom as if she were a stranger in this house. She picked up Tony's pajamas from where he had left them on the floor that morning, wondering if she should exclude his clothes from the wash. And then she saw that that made no sense at all.

Maybe, instead, she should tell him to remove himself to his mother's house and she could talk to him when she had collected her thoughts.

But what, then, if it was a misunderstanding? She would be in the wrong, too ready to believe the worst of a man to whom she had been married for more than twenty years.

She went into Larry's room, examining the large-scale map of Naples that he had pinned to the wall. He had insisted that this was his real homeplace, ignoring her efforts to tell him that he was half Irish and that his father was actually born in America and that his grandparents, in any case, came from a village south of the city.

"They sailed to America from Naples," Larry said. "Ask them."

"I sailed from Liverpool, but that does not mean I am from there."

For a few weeks, as he worked on a class project about Naples, Larry became like his sister, fascinated by detail and ready to stay up late to finish what he had begun. But once it was completed, he had reverted to his old self.

Now, at sixteen, Larry was taller than Tony, with dark eyes and a much darker complexion than his father or his uncles. But he had inherited from them, she thought, a way of demanding that his interests be respected in the house while laughing at the pretensions to seriousness apparent in his mother and his sister.

"I want to come home," Tony often said, "get cleaned up, have a beer and put my feet up."

"And that is what I want too," Larry said.

"I often ask the Lord," Eilis said, "if there is anything else I can do to make my husband and son more comfortable."

"Less talk and more television," Larry said.

In the houses in the same cul-de-sac where Tony's brothers Enzo and Mauro lived with their families, the children, most of them teenagers, did not speak with the same freedom as Rosella and Larry. Rosella liked an argument that she could win by using facts and finding flaws in the other person's case. Larry, in any discussion, liked to turn the argument into a set of jokes. No matter how hard Eilis tried, she found herself supporting Rosella, just as Tony often started laughing at some absurd point that Larry had made even before Larry did.

"I am only a plumber," Tony would say. "I am needed only when something leaks. One thing I am sure of, no plumber will ever make it to the White House unless they have problems with their pipes."

"But the White House is riddled with leaks," Larry said.

"You see," Rosella said, "you are interested in politics."

"If Larry studied," Eilis said, "he could surprise everyone."

Eilis heard Rosella coming in. She wondered if the usual easy banter among all four of them at the table would be possible now. Unless the man's visit had been a ruse of some kind, a part of her life was ended. She wished that he had made some other decision about his wife's pregnancy, one that didn't involve her or Tony in any way. But then she saw how desperate and how futile such wishing was. She could not force the man not to knock on her door just because she wanted that.

As they sat down to dinner each evening, Tony would describe his day, going into detail about his clients and their houses, how much dirt often lay in the area near the sink or the toilet. If Eilis had to tell him to stop, it was only because he was making Rosella and Larry laugh too much.

"That is what puts the food on the table," Larry would say.

"But wait, things were worse this afternoon," Tony would begin again.

In the future, Eilis thought, she would watch him to see what he was concealing.

Having shouted a greeting to Rosella, Eilis went back into the main bedroom and closed the door. She was trying to imagine Rosella's response, and Larry's, to the news that Tony had fathered a child with another woman. Larry, despite his swagger, was, she thought, innocent, and the idea that his father had had sex with a woman in whose house he was fixing a leak would be beyond him, whereas Rosella read novels and discussed the most lurid court cases with her uncle Frank, the youngest of Tony's brothers. If a husband choked his wife and then chopped her up, Frank, who was a lawyer, the only one among the brothers who had gone to college, would learn even more alarming details and share them with his niece. Finding out that her father had been involved with another woman might not shock Rosella, but Eilis could not be sure.

Strangely, she thought, Tony was more prudish than she was. He grew uncomfortable if a kissing sequence on television went on for too long. He and his brothers often nudged one another at family meals and hinted at jokes that could not be told at the table, but it would go no further than that. They would never actually tell the jokes. She liked how old-fashioned Tony was. She remembered his blushes when they had discussed family planning. In the end, having listened in to a conversation between her two sisters-in-law, who seemed to have no problems ignoring church teaching, she had simply put a packet of condoms on Tony's bedside table.

He had smiled when he noticed them, opening the packet as though not quite sure what was inside.

"Are these for me?" he had asked.

COLM TÓIBÍN

"I think they are for both of us," she had replied.

He might have used one of those very condoms to some purpose, she thought, a few months before, thus saving them the trouble that was to come.

She sat on the edge of the bed. How would she even tell Tony that the man had called? For a second, she wished there was somewhere she could go, a place where she would not have to contemplate what had happened.

The extra room they had built onto the house, once Eilis's office, was now used by Rosella and Larry for study, although Larry, in reality, spent little time there.

"I can make you tea, or even coffee, if you want," Eilis said when she found Rosella there.

"You did that yesterday," Rosella replied. "It's my turn."

Rosella had a way of composing herself, not smiling, remaining silent, that set her apart from her cousins. They used any excuse to burst into loud laughter or an expression of wonder while Rosella looked to her mother in the hope that she might soon be taken away from this family gathering to the calmness of their own house. When Tony and Larry set about disturbing this calmness, often by vying with each other in replicating the radio commentary on baseball games, Rosella retired to her study, as she called it. She even had Tony put a lock on the door to prevent Larry from barging in when she was trying to concentrate.

At times, Eilis found it stifling living beside Tony's parents and his two brothers and their families. They could almost see in through her windows. If she decided to go for a walk, one of her sisters-in-law or her mother-in-law would ask her where she had gone and why. They often blamed her interest in privacy and staying apart as something Irish.

But, since Rosella's looks were so Italian, they did not really think there was anything Irish about her. Thus, they could not imagine where her seriousness came from.

10

Rosella tried not to stand out. She paid attention to everything her aunts and cousins said and commented on new clothes and hairstyles, but she had no real interest in fashion. They would have thought her bookish and eccentric, Eilis knew, if she had not been so good-looking.

"All her grace and beauty," her grandmother said, "comes from my mother and my aunt. It passed over our generation—God knows I didn't get any of it—and then came to America. Rosella belongs to an earlier time. And those women on my side of the family had brains as well as beauty. My aunt Giuseppina was so clever that she almost didn't get married at all."

"Would that be clever?" Rosella asked.

"Well, sometimes it would, but not in the end, I think. And I am sure you will be snapped up when the time comes."

Two days a week, between school and supper, Rosella crossed from her own house to her grandmother's and they talked for an hour.

"But what do you talk about?" Eilis asked.

"The reunification of Italy."

"Seriously."

"You know, of her three daughters-in-law, she likes you best."

"No, she doesn't!"

"Today, she asked me to pray with her."

"For what?"

"For Uncle Frank to find a nice wife."

"She means an Italian wife?"

"She means any wife at all. And with his brains, she says, and his salary and bonuses, and the fact that he lives in Manhattan, he should have women following him in the street. I don't think she cares whether the woman is Italian or not. Look what Dad found when he went to an Irish dance."

"Would you not prefer to have an Italian mother? Would it not make life simpler?"

"I like things the way they are."

*   *   *

As Eilis flicked through the books on Rosella's desk, it struck her that the life Rosella took for granted depended on her father and his two married brothers, who worked together, applying themselves to their trade, being diligent and dependable so that people trusted them. Most of their work came by word of mouth. Their territory was so much bigger than a town, but sometimes it seemed more intimate, more enclosed. It would not be long before someone found out that Tony had made a woman pregnant while working in her house. And news would spread in the same way as it might in a village.

So far, she had managed to avoid picturing Tony in his work clothes in the house of this woman. She now had an image of him standing up from fixing a pipe and finding the woman of the house looking at him gratefully. She could imagine Tony's initial shyness. And then he would linger, about to leave. There would be an awkward silence.

"Are you having problems at work?" Rosella asked.

"No, none at all," Eilis replied.

"You seem preoccupied. Just now."

"Things are good at work. A bit too busy."

When Larry arrived, having pecked her on the cheek, he pointed to his feet.

"My shoes are perfectly clean, but I have left them outside the door. And I need to listen to the radio. I will be in my room if anyone is looking for me."

Later, Tony appeared and went straight upstairs, as usual, to have a shower and change out of his work clothes before coming downstairs and seeking out Rosella as he had done each day since she was a baby. Often, if she could manage to listen in on their conversation, Eilis would find out something that neither of them had told her, something that had been said by Rosella's grand-mother, or a piece of information about his brothers that Tony confided to his daughter.

She added potatoes to the stew that she had prepared the pre-vious evening while Larry set the table. She had managed so far to avoid Tony without anyone noticing. He was now in the living room watching television. What she dreaded was his coming into the kitchen, commenting on the delicious smell, or making some joke with Larry. He could fill the air with a presence that was always genial, thoughtful. Her sisters-in-law complained about their husbands' silences and lack of good humor once they were home with the family. Their mother-in-law had asked Rosella how her father behaved at home.

"What did you tell her?" Eilis had asked.

"I said that he finds everything funny and that he is always lovely."

"And what did your grandmother say?"

"She said that you bring out the best in everyone so maybe Lena and Clara could learn from you and then Uncle Enzo and Uncle Mauro might be more cheerful at home."

"She just said that to you. I wonder what she says to other people."

"She never says anything she doesn't mean."

Eilis kept her back to the door, stirring the stew and then standing at the sink washing some dishes. If only this, she thought, could go on. If only Tony could be enthralled by something on the tele-vision and could delay coming to the table for as long as possible.

When he did come into the room, she busied herself drying plates. For a moment, in her confusion, she could not remember in what order she normally served dinner. Was it possible she gave

Tony his dinner first? Or maybe Larry, as the youngest? Or Rosella? She dished out the stew and crossed the room with two plates, putting them in front of Rosella and Larry. Then without speaking or looking at Tony, she went to get the other two. He was telling Rosella and Larry a story about being attacked by a dog while half his body was in a cupboard looking for a leaking pipe.

"As soon as he got the bottom of my trousers between his teeth, the brute began to yank. And his owner was a Norwegian woman who had never had a man in her apartment before."

Eilis stood listening to him. He did not, she was sure, have the smallest idea of what this sounded like to her. It was just another of his stories. Leaving her own plate aside for the moment, Eilis lifted Tony's and crossed the room. Just as she was ready to put the plate on the table, she let it tilt until some of the stew began to spill. Then she tilted it some more. The food fell to the floor near Tony. When he looked up at her alarmed, she stood still with the empty plate in her hand.

Rosella rushed over and took the plate from her mother's hand while Tony and Larry moved the table itself and the chairs so that the floor could be cleaned. Tony began to pick up pieces of the stew from the floor.

"What happened to you?" Rosella asked. "You just stood there."

Eilis kept her eyes on Tony, who had fetched a sponge and a bowl of water. She was waiting for him to look at her again.

"There's more stew in the pot," Larry said.

With the floor cleaned and the table back in place, and with a fresh helping of stew for Tony, they ate in silence. If Tony were to speak, Eilis was ready to interrupt him. She realized that Rosella and Larry must see that there was something happening between their parents. But it was Tony on whom Eilis was concentrating; he must be aware that she knew.

II

On Saturdays, Tony's father's morning ritual was to visit his sons who lived beside him to see if they had been having any problems with their cars. Her father-in-law began to pay more attention to her when Eilis bought a cheap car for herself, and asked her every time he saw her how the car was going.

"It is turning out to be a bargain," he said. "I had my doubts at the time. My wife instructed me to keep them to myself, but now that I have been proved wrong, I can speak freely."

Each time Frank visited, his father came out to inspect his son's car, lifting the hood, checking the oil and the water, despite his wife's insistence that he not get himself dirty.

"The best cars ever made stop dead in the street because their owners didn't check the oil and the water."

If any of the cars needed attention, he recommended his old friend Mr. Dakessian, the Armenian, who, he said, knew almost as much about cars as he did, which was just as well since Mr. Dakessian owned a garage, the best one for many miles, with the most competitive prices and the friendliest service, if you could keep the man from discussing Armenian history.

"The rest of them would insult your car and then fleece you," the old man said. "Any problem with your car, you go to Dakessian."

Since Eilis, at that time, was still doing the accounts for the family business, she dealt regularly with Mr. Dakessian, who looked after Tony's and his brothers' cars. She found him as congenial and dependable as her father-in-law said.

One day when she was getting the oil checked in her car, Mr. Dakessian gave her a book on Armenian history.

"You're Irish," he said. "You'll recognize it all. Around here, people just don't understand these things. Your father-in-law thinks I am making it all up. I tried to give him this book but he wouldn't take it."

As she leafed through it, Eilis asked if Mr. Dakessian, who she imagined was in his sixties, had actually been in Armenia when the killings happened.

"I was born there, but I was three when my parents left. They were warned and got out just in time. I feel sad about it all, more than sad sometimes, especially watching my son, Erik, growing up here and knowing nothing about where he came from."

His daughter, with whom Eilis often dealt since she did the accounts at the garage, was about to get married.

"She is marrying an Armenian and so the whole service will be in Armenian. It will be like we never left. Just for one day."

"Tony's family often behave like they never left Italy," Eilis said.

"They are lucky to have you to look after the money for them. I don't know what I will do when Lusin leaves. Erik has no interest in the business at all."

On her next visit, Mr. Dakessian told her that he had found a book on Ireland, and what happened there was as bad as Armenia.

"I always knew that, but now I have it in detail. I'll give you the book as soon as I have finished it."

Mr. Dakessian told her again about his daughter leaving.

"I don't want to advertise the job and have a stranger coming in. This is a family business and customers have been here for years.

If you ever thought you'd like to move and work with the smell of exhaust fumes and the sound of cars revving, then you would be welcome here. But you'd have to let me know soon."

There and then, Eilis decided that she would accept Mr. Dakessian's offer. She had been having difficulty getting Tony and his brothers to agree to a system of invoicing and accounting that she had devised. Enzo had complained to his mother that Eilis was trying to tell them how to run their business. His mother, in turn, had conveyed this to Frank, who passed it on to his sister-in-law.

"They want you to be more humble," Frank said. "I know what I would do."

"What would you do?" Eilis asked.

"They are my brothers. I love them. But I would not be caught dead working for them."

Eilis knew that she should discuss the possibility of taking the job at the garage with Tony, but she was certain that he would want her to continue looking after the books for himself and his brothers. It would be hard to tell him that she had already made an agreement.

"Start as soon as you can," Mr. Dakessian said. "You can learn the ropes from Lusin before she goes."

"And I would like to come to work at ten and finish at three every day," Eilis said, "as Lusin does, and I would like to have four weeks' holidays, two of them unpaid."

Mr. Dakessian whistled in mock surprise and then mentioned the salary he paid his daughter.

"I suppose you want more."

"We can talk about an increase after the first three months."

Saying they had a deal, Mr. Dakessian suggested that he would go and wash the grease from his hand so they could shake on it.

III

Eilis washed the floor again, making sure that none of the grease from the stew had congealed there. She then made herself busy around the house. When Tony seemed to be following her, she sat at the table with Rosella.

"I think you should see a doctor," Rosella said. "Your hand lost all its power and you just froze. If that happened when you were driving, it would be bad."

"I'm better now," Eilis said, but she could see that Rosella was not convinced.

She went to bed early, lay thinking with the bedside lamp on. When Tony came into the room, he smiled softly and then tiptoed around as though she were already sleeping. As soon as he was in bed, he switched off his lamp and she hers.

She waited, wanting to give him a chance to speak, say anything, even talk about work or what he had been watching on television. He lay on his back and then turned away from her and then lay on his back again. He must be aware that she was awake. She heard him clearing his throat. In the dark, she could let this silence go on for as long as she thought fit. She might even decide not to break it at all, fall asleep beside him and put him through another day guessing what she knew or how she would respond.

But she worried that he might actually fall asleep, leave her awake beside him considering what she might have said. She had to say something now.

"There's one thing I need you to tell me," she whispered, putting a hand on his shoulder.

He did not move.

"Does that man who came today mean what he said? Does he really plan to leave a baby on my doorstep or is it just a way of letting you know how angry he is?"

Still he did not respond.

"If it's just an idle threat, you need to let me know this instant."

When she heard nothing, she sighed.

"You have to—" she began.

"He means what he says," Tony whispered. "There's no doubt about that. He loves making rules and big statements. He has her very frightened."

"I don't want to know about her."

"You can take it that he will do what he says."

"Literally leave the baby on our doorstep?"

"I can tell you for certain that he plans to do that. I have been struggling, trying to find a way to break the news to you for the past few weeks."

"Not trying very hard, Tony."

"I know that."

"You let him do the talking for you."

"I know. I know."

They lay together in silence for a while.

"I need to ask you one other thing," Eilis said eventually, "and I need you to answer clearly and please do not say anything that is not true. Has there been anyone else?"

Tony switched on his bedside lamp.

"There is no one else. There has never been."

"You need to tell me now if there are—" she whispered.

"Nothing. I told you. I promise you. Nothing."

"Just this."

"Just this," he said and sighed.

Once the man had visited her with the news of the baby, Eilis looked forward to going to work each day, getting away from the house. If they were busy, she would willingly stay on later, anything not to go home, where Tony was behaving as though nothing had happened.

Even the conversation at dinner had returned to normal.

A few times, when she wanted to talk to Tony about what they might do were this man to carry out his threat, she felt his fierce resistance to any further discussion. And since Rosella and Larry had no idea what was going on, Eilis alone was carrying the burden. The man, after all, had come looking for her. She had seen his face and heard his voice. No one else knew what that had been like. And there was no one she could tell.

Tony began to go to bed early. When she joined him, he pretended to be asleep. Sometimes, she lay in the dark knowing that he was awake beside her.

One evening, she found Tony in the kitchen. He averted his eyes when she came into the room and mumbled about being tired.

"There's something that I didn't say to you," she began.

He nodded his head slowly as if to say that he had been waiting for this.

"There are no circumstances under which I am going to look after a baby. It is your business, not mine."

"Maybe you don't want to be," he said softly, "but you are married to me."

"It's a pity you didn't think of that when you were out fixing leaks. But I don't want to go over that. I need to let you know that

21

if that man comes with a baby I will not answer the door, and if he leaves the baby on the doorstep, I will not open the door. I am not dealing with this."

"So what are we going to do?" he asked.

"I have no idea."

She stayed up late reading a magazine that Frank had left her, hoping Tony might be asleep by the time she went to bed.

Once she let herself see things from his perspective, the dilemma was clear. If he really believed that this man was going to dump a baby on their doorstep, then he must be feeling helpless. But she had to steel herself from feeling sympathy for him. If she softened in any way, she knew, it could result in her getting up in the night to feed someone else's baby. She was determined that she would not do this.

She could see that Tony was working on her, looking sad and making sure he did not say a single word that could make relations between them any worse. Without her support, he could do nothing.

And then it occurred to her that she could not be sure what Tony's mother would do. Francesca had a way of making everyone in the family, including Eilis herself, feel that they did no wrong. Even when Lena, in one of her rages, tried to run Enzo over in the driveway of their house, her mother-in-law declared that these things happened in the most loving families.

Each time Eilis bumped into Francesca, she studied her to see if there was any sign that her mother-in-law knew about the baby, but Francesca responded to her in the same way as always. Tony, she thought, had not felt free to confide in his mother.

In the garage one day, on a whim, Eilis phoned Frank's law office in Manhattan and made an appointment to see him.

The previous summer, Rosella had spent a month in her uncle Frank's office, sitting with the receptionist, learning about the filing system, getting to know Frank's colleagues. She even got to visit Frank's apartment in Hell's Kitchen, which no one else from the family had ever done. She was going to intern at another law office once the school term had ended.

Frank had spoken to Rosella about her grades and her ambitions and had realized that she would, most likely, be accepted by a good college. If she was, he told Eilis, he would pay her tuition.

"I can't do that for all my nieces and nephews," he said. "But Rosella really should go to college and she wants to. She is dedicated."

"Does she know about this?"

"She does."

"Did you mention it initially or did she?"

"I was telling her about my time at Fordham. And I said I thought she would like it there. She was very hesitant when I offered to help her."

"And then?"

"She admitted that it would be her dream."

That same night, Eilis waited until she and Tony were talking in the dark, whispering about ordinary things, before raising the question of Rosella going to college. She explained that Frank had offered to pay and Rosella had accepted only when he had pressed her to do so.

"No one consulted me?" he asked.

"Nor me either," she said.

"But you know about it now."

"And so do you."

"What will Enzo and Mauro think? They know that we couldn't afford it."

"Well, Frank can't pay for all his nieces and nephews."

"Why is he paying for Rosella?"

"Because she is the cleverest."

"Did you ask him to?"

"Of course I didn't!"

"What happens if the others find out?"

"We can say that she won a scholarship."

He grew silent. It occurred to her that he might feel hurt or undermined because someone else was paying for his daughter's education.

He sighed and moved closer to her.

"I don't know how to say this," he whispered.

It was important, she knew, to say nothing now, to make clear that she would not speak until he did.

"It began as a sort of joke. You know the way Enzo and Mauro behave."

He stopped for a moment as though he was unsure if he should continue. His voice faltered and then became more confident.

"They make jokes about you and Frank," he said, "how much the two of you talk, how he brings you newspapers and magazines, and they wonder why Frank doesn't get a girlfriend of his own."

"Frank is not going to have a girlfriend," Eilis said.

"Why not?"

"Frank is one of those men."

Tony held his breath. He began to say something and then stopped.

"How do you know that?" Tony asked.

"He told me."

"Who else knows? Does my mother know?"

"I don't think so."

"Will you promise me something?"

"What?"

"That you will never say this again. Ever. Not to me or to anyone."

"I wasn't planning to."

"No, no. I want you to promise that you won't. I need to be sure that no one ever says this again."

Frank's law office was a twenty-minute walk from Penn Station. In letters from Ireland, Eilis's mother had often asked about the glamour of New York, the fashionable stores, the skyscrapers, the bright lights. But Eilis never had anything to tell her about the city. She still wrote to her mother regularly and sent photographs of the children.

Her mother would be eighty this summer; Eilis would love to see her one more time. But more than that, she thought, she would regret not having gone were she to get news if something happened to her mother. Martin, her brother, had come home from Birmingham and was living in Cush, on the edge of the cliff, ten miles from the town. He went to see their mother a few times a week, and often wrote to Eilis, in his own rambling style, about the state of her health.

She knew that Francesca as well as Lena and Clara, whose families lived nearby, thought it strange for someone to spend her life so far away from her family. In their world, people came to America in groups. No one they knew had traveled alone, as Eilis did, without family or close friends.

In the evenings sometimes she spoke about home over dinner, especially if a letter had come from her mother or from Martin, and she kept a photograph on the mantelpiece of her sister, Rose, taken in 1951, the year before she died, when she had won the Lady Captain's Prize at the golf club in Enniscorthy. But Tony and Rosella and Larry had no real interest in Enniscorthy, or even Ireland.

In his office, as she told Frank the story of the man's visit and his threat to leave the baby on her doorstep, Eilis hoped that he might be able to reassure her that there was a legal recourse to stop him doing this.

"Obviously," Frank said, "you can't just dump a baby. But the problem is what to do if he goes ahead with his threat. It could take days to get social services or even the law to act, especially if the baby's with its natural father."

"How can anyone prove Tony is the father?"

"Yes, you're right. And eventually the problem would be solved and the man could even be charged and a foster home could be found. But what will happen in the first days, or the first hours even?"

"That's Tony's business."

"But what if you are in the house, or Rosella and Larry are there?"

"Maybe the man is bluffing, but Tony says he isn't. I can't imagine what it is like for the man's wife. Surely, she should have some say in the matter? Surely she should be the one—"

"This man really does feel," Frank interrupted, "that the presence of a child not his would actually contaminate his family. And he also believes that his wife should have no say at all in what should happen."

"How do you know all that?"

"I met him. He came here."

Eilis decided not to ask Frank why he had not told her this the very second she had arrived to see him. He looked self-satisfied as he waited to be asked questions. She had never disliked her brother-in-law before, but she did now. If the silence between them were to go on for an hour, she would not be the one to break it. She studied the window and looked at the shelf of books to the side and then directed her gaze at Frank.

"I thought Tony might have told you that I knew," he said.

"Frank, you didn't think that."

"I don't have permission to talk to you about it at all. When you came in, I didn't feel I could tell you that I already knew the story."

"You know more than I do, it seems."

"If I talk to you, it will have to be agreed that you can never tell anyone what I've said. Do the others know you are here?"

"No."

He must regret, she thought, seeing her at all. His mistake was to allow her into his office.

"Am I speaking to you in confidence?" he asked.

"Who could I tell?"

"I am asking you again if we are speaking in confidence."

"Yes, we are."

"About two weeks ago, my father came to see me. He has never come to my office before. He stayed for less than five minutes. All he would say was that I must do what my mother wanted. I honestly thought they had found me some eligible girl. But he would tell me nothing more. A few days later, when my mother appeared, she told me what you just told me, but added that she had been to visit the couple in question, the man you met and his wife, and she arranged for the man to come and see me here."

He stopped and looked at her.

"It has been decided that my mother is taking the child," he said. "I am trying to work out the best way that this can be done under the law."

"Was Tony in the room for any of the meetings?"

"No."

"Does he know what has been decided?"

"Yes."

"You're sure?"

"My mother told me."

"Did you ask your mother if I had been consulted?"

"Yes."

"What did she say?"

"She said that it would be all for the best."

"That is not what I asked you."

He sat back in his chair and sighed.

"You should talk to Tony, but you cannot tell him that you have spoken to me. You need to work this out between the two of you, but it's hardly my job to tell you that."

"Did you learn to talk like this at Fordham, or does it come naturally to you?"

"I am sorry this has happened."

"Spare me your pity, Frank, if you don't mind. Now, before I go, I need to be clear. The baby will be delivered soon after its birth to my mother-in-law, who will raise it in her house. Is that correct?"

"The baby will be adopted."

"By whom?"

"That is what I am working out."

"By Tony?"

She almost smiled at the thought that dealing with Enzo and Mauro about accounts had been easier than this. She had always admired Frank because he was so unlike the others; he had made his own life. Now she wished he had more in common with his brothers.

"We are working out the details."

"Frank, I know you are taking no pleasure from this, so just answer. Is Tony adopting the baby?"

"The husband wants the matter dealt with once and for all."

"Frank, if Tony is to adopt the baby, will I not be required to sign the forms as well?"

"Tony and you will have to talk."

"I don't want this baby anywhere near me."

"Well, go home and discuss it with Tony. And I repeat: you cannot tell them that you've been here."

IV

In all the years since the extended Fiorello family had moved to Lindenhurst, building four houses in a cul-de-sac, they had lunch together, except in the high summer, at one o'clock on Sundays, a meal that lasted through the afternoon. When they were drawing up the plans, Tony's mother had asked for a very large dining room. Now, with her husband, four sons, three daughters-in-law and eleven grandchildren, she prepared a meal each Sunday and set with elaborate care the long table that Mauro had made for her. Each week, one of the daughters-in-law would help her in the kitchen and then assist her in serving the food and cleaning the dishes later.

"I like it best when it's you," Francesca said to Eilis. "You are always calm whereas that Lena could go off in a temper at any moment. And you don't know about Italian cooking so you don't criticize me, unlike that Clara, who is always sniffing around and disapproving."

Eilis was on the point of asking if she should be flattered, but she liked her time with Francesca and appreciated her mother-in-law's way of keeping everyone as happy as she could.

The Sunday lunches, however, were a strain. Eilis found that the plate of pasta filled her up so that she seldom had any appetite for the lamb or the fish that came afterwards. And she was no good at taking part in the noisy banter and cross-talk at the table. Even into Monday, the irritating sound of all the competing voices was still with her.

Francesca made strict rules for the children once they were old enough to join the table. They must sit quietly and they must display good manners at all times. Francesca's effort to impose discipline was done with much humor and kindness, but she was not joined in this by Lena and Clara, or even by Enzo and Mauro, who would shout at their children and threaten them. Since Tony and Eilis never spoke harshly to their children, Rosella and Larry enjoyed a special status in their grandmother's house.

As the adults had their coffee, the children were free to leave the table. This part for Eilis was the worst. None of the family ever managed to finish a sentence without being interrupted by one of the others. It was pure babble.

One day, Eilis brought her camera to the lunch so she could take photographs to send to her mother. Each time she stood up to take a picture, the adults raised their glasses and smiled, and the children, too, posed for the camera, looking happy. When she had them developed, the photos showed a table laden down with dishes and bottles and plates and glasses; the family appeared festive, delighted to be together as though it were Christmas rather than an ordinary Sunday. Her mother had no grandchildren in Enniscorthy. Martin had no children. Pat and Jack had stayed in the Birmingham area and seldom came home. Her mother had met their wives and children only on a few occasions. Thus, a gathering like the Fiorellos' on Sundays was something her mother had never known. Eilis decided not to send these photographs to her. They would make her too sad.

At the meals, her father-in-law presided at the head of the table. If there was lamb, he performed the carving as a sacred duty. He arranged on each Sunday for one of his sons to sit on his right-hand side. He would slowly turn the conversation towards what happened to his mother on Ellis Island when she came to America from Italy.

Eilis remembered Tony telling her the story soon after they married.

"They sent his mother back. There was something wrong with her eyes. She was in quarantine first, but then they put her back on a ship to Naples. My father tells it like it happened yesterday. The same story."

"And how long did she go back for?"

"She didn't make a second journey. She stayed in Italy."

"So he never saw her again."

"Every Christmas she would go into some town and have her photograph taken. She would send a photograph. Enzo says if he has to hear about it all one more time he will go into quarantine himself. It used to make Mauro cry, but now he says he doesn't listen, he just nods his head."

"What do you do?"

"I listen. If I didn't, I'm sure he would notice."

When, a few years earlier, the television had been showing news of student marches and sit-ins against the war in Vietnam, Eilis's father-in-law had denounced the protestors and said that the police had been too lenient with them.

"But aren't they very brave, the protestors?" Eilis asked.

"I would like to see them all in uniform," her father-in-law said.

"I would hate a son of mine having to go to war," Eilis said, "so I think they are protesting for me."

By this time, most of the children had gone out to play. Tony put his head down. Enzo made signs to Eilis that she should stop.

"I can't think of anything that would make me more proud," her father-in-law said.

"To have a son or a grandson in the war?" she asked, looking at Frank, whom she had heard denouncing the war many times.

"Fighting for his country. That's what I said. It would make me proud."

Eilis hoped that someone else would speak. For a second, she thought it best to say nothing more, but then she felt a flash of anger at Tony and Frank for not supporting her.

"That is not an opinion many people would share," she said.

"Do you mean Irish people?" her father-in-law asked.

"I mean Americans."

"What do you know about Americans?"

"I am as American as you are. My children are Americans. And I would not want my son to be sent to fight in Vietnam."

She looked directly at her father-in-law, forcing him to avert his eyes.

Enzo interrupted first by making a sound under his breath that rose into "Whoa" and then became louder. He pointed at Eilis.

"Keep quiet, you!"

Everyone watched Eilis except Tony and Frank, who kept their heads down.

Francesca, eventually, stood up.

"I think it's a day for grappa," she said. "We will all have a little something with our coffee. Now can someone help me get the glasses?"

Even though it was her turn to help, Eilis did not move. Both Lena and Clara seemed relieved to be able to stand up from the table.

"Can you not control her?" Enzo asked Tony, as though she weren't there.

"Enzo, don't start," Mauro said.

Frank stacked plates so they could be taken to the kitchen.

On the walk back to their house, with Rosella and Larry coming behind them, Eilis felt almost sorry for Tony. Clearly, he should have supported her at the table, or turned the conversation to some other topic. But he could not go against his father.

*   *   *

A few days after the argument, when she was alone in the house, her mother-in-law arrived with an apple pie. At first, they had discussed Rosella and Larry, Francesca praising both for their exemplary good manners. Then Francesca spoke about the Sunday lunches.

"It was my dream that we would all do different things during the week and then we would come together on Sunday. And the children would be at the table and get used to sitting quietly and that nothing said at the table would be unfit for children's ears."

Eilis wondered if she was going to be asked to apologize. She was preparing to use the same sweet tone as her mother-in-law and say that she had enjoyed the lunch immensely and did not regret a single word she or anyone else had said.

"I often worry about you," Francesca went on. "I often think you get homesick at our big gatherings with all the Italian food and all the Italians talking. It often strikes me that you might sometimes dread the lunches. I know how I would feel if everyone was Irish."

Eilis was not sure where this was leading.

"And you are so polite and you fit in so well that I often wonder what is really going on in your mind. I don't mean anything bad is going on in your mind! I mean that you have thoughts of your own in a way that Lena and Clara don't. I often believed that someone like you would marry Frank, he is so educated, but you married Tony and the children are a credit to you. All four of you are wonderful. Life is full of surprises."

Eilis wished the phone would ring or someone would come to the door.

"Do you know what I mean?" Francesca asked.

Eilis nodded and smiled.

"It struck me that you would be much happier if you didn't have to suffer through those long Sunday lunches."

Eilis pretended that she had not heard. She wanted Francesca to spell out what she meant.

"It struck me that you would love a break from us. And, of course, Tony would still come, his brothers would miss him too much, and Rosella and Larry too."

Eilis was ready to ask if Francesca thought that no one would miss her. Instead, she asked, "Have you spoken to Tony?"

"No, but I will."

"And what will you say?"

"I will say that I have been thinking about our Sunday lunches and wondering if it is not all too much for Eilis."

"Too much for me?"

"Too boring, too loud, too many people talking at the same time."

Francesca appeared to swallow hard as though saying all this had been an ordeal. If she accepted the suggestion that she no longer come to the lunch, Eilis wanted it to be clear to everyone, especially Tony, that the proposal had come from Francesca and not from her.

"I would not like anyone to think that I did not enjoy their company," she said.

"But we see you all the time!"

"Tony would be hurt if I didn't come with him."

"I will assure him that it was my idea."

"Well, it certainly wasn't mine."

"I would not like to have an argument with you," Francesca said. "You would always win."

"I am not arguing with you."

"I know that. And, of course, if you really did want to come for lunch on Sundays, I could make sure that you enjoyed yourself as much as everyone else does."

Eilis began by ordering the Sunday edition of *The New York Times* to be delivered. Up till then, she'd had to wait until Frank had finished with his copy and hope that he remembered to bring it.

34

All the family went to ten o'clock mass, often sitting in different parts of the church but waiting until Mr. Fiorello and Francesca appeared in the line for communion before any other member of the family joined it.

Just as Tony's parents wore their best clothes and Lena and Clara treated the ceremony as a fashion show, Enzo and Mauro wore suits and ties and their good shoes. Eilis saw no need for Tony to wear a tie, and did not dress up herself, using a simple mantilla rather than a hat and not wearing high heels.

Eilis loved it when the time approached for the others to go to Sunday lunch and leave her to read the paper, listen to the radio and idle in the house. Once it was established that she no longer attended, no one questioned her about it except Rosella, who believed she had been banished for arguing with her father-in-law and thought it unfair.

"When you get to my age," Eilis said to her, "you love time on your own."

"But I feel there's an empty chair at the table," Rosella said. "And all you said was that you don't want Larry to have to fight in a war."

"I love my Sundays," Eilis said, "so I am not complaining."

V

Eilis tried to put the man's visit out of her mind, but his voice came to her in odd moments. It was like a change in temperature, or a shift in the light, and it made her shiver.

Tony still did not tell her what he and his mother planned to do. As the days were growing longer, she suggested that they take a walk around the neighborhood once he had cleaned up, hoping that he would talk to her about it. When this had happened a few times and she was getting nowhere, Tony too taken up with examining any house they passed that was undergoing repairs, she was tempted to tell him everything that Frank had shared with her and was dissuaded only by the thought that she might need Frank to tell her more in the future. So she did not mention the baby or the specter of adoption but she listened to Tony's stories and his jokes and followed his comments on the houses. Anyone seeing them, she thought, would believe they were the perfect married couple.

One day she took her camera to work so she could take pictures of Mr. Dakessian and his son, Erik, and some of the mechanics and also of her own office.

"I will send them to my mother," she explained. "When I write to her, I enclose photographs in each letter."

"And what does she send you?" Mr. Dakessian asked.

"News from home, if there is any."

"You must miss her."

"Yes, I do, especially when I don't get a letter for a while, and then I worry about her."

"Why don't you invite her over?"

"I don't think she would come. She is almost eighty."

"How long is it since you have seen her?"

"More than twenty years."

"She has never seen your children?"

"No."

"That must make her very sad."

The next day, when Eilis got home, Lena was standing in her doorway.

"I thought I might find you," Lena said. "I slipped over because no one was looking. But you never know. They see everything here."

Inside, they sat at the kitchen table, Lena refusing any refreshment.

"I came over to say that if you need anything I am ready to help. Anything. If you need money or advice, or just need to talk. And Clara says the same. She didn't want to come too because it would crowd you out and then Francesca would launch an investigation into why two of us had come over here. We are shocked about this awful baby. That is what I came to say."

She stood up then and put her finger to her lips.

"Don't say a word to anyone, or Enzo will find out I came here. He is sleeping in his parents' house for the moment until he learns manners."

Before Eilis could ask her what she meant, Lena had departed.

*   *   *

On the hall table, she found a letter from her mother, and when she opened the envelope she smiled at how her mother had reverted to a system she had adopted when Eilis first came to America. She simply listed all the people she had met in Enniscorthy over the past few weeks who had asked how Eilis was and had sent best wishes to her. They included every type of person from shopkeepers to neighbors to girls she had been to school with, including Nancy Sheridan, who had been her best friend.

The name that was missing, Eilis saw, was Jim Farrell. Surely, her mother might have run into Jim at some stage, since he lived in the town center over the bar that he owned!

If their paths crossed, they would remember the return of Eilis from America more than twenty years ago after her sister, Rose, had died.

That summer, in Enniscorthy, Eilis had a romance with Jim Farrell. No one, not even her mother or Nancy, and certainly not Jim, knew that she was, by that time, married to Tony. They had got married in Brooklyn. Eilis had wanted to tell her mother as soon as she arrived home, but it was too hard because it meant that, no matter what, she would have to go back to America.

So she told no one, no one at all. And then, at summer's end, she had abruptly left, just as Jim was making clear that he wanted to marry her.

Once she had come back to Brooklyn and settled down with Tony, Eilis had put that whole summer out of her mind. It was strange to be reminded of what had happened by the absence of Jim Farrell's name on a list of people in the town, some of whom she barely remembered.

The late May days were blustery, often threatening rain. It was like Ireland, she thought, or Wexford anyhow, when hints of summer would be dulled by a faint chill in the wind. The raked light forced her to concentrate harder when she drove.

One afternoon, close to the turn for home, she made the decision to drive on. She would go to Jones Beach to walk by the sea.

The first summers when the Fiorellos moved to Lindenhurst from Brooklyn, Tony and Eilis often arrived at Jones Beach early on a Sunday, carrying a cooler with drinks and sandwiches and a large sun umbrella that, with its yellow and blue stripes, stood out so that Tony's brothers and their friends could easily locate them. At that time Enzo was with Lena but Mauro had not met Clara.

By lunchtime on those Sundays, a crowd of friends would gather around their umbrella, holding space so that others could come and join them. Some old friends of Tony and his brothers came from Brooklyn, young men perfectly dressed for summer and the women wearing the most fashionable sunglasses and beach shoes and swimsuits. Usually, the men went swimming together, leaving the women behind. They played ball at the edge of the water and then came back exhausted and lay flat on the sand.

At the beginning, as the only married man among the group, Tony was loath to leave Eilis on her own. When the others shouted at him to follow, he seemed doubtful.

"She will be well looked after," Lena called out to him. "And we want to know the secrets of married life."

Hesitantly, Tony joined his brothers and their friends, coming back a number of times to check that she was all right.

"He is a devoted husband," Lena said. "If I get half of that from Enzo, I will be content."

All of the young women who came on those Sundays saw the story of Eilis and Tony as a great romance.

"I think you were destined to meet," Lena said to general agreement. "Even if he had not gone to that Irish dance and found you there, you would have met somewhere else."

"And getting married secretly! You must have been so happy!" another said. "It makes me believe in love at first sight."

It struck Eilis as strange how little they all knew about her, but she told them nothing.

At some point in the afternoon, Tony would edge away from the group and ask Eilis if she would come for a swim with him. By this time, the heat was sweltering and every inch of the beach would be taken up. They had to step around people and then work out a way to circumnavigate the next group. Tony held her hand as though they were just boyfriend and girlfriend.

He didn't seem to mind that she could swim better than he, and that she would drift away from him out into the deeper water. Tony was nervous about following her; he stood up to his chest in the water, jumping to avoid each wave, watching her, smiling, seeking her attention. When she came back and stood close to him, he shyly kissed her.

From then on, Tony did not leave her side. They found a place to be together under a smaller umbrella. The others left them alone.

Eilis drove to the parking lot near the water tower at Jones Beach. On weekend days in high summer, there would not be a single space free; instead, there would be cars circling, looking out for anyone who gave a sign they might be leaving.

When the children were born, they had tried to go to the beach as usual. But it was often too hot or too crowded. So, instead, they began to go in the evenings when everything had quietened and they would settle down for an hour close to the shoreline.

Eilis remembered one of those evenings, the heat still heavy in the air, the beach half-deserted, the water the warmest it had been for a while. She had gone in for a swim on her own, leaving Tony to look after Rosella and Larry, who was still a baby. As she waded out, she turned several times to wave at them. And then she swam away from the shore to beyond the breaking surf, where the water was calmer. When she lifted her head, facing the beach, she saw that Tony had Larry in his arms and Rosella by his side and he was pointing her out to them and laughing. She swam in towards them. When Tony put Larry down, Larry began to crawl in her direction. She presumed that he wanted to be picked up, but discovered instead that he was determined to make his own way towards the water. She and Tony and Rosella stood back and watched him, his pure determination.

It was nothing, she thought, except a picture of contentment that seemed complete.

Now Eilis looked up and down the beach, trying to gauge where she would have stood and where Tony might have been. But the beach was too long. It could have been anywhere along this stretch. She stayed still, looking out at the waves, dreaming of Tony standing with the children, imagining that they were waiting for her to come back from her swim.

As May went into June, Tony still did not reveal to her the plans he and his mother had. His easy manner and his good humor when he came in from work were, she thought, designed to seem unforced and natural. Watching his efforts to conceal his intentions made her wish that she did not have to sit opposite him at the table or sleep beside him at night.

One afternoon when she had just come back from work, she saw Francesca approaching across the lawn towards the back door.

Once they were seated and had tea and biscuits on a tray on the small table, Francesca came straight to the point.

"Tony has told me about the baby. I am annoyed that he waited so long."

Her mother-in-law left silence. When Eilis said nothing, Francesca continued.

"It's a very big shock for all of us. Now, what do you think we should do about it? I hoped that you might have come to talk to me."

Eilis saw how easily she could now be put in the wrong with the suggestion that it was her inaction that had caused her mother-in-law to feel that she had to intervene.

"I told Tony two things at the beginning," Eilis said. "One, this has nothing to do with me, it is for Tony to deal with. And two, I will not have the baby in this house."

"So what will we do if this man comes, as he promises, and leaves the baby on our doorstep? Now maybe it won't happen. Maybe he will see sense."

"If he leaves it on mine, I will expect Tony to return it since he knows the house where it was conceived, or he can take the baby to the police or to whoever looks after abandoned babies. But, as you say, maybe the man will see sense."

"Tony could not take his own baby to the police."

"It is not my baby."

"The baby will be a member of the family whether we like it or not. Tony is the father."

"It will not be a member of my family. I don't care who the father is."

"Do you want it put into an orphanage?"

"I have no interest in talking about it. I told Tony my views on this. They haven't changed and they won't change."

She was deliberately making things difficult for her mother-in-law.

"What would Rosella and Larry feel if they knew that their half sister or brother was to be put into an orphanage? Have you taken them into account?"

"Leave them out of this. How they feel is none of your business."

Eilis realized that she had gone too far.

"No one has ever said anything like that to me before about my grandchildren."

Eilis was tempted to ask Francesca to leave, but then thought that, since she was unlikely to want to discuss this again with her mother-in-law, then she really did need to hear everything in this meeting.

"I will not have the peace and happiness of this house disturbed, or my children—"

"What's done cannot be undone," Francesca interrupted.

"It is not my responsibility."

"You are married to him."

"Yes, and I have told him as his wife what my feelings are. Since he spoke to you, I am surprised that he did not let you know how I feel about this."

"Oh he did, he did. But that isn't going to solve the problem."

"Do you have a solution?"

She had, she hoped, opened a door for Francesca. She could now declare what she had in mind.

"No, I don't. I just don't know. It's as simple as that. And I feel sorry for you. When Tony told me, that is the first thing I said to him. And, of course, I didn't think it was true! I thought that Tony could never be so foolish. He should be ashamed of himself. And then I could not believe that any man would not let his wife keep her own baby. But Tony says we have to take the man seriously. I think this is a really sad situation for all of us. And I came to see what you thought."

Francesca seemed, Eilis believed, to have closed the door she had opened for her. She would not help her again. She looked at her coldly.

"If he comes here with a baby," Francesca asked, "what will you do?"

"Nothing. I will not answer the door."

"And if the children are here?"

"The baby will not pass the threshold."

"Even if it's lying on the ground outside?"

"I will call the fire brigade if I have to."

"And what if Tony has a different view?"

"You can take it that Tony's view is the same as mine. Unless he has told you something different?"

Her mother-in-law looked at her quizzically.

"I am sure he didn't say anything different to me than to you."

"So you know my position, then?"

She could see Francesca trying to work out how to answer this.

"I think all of us will stand with you and help you."

"There is no help you can give me other than listen to me when I say that I will not look after another woman's baby."

"What if I looked after it?" Francesca asked, and quickly added before Eilis could interrupt her, "If the man does come I can deal with it, and I fully understand you when you say you don't want to."

"I have told Tony he must not get involved with the man or the baby. That also applies to anyone else."

"Am I anyone else?"

"It is very kind of you to offer to help. But I need to make clear to you that I don't want this child anywhere near us. The problem had best be resolved as soon as it arises."

"How?"

"By returning the baby to its proper address or by calling the police."

"I meant that I would deal with the father if he should come with the baby."

"I don't understand you. How would you deal with him?"

"Do you not trust me?"

"I need to know what you mean."

"I guarantee that you will not be further troubled by this."

"I need you to spell out what your intentions are. I also need you to know that you and Tony have no right, none at all, to make any plans behind my back."

"I'm his mother."

"What does that give you permission to do?"

"Eilis, I will do my best. That's all I can say."

45

In the silence that followed, Eilis saw that she had been trapped. Even if she were to tell her mother-in-law that she knew the plan, all Francesca had to do was deny it. As she sat in the living room, she saw what was ahead. She would look out the kitchen window and see Tony's child being raised by its grandmother, taking its first steps on a lawn on which there was no fence to divide Eilis's house from Francesca's. If only she could think of one thing to say that might prevent this!

"I won't tolerate," Eilis said, "any threat to the children's happiness and well-being."

"No one is threatening anyone."

"And just in case this is in anyone's mind, I will not tolerate this child being brought up in your house, in plain sight of us here."

"But who has said that is even a possibility?" Francesca asked.

Eilis realized that the conversation had gone as far as it could. Her mother-in-law was setting out to deceive her.

"I will do my best," Francesca continued.

Eilis was going to ask her if she could oblige her by doing nothing at all, but then thought better of it.

"We don't see each other enough," Francesca said. "We should make an arrangement to meet more regularly."

Francesca stood and waited for Eilis to stand up too and accompany her out. But Eilis remained seated. Francesca left the room and made her way alone to the front door. Since her mother-in-law was a stickler for form, Eilis knew that this studied insult would not be forgotten. As much as anything she had said, it would create a chasm between them that would not be easily bridged and that made her feel satisfied that something, at least, had been achieved.

Having checked the time, Eilis rang the garage. Erik Dakessian answered the phone and confirmed that his father was there and would likely not be closing up for a while. Eilis said that she would drive down to the garage immediately.

Later, as she worked in the kitchen, Tony came and joined her.

"Was my mother here today?"

"Oh yes, she was," Eilis said. "It was lovely to see her."

"I think she was worried about you."

"We had a nice talk."

"So there is no problem?"

The idea that she was standing beside a drawer of knives gave Eilis pause for thought.

"Why are you smiling?" Tony asked.

"Just something funny your mother told me."

"About what?"

"About Lena," she said. "But I promised to keep it to myself."

If they could tell her lies, she thought, she could tell them lies too.

Once the light was off, she waited for a while and then, afraid that Tony might fall asleep, touched him on the shoulder.

"I am going to Ireland," she said. "I am going to see my mother."

He did not move.

"I spoke to Mr. Dakessian today and we agreed that I can go."

"When are you going?" he whispered.

"Soon."

"For how long?"

"My mother's eightieth birthday is in August. I am going to train Erik to do my job and I will be back to take over again just as he gets ready to go away to college."

When she heard him whispering something after a while, she was not sure at first that she had heard him properly. She had to ask him to repeat whatever it was.

"Will you promise to come back?" he whispered.

The question itself and the plaintive tone surprised her.

"I am sorry for all this," he continued. "I am sorry."

She did not reply.

"Will you promise to come back?" he asked again.

"Maybe you will promise that I will never have to see this baby and that no one from your family will become involved in bringing it up?"

He sighed.

"I don't know what to do," he said. "That husband means what he says. He is a brute. He is going to leave the baby here."

"I am waiting for your promise."

"I will do what I can," he said.

"On Saturday, you will go with Rosella to her game and leave Larry with me. I will tell him while you are away and I will tell Rosella when you come back."

"Is it not too soon to tell them?"

"They need to know now."

On Saturday, when Tony and Rosella had gone, Larry appeared in the kitchen to complain about Eilis's order that he was to stay in the house.

"I need you here," she said.

"Why?"

She indicated that he should follow her into the living room.

"What's this about?" he asked.

"It's about your father."

"I know all that."

"What do you know?"

"I was sworn to secrecy."

"By whom?"

"By everyone."

"What is the secret?"

"He has a girlfriend."

"Who told you that?"

"On Sunday there was a big row at the table because Uncle Enzo and Uncle Mauro were laughing, pointing at Dad and making jokes. Uncle Enzo imitated a man holding a baby. And then when Aunt Lena found out what the joke was, she walked out and Uncle Enzo is sleeping in Grandma's."

"Dad does not have a girlfriend."

"That's what I thought, but it's not what they are saying."

"There is a woman who is going to have a baby and Dad is the father."

"She is his girlfriend, then."

"She is not and never was. He was doing a job at her house."

"And they are having a baby together?"

"She is having the baby. The woman's husband says he will not have the baby in his house, so he wants to drop it here on my doorstep."

"And what are you going to do?"

"I am going to Ireland. My mother's eightieth birthday is on the fifteenth of August. I want to be there for that, but I am going very soon."

"Is Dad going with you?"

"No, he certainly isn't."

"Can I come with you?"

"Do you want to?"

"Yes. I have only met one of my grandmothers. I would like to meet the other one."

"Does Rosella also think that Dad has a girlfriend?"

"No, they didn't know I was listening when they talked about it. Rosella had already gone home to study."

As she waited for Tony to return with Rosella, Eilis realized that this was what she dreaded most. She knew how close Rosella was

49

to her father. She waited for a while when she heard Tony's car and then found Rosella in her bedroom.

"I knew there was something," Rosella said. "But I couldn't think what it was. Are you sure?"

"Sure?"

"Could the man not be——?"

"No, seemingly he means what he says."

"And the baby is definitely Dad's."

"That's what I am told."

Rosella sat on the edge of the bed.

"I wish I hadn't heard this. I know that sounds stupid but that's what I wish."

She began to cry.

When Eilis let Rosella know that Larry was traveling to Ireland with her, Rosella said that she too would come.

"Of course I will. I don't want to stay here. But my internship won't be over until the end of July."

"You and Larry can join me then."

They sat in silence until Eilis went to find Tony.

"Rosella and Larry are coming to Ireland as well," Eilis said. "I will go on my own at the end of this month and they will come later. We might need to get a loan from the bank."

"So that's all decided, then?" Tony asked.

"Yes, it is," she said in a voice she might use on the telephone to a customer.

"Do I have no say in this?"

"None."

Rosella and Larry appeared together in the doorway.

"What if I say I don't want you to go?" Tony asked.

"You are the one who caused all this. It wasn't easy for me to tell your children about you."

"I've said I'm sorry," Tony said.

He turned to Rosella and then to Larry.

"I've told your mother I'm sorry."

"We are sorry too," Eilis said. "And we will start making our travel plans on Monday."

Rosella crossed the room to embrace her father. When Larry glanced at Eilis, she indicated that he should do the same. She stood back and watched, waiting to see if Tony would do anything to dissuade them from going to Ireland by making them feel sorry for him, the one left behind.

In the bedroom later, Tony moved awkwardly around. She knew that he disliked being alone, how if she and Rosella and Larry were not there he would go to one of the other houses rather than stay on his own. In all the years, they had shared a bed every night except when Eilis was having the children. She remembered that after Larry's birth, which was difficult, she had to stay some extra days in the hospital. When Tony heard that news, he was forlorn. He wanted her back home. He loved how things were, living with his family, having his parents and his brothers close by. She knew that he must dread her going. If he really did not want her to go, she thought, all he had to say was that she would never see the baby and never have to worry about its being brought up by his mother. But it was clear to her now that he would not say that.

Tony had asked her to promise that she would come back. Until then, it had never occurred to her that she might do otherwise. Tony was still moving around the room. She went to the bathroom and stayed as long as she could. When she returned, he was not yet in bed. She did not want him to come towards her or embrace her. She caught his eye for a moment; they exchanged a look that was filled with regret. She was glad when, eventually, they got into bed and the lights were turned off.

PART TWO

I

The smell of cooking oil filled the chip shop. Nancy was wringing out a dishcloth to clean the counter before she opened for business. Trying to think who else was in the house, she realized with relief that her daughter Miriam was out. If Miriam were here, she would come running down from her bedroom to say what she always said: that the smell was eating its way into the upper stories of the house and getting into her clothes and into the very pores of her skin.

Nancy shouted up into the stairwell in case Gerard was upstairs, but there was no reply. Now that the chip shop was thriving and there was money in the bank, he liked to go to Stamps on the opposite corner of the Market Square or Jim Farrell's in Rafter Street and have a drink with others who ran businesses in the town. As she made her way quickly downstairs, she wished her son were here.

The air in the chip shop was getting even thicker with the fumes. She switched on the fan, which began with a clatter and then continued with the loud rhythmic buzzing sounds that often caused her neighbors to complain.

But when the fan proved ineffective and her eyes were still watering from the acrid fumes, the only solution was to open the door to the Market Square and let the smoke out. She hoped that no one she knew might be walking by.

Some months before, when a motion had been passed at the monthly meeting of the Urban District Council denouncing the disturbance caused by businesses such as hers, she had agreed to close the chip shop before the pubs did on Mondays, Tuesdays and Wednesdays. But these were not the busy nights. The chip shop did most of its business at the weekend, disturbing the peace enjoyed by the families who lived above their shops and offices.

As she was wiping down the countertop, she became aware that two people were looking at her through the window. It was June and still bright outside. She ignored whoever was peering in and carried on working, but when she looked up again she saw it was Mr. Roderick Wallace, the manager of the Bank of Ireland, whose premises were across the square, and his wife, Dolores. Wallace, who had resolutely refused Nancy a loan when she was closing the supermarket and fitting out the chip shop, was prominent among those who complained about it. And at a hop in the tennis club his daughter had made a snide remark to Nancy's two daughters about their mother and her grubby chipper.

Now both Roderick and Dolores were standing in the doorway.

"The place is as grimy as ever," Roderick said in a loud voice.

When Nancy glanced up, Dolores addressed her directly.

"We usually don't pass this way because of the odor," she said. "And this evening it is noxious."

"You're in breach of the planning regulations, I'm sure," Roderick added.

Nancy began cleaning the surface of the narrow ledge that ran along the wall opposite the counter. The air in the shop was better now. In a short time, she would be open for business.

"If your husband was alive," Roderick went on, "I'm sure he would join with the rest of us in deploring this."

Nancy stood still for a moment before moving towards the door and brushing past Roderick and Dolores until she was on the footpath.

"I believe you are to be transferred soon," she said. "And a lot of people in Enniscorthy will be happy to see the end of you both."

She looked at Dolores and then directed her gaze at Roderick.

As they began to edge away from her, she noticed a group that included her son Gerard observing this scene closely from just across the Square.

"You can shag off back to Cork," she added, "or wherever it is you come from, the pair of you!"

Roderick turned.

"I dare you to repeat that."

"No problem at all! Shag off back to Cork, the pair of you."

Later, when Gerard had gone with his friends to Wexford and Miriam said that she wanted an early night, Nancy worried that if people heard about the altercation with the Wallaces, they would surely blame her rather than them. It would be another example of the low tone that she was bringing to the Market Square.

Business was slow and she closed for the night a few minutes early. The fan was still making too much noise; she turned it off and kept the door open to get the last fumes out of the shop. When she went outside, she noticed that the chill that had persisted until recently had softened. The night was warm.

With the door locked and the lights dimmed, she was doing a final clean-up when she noticed another two figures, also a man and a woman, at the window. She smiled at the thought that this might be the Wallaces come back to order burgers with onion rings and plenty of ketchup or to request that she repeat once more what she had said to them.

Because it was dark outside, she could barely make out who they were, but when the couple moved away slightly, she saw them perfectly. Although she didn't know their names, she was sure that they lived up by Summerhill in one of the soldiers' cottages.

They had a string of children. They were barred from most of the pubs in town. Often, they came in a drunken state to buy chips for three or four nights in a row and then disappeared. She wondered if they stayed at home in between bouts of drinking. When they had alcohol taken, she knew, the wife, whatever her name was, became even more belligerent than the husband. On a busy night, they had no patience, pushing through the crowd, demanding to be served out of turn. A few times, not understanding that she closed early midweek, they had come after the pubs shut demanding service, but it was too late and she had not let them in.

They shaded their eyes with their hands and stood right up against the window. Then they began to knock on the glass to get her attention. She ignored them at first, but they continued to bang on the window even when Nancy turned on the main light and mouthed the word "closed." The man made a sign to her that she should open the door. She shook her head and carried on working.

Still they did not give up.

"We'll go," the woman shouted, "as soon as we get the chips."

Nancy pointed to the deep fryer and put her hands in the air to let them know that there was nothing she could do at this late hour.

"Will you open up, for fuck's sake," the woman shouted. "We're starving."

Her husband banged forcefully on the glass.

Nancy turned off the lights at the back of the shop and moved to put the four high stools neatly against the wall. It occurred to her that her neighbors must be listening closely. She wished one of them would appear to give her some support, or that Gerard would come back from Wexford. Since Miriam slept at the back of the house on the top floor, she would be unlikely to hear what was happening. And Nancy would never dream of waking her up to look for help. Miriam, who was getting married in July, would be glad, Nancy thought, to see the end of this house. Laura, her other daughter, almost qualified as a solicitor, could hardly visit from Dublin without making a disparaging remark.

"Open up outta that, or I'll kick the fuckin' door in," the woman shouted.

When Nancy went upstairs, she could still hear the sound of fists banging against the glass. Without turning on the light, she went to the front window hoping not to be seen, but the woman, now standing on the roadway, spotted her immediately.

"Come down outta that, you!"

If she phoned the Guards, she thought, they might want to press charges against the couple. In that case, she would be called to give evidence and the story would be in the local papers and her chipper would be further associated with unruly behavior and unsavory people.

She decided to phone Jim Farrell. He would still be in the bar in Rafter Street cleaning up.

He answered the phone on the first ring.

"I'll be there in one second," he said.

When Jim appeared, Nancy stood at the window listening as he spoke to the husband and wife. He sounded like a Guard on duty or someone in authority. Since he owned a popular bar, she supposed, he must have learned how to manage a situation like this. Having ordered the man to stop banging on the glass and the woman to stop shouting, he began to talk to them, his voice subdued.

Eventually, the couple walked away. Nancy went down and found Jim, who followed her upstairs, but since the living room was being redecorated in preparation for Miriam's wedding, they sat in the kitchen. Jim had a way of not smiling and not saying much that she had come to appreciate. It always took a while for him to become comfortable.

He told her that he had got a promise from the pair that they would not return to harass her.

"Are they still barred from your pub?"

"Yes. But they know why and they accept that."

She heard Gerard on the stairs. He looked into the kitchen for a moment.

"Any news?" he asked.

"All quiet," Jim said.

"Did you hear about my mother and the bank manager?" Gerard asked.

Jim made clear that he did not know what Gerard was talking about.

"It was nothing," Nancy said. "They complained about the smell from the oil."

"You gave him a lot to think about, anyway," Gerard said before wishing them both good night.

They listened to him going up the stairs and heard him in the bathroom. Jim signaled to her without saying anything that if he went back to his own house she might soon follow. She smiled.

"I'll see you in a while," he whispered.

She had been having an affair with Jim for almost a year now, although she wondered if "affair" was really the word. They had never appeared in public together. But sometimes, when the chip shop and the pub had closed, Jim would phone, and Nancy would cross the Market Square and slip into Rafter Street and find the side door to Jim's quarters above the pub on the latch. It was strange, Nancy thought, for two people in their mid-forties to behave like furtive teenagers, but soon that was going to change.

She still liked the idea that no one, no one at all, knew about them, and no one, she believed, even guessed.

Usually, when she had left his bed, she would sneak out of his house, with him checking beforehand that there was no one on the street. She was careful. Anyone who saw her might ask themselves what Nancy Sheridan was doing walking around the town of Enniscorthy as the cathedral bell rang out three o'clock in the morning. And she tried not to make a sound as she ascended the stairs to her own bedroom.

She remembered leaving her own house late on Christmas Day and finding the Market Square empty, knowing that Jim would, once more, be waiting for her upstairs in the house on Rafter Street.

She found him sitting that night in an armchair with a gin and tonic poured for himself and a vodka and orange juice with plenty of ice on a small table beside the other armchair. She noticed a plate of mince pies. They spoke casually for a while, even discussing the weather and the quality of the Christmas dinner in Jim's cousin's house in Monart. She saw that he was blushing and looking at the floor and then glancing nervously at her.

"It struck me," he said and then stopped and sipped his drink.

"It struck me . . ." he began again and sighed and looked at the floor. "You know, I've been thinking."

"What?"

"That it wouldn't be good for you if anyone noticed you coming here."

He was going to end it, she saw. He would use his own concern for her reputation as an excuse. She determined that she would leave as soon as she could. When she sipped her drink, it was clear that he had put too much vodka into it.

"I know you're very independent. You're independent and have your own way of doing things." Jim was looking towards one of the tall windows that gave onto the street. It occurred to Nancy that it might be best if she stood up now.

"It struck me . . ." he began again. "I thought it would be nice if we were actually living together."

Nancy set about detaching one of the mince pies from its silver casing.

"I have been thinking about it for a while," Jim said. "I thought, if you liked, we could become a bit more serious."

He sighed again and stirred the ice in his drink with his finger.

"I suppose by agreeing that we wanted, you know, wanted . . ."

He looked at her as if she might finish the sentence for him.

"Wanted?"

"I suppose eventually to see each other more."

She winced when she took a gulp of the vodka.

"What's wrong?" he asked.

"Nothing. You just put too much vodka in the drink."

"Do you need——?"

"No, it's fine."

"I'm going the wrong way about this," he said.

"I'm listening."

"I know it's a bit unusual because we have always known each other. It's not like we're twenty-one."

He was speaking as though to himself.

"What do you think?" he asked.

"Well, I'm not twenty-one anyway," she said.

"Nor me," he replied.

She nodded and held his gaze.

"I'd like to know that we are both serious," he continued.

"Jim, could you spell out what you mean?"

"We'll talk about it another time. But I think you get my drift."

She came to his house over the next few nights. They discussed arrangements they might make, working out how a widow aged forty-six with three children, the youngest almost twenty, might marry a bachelor of the same age whom she had known all of her life and who had, during a summer many years before, been in love with her best friend, who had let him down badly by going back to America, abandoning him and Enniscorthy without warning.

"I can't imagine getting married in the cathedral with the whole town looking at me. I am not sure the children would welcome the sight of their mother in a wedding dress."

"We'll suit ourselves," Jim had replied. "We won't do anything we don't want to do."

That was as far as they had got with the arrangements when Miriam, Nancy's elder daughter, announced her engagement to Matt Wadding on New Year's Eve, with plans to marry in the summer.

"Let her have her big day," Jim had said. "Let them get married first. We'll wait until they're settled. We'll tell no one about our plans until they are well married."

Once Miriam set the date of her wedding for the last week in July, Jim declared that it would be only decent for her mother and himself to wait until September to make any announcement.

"No one will believe us," Nancy said.

"They'll get used to it quickly enough."

It was strange, Nancy thought, that it did not strike Gerard that his mother and Jim were actually making plans to marry, even though Gerard often went to Jim's pub when Jim might not be busy so they could discuss the day's news. Even finding his mother and Jim together in the kitchen after midnight did not stir his curiosity.

"I suppose it is too strange," Nancy said.

"Gerard is smart enough," Jim said, "but he knows only what he sees."

The day she and Jim were married, Nancy thought, would be a happy day for her. But the day when word began to spread in the town that she had become engaged would also be something to enjoy. Jim was solid; people liked him. In recent years, his pub had been doing a good trade. It was where all the young teachers and solicitors and bank clerks drank now. And Jim had managed to make his new clientele welcome without losing any of his old customers. He had a barman, Shane Nolan, who had been with him for years. Nancy knew how Shane and his wife, Colette, looked after Jim.

"You'd be lost without them, but I wonder if they won't be a bit put out by the idea of a new woman coming into the house."

"Shane takes everything in his stride."

*   *   *

As Nancy left Jim's house on the night she had called him to help get rid of the boisterous couple, she calculated how long it would be before her life changed. In ten weeks, they would be able to announce their engagement. She imagined herself at eleven o'clock or twelve o'clock mass in early September, people watching her in the church. Maybe she would be wearing a new suit, something she might have bought in Switzers or Brown Thomas's in Dublin, with a hat, perhaps one that had a light veil in front. People would congratulate her when the mass was over as they gathered in front of the cathedral. She wasn't sure what sort of engagement ring she wanted. But something plain. Since Miriam's was so beautiful and dazzling, she did not want her daughter to think that she was competing with her.

She stood on the street for a moment, hearing Jim lock the door from inside. It occurred to her how strangely time moved on the nights when she saw Jim. Just now, as she decided to take the long way around to the Market Square, her altercation with Roderick Wallace and his wife seemed like a long time ago, as did the arrival of the husband and wife demanding that she reopen to serve them. The time she spent with Jim made her feel lighter and happier. When George died, she had resigned herself to being a widow. She sometimes sat up late in the kitchen dreading the prospect of the night ahead, the fitful sleep.

When she had made her way along Castle Street and was at the top of Slaney Street, she realized that she did not want to go home yet. She was enjoying the solitary walk through the deserted town. For all of her life, everyone had known her. There was no mystery. And now, should a car pass or a lone stroller appear, they would have no idea where she was coming from, what she was thinking about, what plans she had.

It seemed unlikely to have Jim as a partner in subterfuge. He was so plainspoken and straightforward. From the beginning, she had wanted to ask him if these encounters were something that really had begun casually or if he had been thinking about meeting her like this, even planning it, for some time.

She remembered a Sunday in the summer many years ago just before she had married George when she had gone with Jim and Eilis Lacey, who was home from America after her sister died, to the strand at Cush. Jim was in love with Eilis, and George with Nancy. They were not just four friends; they were two couples. Did Jim ever think of her back then? She would like to ask him when he got the idea that they could be together. It would be reassuring if he told her that he had always noticed her, always thought of her. Or if there was a day when he had seen her on the street, or in her car, and had come to view her in a new way.

Even though he was shy, he was also confident, sure of himself. He had a way of standing apart without causing anyone to dislike him.

She walked down Castle Hill and into Castle Street. If Jim was interested in settling down, she wondered why he didn't look for someone younger, someone glamorous. She had put on too much weight since George died. As she passed the Cotton Tree, she resolved that she would go on a diet. She had kept some magazines with articles on how to get her figure back.

In the morning, she heard Miriam letting the decorators in, and then the sound of Gerard's voice as he made some joke with them. By the time she got up, Miriam had left for work and Gerard must have gone out somewhere.

Because they expected that many people would call with presents in the weeks before Miriam's wedding, and since the main room over the chip shop had become shabby, then it needed to be redecorated. Miriam and Laura, her younger daughter, had insisted that every single item of furniture in the room be thrown out. And instead of wallpaper, they said, the room should be painted. And instead of a patterned carpet, there should be a simple gray one.

"Everything must go," Laura had said.

"Even the television?" Nancy asked.

"Especially the television and the awful stand it's on," Miriam had replied.

"We have had to live for years with the place half falling down," Laura said.

"It wasn't half falling down."

"And the smell from the burgers and the onion rings gets into my wardrobe and into my clothes. I swear it's in my shoes."

"It pays the bills."

"Great," Miriam said. "Then it can pay for a van-load of nice new furniture that we've seen in Arnotts. And the walls are going to be painted white, or a sort of off-white."

"And we bought prints that we are going to have framed," Laura added. "And the windows are going to be cleaned for once. And we've found an air extractor for the shop that might actually work."

"You've everything planned," Nancy said.

No matter what day it was, there was always something to be done in the chip shop. Once she and Jim were married, she thought, Gerard could collect orders, deal with invoices and go to the bank. At the weekend, he was always by her side in the chip shop as well as a girl called Brudge Foley, whose mother had been in school with Nancy. She worked in the shop on Friday, Saturday and Sunday nights. On Saturdays, they stayed open until two o'clock in the morning, although Nancy had agreed with her neighbors that they would close at one.

She would love to move out of the town to a place where people could not see her every time she came out of her own door. Helena Hennessy across the Square had moved to a nice bungalow near Davidstown. It was she who had let Nancy know that there was a site for sale at Lucas Park.

Nancy had almost put in a bid for that site, but then realized that she could not do so without consulting Jim. She had not even mentioned her plan that they would live outside the town, leaving the house in the Market Square to Gerard and perhaps renting out the floors over Jim's pub. It would be more private for them, she thought; sitting in a garden in the summer would be like something out of a dream.

What she loved doing most now in the morning was making tea and toast and fetching the artist's sketchbook that she had bought in Dublin with some rulers and plastic triangles and T-shapes and colored pencils, and making a plan to scale of the house she hoped to build.

Since Miriam and her husband were going to live in Wexford, a half hour's drive away, and Gerard would also be living locally, she would have to think about having a house where future grandchildren could come regularly. She made space in the plan for a big kitchen where she could cook while the children watched television.

When the doorbell rang, she looked at the clock and saw that it was almost eleven thirty. She had become lost in measurements and drawings. The morning was practically gone. There were several deliveries due and she went downstairs in the expectation of seeing one of her usual suppliers. Instead, there was a woman at the door who broke into a laugh when she saw her.

"I hope you don't mind me calling like this."

The voice was unmistakably that of Eilis Lacey. And when Eilis lowered her gaze and lifted it again, Nancy saw that she had not changed. Her face had become thinner and she seemed taller. She was more composed. That was all.

"Come in! Come in!"

She explained about the decorators, telling Eilis also about the wedding.

"It seems like yesterday, or maybe it doesn't, when you were at my wedding. And now Miriam is getting married. I wasn't expecting it when she got engaged. They both have jobs in Wexford. They are very sensible. I wouldn't be surprised if they'd signed up for a pension scheme already."

They had ascended the stairs and were standing outside the door of the living room. Nancy was worried that she was talking too much. She felt as though she had to explain herself to Eilis. When she realized that, really, she didn't, she laughed. But the laugh was too loud. She led her visitor into the kitchen at the back of the house, quickly putting the sketchbook and the ruler and the pencils away.

"And how long are you home for?" she asked when they were sitting at the kitchen table. She looked at Eilis's arms, bare in her short-sleeved dress, and observed how smooth the skin was. And then she noticed her slim wrists and her manicured fingernails. She studied her face again: Eilis did not seem younger than her years, but fresh and unworn nonetheless. Her eyes were bright; there were very few wrinkles on her neck. Nancy was examining her so closely that she realized she had not been listening. She had to ask Eilis again how long she was staying.

"I'll probably go back at the end of August."

"You'll be here for the wedding, then. Miriam's wedding is next month. It would be so great if you could come!"

They spoke for a while about their children. For a moment, Nancy was going to ask Eilis about the man she had married in America, but then decided to wait and see if Eilis would bring up his name. She thought it strange that her friend did not mention him.

"How is your mother?" Nancy asked.

"She speaks her mind much more than before. It takes getting used to. Maybe it's a good sign. I don't know."

In asking after Mrs. Lacey, Nancy had thought Eilis would say that her mother was as well as could be expected for a woman of eighty, or some sort of customary answer. She was surprised by the tone of exasperation in her reply.

They spoke of teachers they remembered and dances they had attended. But they did not refer to the summer Eilis had returned when she had been two years in America, the summer when it was clear to everyone how much in love she and Jim Farrell were, the summer that ended when Eilis returned without warning to America. Jim told no one what had transpired, and Eilis's mother, it was said, did not appear in the street until after Christmas that year. But Nancy had finally found out that Eilis had been married all along, she actually had a husband in Brooklyn. She had told no one, not even her own mother.

When she discovered the truth, Nancy went through every encounter she'd had with Eilis that summer. She recalled Eilis at her wedding, with Jim as her partner, Jim who believed he had found the love of his life, encouraged by Nancy and George to propose marriage to Eilis before she went back to America.

Nancy was pregnant, she remembered, when she met Mrs. Lacey for the first time after Eilis's departure. She was buying a newspaper in Godfrey's close to the supermarket when Mrs. Lacey came in. Because the interior of the shop was dark, Nancy thought she could pretend that she had not seen her.

"Are you avoiding me, Nancy Sheridan?" Mrs. Lacey had asked. "Is the whole town still avoiding me?"

"Oh God, I didn't see you, Mrs. Lacey."

"Well, I saw you, Nancy. And maybe the next time we meet you can work out a way of seeing me, too."

She walked out of Godfrey's with an air of grievance.

Eilis was looking at her now, puzzled.

"Nancy, you're not listening to me!"

"What did you say?"

"I said you must be excited about the wedding, but you are miles away."

"I am excited," she said. "When George died, the only thing that kept me going was the children. Seeing Miriam happy and settled is a great relief. And Laura is going to be a solicitor."

COLM TÓIBÍN

Eilis's dress, she thought, was cotton, but it was a heavier cotton than she had ever seen before, and the pale yellow color was new to her as well, but the strangest part of it was the waist, how the waist was held in by a belt in the same cotton and the same color. She was tempted to ask Eilis what her waist measurement was and how she managed to keep her figure.

"What are you thinking about?" Eilis asked.

"I was trying to stop myself asking you how you keep your figure."

"I have two sisters-in-law and they spend their lives going on diets. If I put on an ounce, they notice."

"I really need to lose weight before the wedding," Nancy said. "But it's only five weeks away now. I should have started in the New Year. Can you really come to the wedding?"

"I would love to."

"The reception is in Whites Barn. I hope it will be a great day."

Nancy told her then about the chip shop, surprised that Eilis's mother did not seem to have mentioned it, and about Gerard's interest in taking over the business and perhaps opening another shop in Wexford or Gorey, or maybe Courtown in the summer. Eilis, in turn, asked her about the best place to buy a new fridge and washing machine and cooker for her mother's house.

"She hasn't done a single thing to the kitchen."

As she was getting ready to leave, Eilis seemed to hesitate for a moment before she asked, "How is Jim Farrell?"

"Oh, he's fine, fine."

"I mean, did he ever . . . ?" She stopped for a second.

"Marry? No, he didn't."

Eilis nodded and looked thoughtful.

"But he's doing a strong line with someone in Dublin," Nancy said. "Or so I believe. He's keeping it quiet, but it's hard to keep anything to yourself down here."

Eilis indicated that she was well aware of that.

Nancy wondered why she had just made up this story about Jim. It would have been better just to have said he wasn't married.

When Eilis had gone, Nancy felt a sudden resentment against her for how she had treated them all, never giving them any explanation of why she had to go back to America, fooling them for that whole summer.

She went back to the kitchen and noticed, as though for the first time, how shabby it looked. All the Formica was chipped and there were dirty plates and utensils on the draining board. The window needed to be cleaned.

Nancy took the plates and busily set about washing them as though that would make any difference. She wished that Eilis had come back in a year or two after she and Jim were married. She would like Eilis to visit her in her new bungalow, sit with her in the bright kitchen she was dreaming about.

It occurred to her then that she should not have asked Eilis to the wedding without consulting Jim. She had been so flustered at Eilis's appearance at her door that she had said too much, too quickly. She thought she should not tell Jim immediately; instead, she would allude casually to Eilis's visit and then judge his response. She tried to think where she might seat Eilis. She must look at the table plan again. There would be many at the wedding who would remember Eilis Lacey and want to see her. She would stand out. Everyone would notice how well she looked, and how glamorous. Nancy was sure of that.

She caught a glimpse of herself in the mirror on the landing. In the future, she resolved, she should make an effort to dress more carefully during the day, not just put on anything she found in the wardrobe that still fitted her. Eilis must have observed how badly dressed she was and the pair of old house slippers she had on. She would go upstairs now and put on something decent.

II

Eilis was in the kitchen with her mother when the deliveries came. Martin, her brother, must have been doing something in the hallway, because he was the one who answered the door. The two deliverymen had already unloaded the fridge, the washing machine and the cooker from the van. When Eilis went to the door, she observed some of the neighbors watching the scene closely.

"The plumber is on his way," one of the men said. "So we'll need to find a place in the kitchen for the washing machine. The man for the cooker will be here tomorrow. He's in Bunclody today."

It was only when she saw the sheer size of the deliveries that it occurred to Eilis what a mistake it had been not to consult her mother before ordering these items. In her excitement at being home, in an urge to do something special for her mother, she had imagined this as a surprise. She could not believe that nothing at all had changed in the house since she had left more than twenty years earlier—the same wallpaper, the same curtains and lino and worn rugs, the same blankets and eiderdowns on the beds, and still no fridge in the kitchen and an old cooker that depended on bottled gas, and no washing machine. Her mother had the sheets and towels done at the laundry but washed her own clothes by hand, using a washboard that could, Eilis thought, more usefully be put into a museum or maybe just thrown out.

Her mother shouted from the kitchen.

"What is happening out there?"

One of the deliverymen walked down the hallway to the kitchen, followed by Eilis.

"We can drag the old cooker out now," he said. "It will just take one second."

"One second to what?" her mother asked.

The man ignored her and called to his colleague.

"Best to put the stuff where it's going to stay, so they won't have the trouble of moving it again. It would be great if that plumber came sooner rather than later."

"What plumber?" her mother asked and stood up.

"To connect the washing machine."

"I didn't order any washing machine."

"I did," Eilis said. "I ordered some things for the kitchen."

"What things?"

"What they are delivering now."

Her mother walked slowly along the hallway to the front door, with Eilis following. Martin was standing beside one of the deliverymen.

"Now, what might I ask is all this?"

"Well," the man said, "this is a fridge, that is a cooker and this here is the washing machine. We are waiting for the plumber."

"Then you are at the wrong house."

"Mammy," Eilis asked, "I wonder if I could speak to you inside for a minute?"

In the sitting room, she explained to her mother what she had done.

"Without consulting me?"

"I thought it would be a surprise. It would be really lovely to have a fridge and a washing machine."

"If I had wanted them, I would have ordered them myself. I was not sitting here waiting for you to come home and put everything right. And I was lucky, because I would have waited a long time."

74

"They've already unloaded everything and it's paid for."

"Is there a law saying that they can't take it back to where they found it?"

Before she had left for Ireland, Frank, her brother-in-law, had phoned her at work and arranged to meet her in the parking lot of a shopping mall. He had chosen a quiet place for them to talk.

"If you're asking me," Eilis said, "to see things from Tony's point of view, or your mother's point of view, then you're wasting your time."

"I wanted to get an address for you so I could keep in touch."

"Are you the one designated to keep me informed?"

"No one asked me to inform you of anything. But there is something else."

"What?"

He handed her a thick envelope filled with twenty-dollar bills.

"What is this for?"

"For you. For your trip."

"How much is here?"

"Two thousand."

"Why would I need that amount of money?"

"My grandfather went back to Italy once. He went to implore his wife to come to America, try to make the trip one more time. He barely had the fare. But when he arrived in the village, both his family and my grandmother's family held big parties in his honor. And then the next day they showed him the fields they had chosen to build new houses in. It was all ready to go. They presumed he had come home loaded. When he spoke, it sounded like dollars to them. When they discovered he was broke they had no further use for him."

"What has this to do with me?"

"I thought it would be best for you to have some money in case you need it. Maybe go on a road trip with Rosella and Larry, rent a car or buy a present for your mother. You have always been kind to me. It's the least I can do. No strings attached. It's not a loan. I don't want it back."

"But you have already been so generous, paying for Rosella's tuition."

"It's a hard time for you. This is just to help you out."

Eilis could see that her mother was trying to decide what to do. For a second, she wondered if there was one more thing she might say. While her mother moved slowly and seemed to be in pain some of the time, especially when going up the stairs, or when she had to stand up, she had developed a strength and determination when she spoke that had not been there before. She used to be gentler and easier.

Her mother returned to where the deliverymen were standing. The fridge, oven and washing machine were blocking the hallway. Martin was still talking to one of the neighbors. When she heard his high-pitched laughter, Eilis wished that her brother would move inside the house.

"Is all this paid for?" her mother asked the deliverymen.

"Yes, paid for and delivered."

"Well, I'm not sure where I want it or what I want to do with it, so if you just leave it in the hallway for the moment and let me think about it. And maybe you can tell the plumber that he won't be needed?"

"He's on his way, ma'am."

"Well, I'll tell him when he comes."

When they had gone, Eilis sat in the kitchen with her mother and Martin.

"And who might pay the electricity bill for all these machines?" her mother asked. "They would eat electricity. Eat it! The fridge would be on day and night running up bills. When you are back sunning yourself in America, I will be here paying bills."

While her mother had become more assertive, Martin appeared nervous, jittery, unable to stay still. He had an old Morris Minor that often took time to start. When he came home from England first, with compensation money he had been awarded for a fall at work, he had bought a small house in bad repair at the edge of the cliff at Cush, ten miles away. Every day he seemed to move between there and his mother's house. If he was in the town during the day, he went out regularly to take a stroll or visit a pub. If he was there at night and sober, he could, in the middle of a sentence, stand up and announce his departure, made all the more dramatic by the dry sound of the ignition of the car failing, and then the engine eventually starting, and the noise of loud revving.

Eilis asked him, when she found him alone, if he agreed that their mother had changed.

"She's only like that with you," he said.

"Why?"

"Who can say?"

Slowly, she understood why her mother did not miss having a fridge in the house. It meant that she had to venture out often to buy groceries, getting some things in Hayes's in Court Street and others in Miss O'Connor's opposite, or going farther to Jack Doyle the butcher's, or Billy Kervick's in the Market Square. Now she insisted that Eilis come with her, both of them struggling to get past the bulky objects in the hallway. Eilis had tried to convince her mother that she should at least agree to have the washing machine installed, but her mother told her that she needed time to think about it.

"When I decide what to do, I will let everyone know."

For every trip to the shops, her mother dressed up, wearing her good shoes and putting on a hat and then standing in front of the mirror as she inserted an old-fashioned hatpin. She demanded that Eilis, too, should look her best. And then, on the street or in shops, people remarked on how well Eilis looked or said how glad they were to see her, and her mother kept the conversation going for as long as she could.

"We'll have met the whole town before long," Eilis said. "And they look at me like I'd come from the moon."

"It's nice to see them all so charming," her mother said.

When she informed her mother that Nancy had invited her to Miriam's wedding, her mother was not impressed.

"God knows who will be there."

"What do you mean?"

"Every type of latchico is to be found outside that Nancy's chip shop. They drink first in any pub that will have them and then they come to Nancy for fish and chips, and the next thing is a pool of vomit, or worse, if there is worse."

"I'm sure that's not Nancy's fault."

"She turns no one away. She likes money. Speaking of which, there is something I would like to show you."

Her mother left the room. Eilis could hear her slowly ascending the stairs. Tomorrow, she thought, she would think of subjects that would please her mother more.

Her mother returned with a bankbook that she opened and showed to Eilis. In her deposit account, there was a large sum of money, much more than Mrs. Lacey would have been able to save from her meager pension.

"I don't need to be rescued from poverty," her mother said.

"But where did this money come from?" Eilis asked.

"It's mine. It's nobody else's."

"But how did you . . . ?" Eilis was unsure how to finish the question.

"Jack, your brother, bought this house from me. I made an arrangement with him when he was home from Birmingham two years ago that the house is mine to live in the rest of my life and then Martin can live here until it is his time to meet his maker. And then it will belong to Jack or his family. It is an arrangement that suits everyone, since Jack has plenty of money. When business is good, he has more than fifty men working for him. And I thought I would let you know for two reasons. One, so that you don't think I am in need of charity. And two, so that you don't expect a share in this house when I have passed on to my reward."

"I didn't expect anything."

"So we're happy, then."

The days were hard to fill. The car Eilis had rented at Dublin Airport on arrival, using some of Frank's money, was parked outside the door. When she suggested going for a drive, her mother demurred.

"Getting into a car might be possible, but I know I would never manage to get out of one. And what would we do then? I would be a holy show."

At first, Eilis found the conversation at the table between her mother and Martin intriguing. There was a woman called Betty Parle living in St. John's Villas who worked in an insurance company on Main Street. Every morning she passed the house in Court Street. Usually she carried, with some style, an elegant umbrella. Her clothes, too, were elegant. Her hair was dyed pitch black and there was a cake of makeup on her face.

"Do you know what I heard?" Eilis's mother asked. "I heard that Betty Parle wrote to the pope. Oh, it was after her mother died and all the family had left the town and she was on her own, with just her umbrellas and her costumes and her makeup and that dyed hair of hers, and she was lonely, as you would be, and sad. But what did she do then? She wrote to the pope! And told him all about herself. Can you imagine them all in the Vatican on a busy day? They would wake the pope early. Get up, there's a letter from Betty Parle."

When her mother told the story a second time and then a third, with Martin laughing each time, egging her on, Eilis realized that he had heard it many times before.

By the end of the first week, most of the stories her mother told had been repeated more than once. Often, however, she found new people in the town to discuss and denigrate.

"Josie Cahill stopped to talk when she was passing, which she doesn't usually do. And I wondered why until I realized it was to boast. Her son, the second boy, is studying to be a doctor. He has finished his first year. None of those Cahills had a brain in their heads. I almost said it to Josie straight. And none of her side either. I remember her father delivering coal and there's a brother of hers who used to walk greyhounds."

"Isn't it great that the boy is going to be a doctor?" Eilis asked.

"But no one in the town will go to him if he opens up here."

"Maybe he'll practice somewhere else?"

"I hope so. I wouldn't like one of the Cahills prodding at me."

Her mother rose at eight and had the breakfast things cleared away by nine. At one thirty they had the main meal of the day. When it was over, there really was nothing to do. Eilis did not feel that she could go for a drive on her own, or even a walk. She had come home to be with her mother.

One evening when her mother had gone to bed early, as she often did, Eilis heard Martin arriving. She had learned that he remained sober once there was a chance that he might drive anywhere. The previous year, her mother had told her, he had been stopped by the Guards and banned from driving for six months.

This evening he seemed less agitated than usual and he agreed to have a cup of tea with her. When she asked him about the pubs in the town, it was a way of making conversation, but as he went through his favorite haunts, she realized that she would soon be able to ask him about Jim Farrell and make the question seem natural.

"My mother says you broke his heart," Martin said.

"My mother says a lot of things."

"He's doing a good business in the pub. He opened up a big space in the back and brought in a young fellow to be a barman to add to Shane Nolan. I have never met anyone who dislikes Shane Nolan."

"And Jim Farrell himself?"

"He has all the old-timers and then the younger crowd in the big back room. It's roaring in there sometimes. Standing room only at the weekends in the back. I go there midweek."

"I hear Jim has a girlfriend in Dublin," Eilis said.

"He goes to Dublin on a Thursday but he's back by nine, and he works all weekend, so I don't know when he'd have time to see her."

"You follow everyone."

"That's what I like about here. I know them all."

If their mother had been present, Eilis thought, she would not have been able to ask so many questions about Jim Farrell. She deliberately left silence now in case Martin had more to say about him, but he soon set off for Cush without telling her anything else.

Her mother did not mention Jim. Nor had she been eager to hear news of Tony and his family, and even Eilis's efforts to talk about Rosella and Larry had not met with enthusiasm. In letters, she had told her mother about Mr. Dakessian's garage, but when she had referred to it on one of her first days home her mother did not appear to know what she was talking about. Over time, she hoped, it would change, but she realized that, for the moment, her mother did not want to hear about her life in America.

When her mother showed her photographs of Jack's big house on the outskirts of Birmingham and then his wife and children at various celebrations, she wondered what had happened to all the photographs that she had sent of Rosella and Larry. Her mother crossed the room to find another album of photos but they were of Pat and his family in a more modest house in Bolton. For the rest of the day, the lives of Pat and Jack and their families in England became her mother's main subject. Eilis learned about the different schools her nephews and nieces attended, the holidays they went on, the fact that Jack's eldest daughter was in university studying science and Pat's eldest boy was a wizard at maths.

She should not, Eilis realized now, have come home so early. She tried to remember how the decision to come a month before the children had been made. It was partly to get away from Tony and his mother before she found out anything more about the plans they had. But she had not put enough thought into what the days would actually be like, how long the afternoons and evenings would be, and how little there would be to do.

On her first day, she wrote a brief note to Tony to let him know that she had arrived safely. She did not tell him about the rented car in case he would worry about the cost of it. She tried not to be too cold, but she did not say that she missed him.

A few days later, it was easier to write at greater length to Rosella and to Larry, and also to Frank. As she was writing, she imagined an ordinary morning in their cul-de-sac at Lindenhurst. On a summer's day like this, she would wake earlier than the others and often would have finished her breakfast before anyone else got up. How easy it would be now to wake in that house! And then be greeted by Mr. Dakessian with an account of some history book he had been reading and meeting the regular customers and making calls to have a spare part delivered as speedily as possible. And all the time aware that there were rooms waiting for her—her bedroom, the kitchen, the living room—and noises she was familiar with—Larry playing with his cousins or Tony's car reversing into the driveway or Tony's voice as he came in the door.

She wondered if she would ever have all this back again. She found herself wishing that a letter would come from Tony or his mother or Frank to say that they had begun to see things from her point of view, or that the man had returned to say that he and his wife had decided that they would raise the child themselves.

She wished that Rosella and Larry were coming now and not weeks away. She wished her mother would let her talk about them.

But she barely let herself think about what she wished for most—that she were not in her mother's living room trying to write a letter, hearing her mother move with difficulty in the room upstairs, but rather at home, waking to the soft light of early summer that appeared through the curtains of her bedroom on Long Island.

In her letter, she told Rosella about Miriam's wedding, adding that she was hoping to buy a new dress or even an outfit to wear if she could find something she liked. She wrote that her mother never missed the six o'clock news on television and complained, when it came to the nine o'clock news, if the headlines had not changed. She was going to write about Martin and his constant moving between the house on the cliff and his mother's house in the town, but she decided she would save that for her letter to Larry. To Frank she hinted at how strange she felt in a house that had once been so familiar. She did not mention Tony in any of the letters. She did not want to say anything about Tony.

To none of them did she say that she, her mother and Martin had to edge past the fridge, the cooker and the washing machine, still in their packaging in the hallway. The longer they remained there, she believed, the more impossible it would be to return them.

In the morning when she woke, the room was in shadow. She tried to think what was making her dread the day to come and then she realized that it was nothing. She was in her mother's house, that was all. It occurred to her, as she lay there, that she would like to change the bed. She was sure that the mattress was the same one she had slept on more than twenty years earlier. Now it was thinner and it sagged in the middle. The sheets had a strange satiny, waxy feel to them and the blankets slipped off them through the night.

She wondered where Rosella and Larry were going to sleep when they came. She herself was in the room she used to share with Rose. Martin slept in the room he had once shared with his brothers. There was a spare room in the attic that could be reached by a ladder but that had never been used. There was no other bedroom, except her mother's.

One evening after the nine o'clock news, she raised the subject of her mattress and the sheets. She did not expect her mother to respond warmly, but she thought it best to mention it now and perhaps soften her mother up on the subject before Rosella and Larry came.

"And what's wrong with it all?" her mother asked.

"It might be nice to get some new mattresses and bedclothes. It might be nice for Rosella to sleep in a new bed in my room and maybe we could get a bed for Larry and put it in the attic room."

"Why can't he sleep in one of the beds in Martin's room?"

"Martin comes in and out at all times of the day and night."

"Have your children asked for new beds?"

"No, they've said nothing."

"So, why don't we leave things as they are?"

Eilis did not reply.

"I notice," her mother went on, "that people pamper their children nowadays. They want a new this and a new that. And often it's not actually the children who do the wanting, it's the parents. They don't spend enough time with their children because they are out working and gallivanting, and then they compensate by buying luxuries that no one needs. I heard someone talking about it on the radio."

Eilis decided to change the subject as quickly as she could.

"You must be looking forward to your birthday," she said. "And Jack and Pat coming. We'll all be here."

"I don't think about it at all. I would like no fuss."

"Well, that's why Rosella and Larry are coming and that's why Jack and Pat are coming, and Martin says some of their children might even come too."

"You must remember the old woman who used to live in number forty-seven," her mother began. A look of satisfaction came over her face.

"Miss Jane Hegarty, she was always called," her mother continued. "She was very noble and kept a beautiful house. Miss Jane Hegarty was a very polite, well-spoken person. When she got older, a priest, a friend of the family's, used to visit once a week to give her the sacraments. And for a while a nurse came, but she took against the nurse. And then it was discovered that she was going to be a hundred years old. And we all got invited to a party in her house. I went only because I believed she had invited me. How could I not go? But the people who organized the party were a low crowd. Not all of them, mind. But enough of them to make it into a free-for-all. Word spread that there was drink to be had. Louts descended on her house. And of course they not only fed themselves lashings of vodka, if it wasn't gin, but they fed Miss Jane too, and in her innocence, Miss Jane drank it, topped up with lemonade. And they drank and she drank until someone put her to bed. And she died the next day. She died of the party. Vodka and good cheer one day and a coffin and a hearse the next. And if anyone thinks this is happening on my birthday, they can think again. I will bar the door."

"It will be just for family," Eilis said.

"Families are often the worst," her mother replied.

Eilis stood up.

"I think I might go for a stroll," she said.

"At this time of night?"

She thought of going somewhere in the car, maybe drive to Wexford and take a walk along the main street there. It was a warm night and there was still a glow in the western sky. She decided to walk down to the Market Square and perhaps down Slaney Street to the river in the last light. She would decide then what she would do. In the morning she might ask Martin to give her a phone number for Jack or Pat and ask them for advice. But they could easily reply that it was her own fault for ordering the fridge and the oven and the washing machine without consulting her mother and it was her own fault for staying away for so long. And they could add that, since their mother was old and since her life had not been easy, then the least Eilis could do was not complain about her.

She passed Aspell's and was tempted for a moment to go down Church Street but instead she continued along Rafter Street towards the Square. Maybe, she thought, she should work out a way of listening to her mother, enjoy her stories even if she told them more than once. It must be hard to be eighty and a widow of thirty years.

As she wondered about how she might set about persuading her mother to come for a drive with her some day, she saw a figure standing at the door of Jim Farrell's pub. Instantly, she realized that it was Jim himself. She did not know if he had seen her. He was looking in the other direction but he might have averted his gaze precisely because he had spotted her coming towards him on the opposite footpath.

Even though she put her head down, she was sure that he would not be able to avoid noticing her. There was no one else on the street. If she were to turn her head and glance across, their eyes would connect. She would not know what to do and she could not imagine how he might respond. Maybe he had not actually recognized her. But if he had seen her, they could hardly just nod to each other, or say a polite hello.

The best thing would be for her not to look across at him again and to proceed to the Square without glancing behind. An encounter like this was always bound to happen. She had never imagined, however, that if she were to see him, she would actually feel an urge, as she did now, to approach him, speak to him, hear his voice. But it could not be done.

She would have to continue on her walk through the town as if he were not standing watching her from the door of his pub.

III

Jim wanted to call in her direction, loud enough to make her look over so that he could be sure it really was Eilis Lacey. He was almost certain that she had seen him because she had suddenly turned her face away as if to avoid his gaze, but not before he had caught a glimpse of her.

People who knew the story of his time with her came to the bar regularly. Surely someone might have told him she was back! He knew her mother; he often saw Mrs. Lacey on the street. In the first while after Eilis's sudden departure, they had barely acknowledged each other, but nowadays she gave him a friendly smile when they met. And Martin, of course. Martin liked coming into the bar early in the evening. But he never got into a sustained conversation with anyone and he never stayed for long. Jim could not think when he had last had a conversation with Martin.

Shane Nolan was behind the bar. Andy, the new young barman, was collecting glasses. Since this was Friday, it was busy. For the last hour of opening, Jim worked hard, wishing, as he always did, that there was some way of stopping customers from ordering rounds of drinks in the five minutes before closing time. Soon he would have to stand over them demanding they finish up, or he would have to restrain young Andy from snatching half-drunk pint glasses from them.

Andy was impatient and often cheeky, and Jim found him difficult to get used to. He would not work on Saturdays and Sundays
until the evening, as he was involved in rugby and soccer as well
as hurling.

"He brings a whole new crowd into the bar," Shane said. "We
can't stop him playing."

"I don't mind him asking me for time off," Jim said, "but I don't
like him telling me, like he was the one in charge."

"You can trust him with keys and cash and that's the main
thing about him."

"How do you know?"

"Do you think I would have recommended him if it wasn't true?"

"But how do you know?"

"I know all belonging to him in the Duffry Gate."

The pub Jim had taken over from his father had been a quiet place,
with a regular trade, busy at the weekends. When women began to
go out to bars in the late 1960s, a few places in the town had added
a lounge, putting in a carpet and better seats. Jim had thought
about this for a while, even had plans drawn up. And then he didn't
do it. The establishment thus remained untouched since the 1920s
when his grandfather had bought it. Some of the woodwork, he
thought, might be even older.

Slowly, the clientele changed. A few teachers began to drink in
his pub during the week and then it became their local. On weekend nights, Jim had to reserve space for his regular customers near
the front door. Within a short time, the more recent arrivals knew
that they must not invade this territory, no matter how crowded
the bar was.

Now, since Jim had opened up a space at the back that had
been unused for years, young sports enthusiasts who were friends
of Andy's had become regulars. Jim took Thursdays off, driving

to Dublin in the morning but always back by nine for the last few hours of business.

On the night he saw Eilis Lacey, when the last customers had gone and Shane had left early, Jim decided to ask Andy to clean the place and lock up.

Jim went upstairs and sat in an armchair in the living room. He made a sandwich with ingredients that Colette, Shane's wife, had left for him. He had noticed that she did not come to the pub as much as she used to. She still made him a cake of brown bread every few days but gave it to Shane to take to him.

Before, Colette would appear, if she could, at a time when Jim was upstairs. He would hear her shouting his name, having opened the door from the bar that led into the hallway. She would have tea with him, always pretending that she was actually on her way somewhere else and could not stay for long.

She was, he saw, like a player moving up a field with a ball, waiting for an opportunity, as she moved the conversation from the ordinary, from inquiries about Andy's mother, who had taken over the cleaning of the house, to news about her children or people in the town, to talk about Jim himself, until that led, inevitably, to a discussion of his bachelor status. She wanted to encourage him to find a wife.

"Who would have me? I'm nearly fifty years old. And how would I meet anyone? I'm in the bar until midnight five or six nights a week."

"There are plenty of women who would be delighted to meet you."

"Name one of them!"

He stood up and stretched, making clear to her that she should go.

"You see, there isn't anyone," he said.

He liked how she made no reference to his failed love affairs, the ones she knew about. She tried to give the impression that she was just making conversation. He would leave it to her to decide when this topic should be mentioned no more.

The next time she brought up the subject even before he had asked her to sit down.

"I've thought of someone," she said. "You are not to laugh. And you are not to dismiss it out of hand. I have thought about it and I have a name."

"Have you discussed this with Shane?"

"Certainly not! I never tell him anything."

"Tell me the name, then."

"I'm afraid if I say it, it won't sound right. I'd prefer to write it down."

"I'll fetch you a piece of paper. Just to get this over with."

"I already have it written down. It's here."

She handed him a piece of paper, which he unfolded.

When he saw the name, he looked sharply at her.

"I've known her all my life."

"I was sure you were going to say that."

"We had every chance, but neither of us had any interest."

"You're older now, and wiser, and so is she."

"Why would she even consider it?"

"Jim Farrell, look at you! You are handsome, you are kind, you are hardworking. She is a good person and you are lonely."

"Is that enough?"

"I have never heard anyone say a bad word about her. Her children are grown up. She really is lovely, Jim. She has a lovely smile. And she's had a very hard time."

"And you want me to marry her? Does Shane know this?"

"I told you already he doesn't. No one knows. I just think you're sad here on your own. If you sit here waiting, you'll never find the right person."

"Is Nancy Sheridan the right person?"

"She's perfect."

Colette did him the favor of not mentioning Nancy's name again. And he put no thought into it for a while.

He'd found himself thinking about some of the young women who had recently begun to come to the bar, teachers and bank clerks. He worried that he looked at them too closely when they came to order a drink. Now he began to think about Nancy Sheridan. Once, years before, the time Eilis Lacey was home, they had gone for a swim on a Sunday. He remembered Nancy changing into her swimsuit, even though most of his attention was on Eilis. He had an image of her starting to dry herself with a towel, the goose pimples on her skin, and her pulling down the straps of the bathing suit.

She was older now. She had put on weight. He thought about what it would be like if she was in the room, slowly undressing, and then coming to bed, turning towards him as she pulled the sheets around them.

At night when he had finished work, he imagined her in the living room waiting for him, everything tidy, the curtains drawn, the fire lighting.

What satisfied him was the knowledge that this was not a mad idea. The young women who came to the bar had no interest in him and never would have. But it was possible that Colette was right, that, if it came into Nancy Sheridan's mind that he was thinking about her, it was not impossible that she would respond favorably.

A few times, when he saw Nancy on the street, he stayed talking to her for longer than ever before. She knew that he was on her side against the residents of the Market Square about the chip shop and that he had spoken in support of her at the Credit Union when she had sought a loan. So she had, he noticed, felt free one day when they met on the corner of Rafter Street and the Square to tell him how hard it was to deal with some of the drunken customers.

"You ask them if they want salt and vinegar and when they say yes, you give them what they asked for, and then, when it's too late,

they announce that they didn't want salt and vinegar at all. And
then they call you names you wouldn't believe. And they won't
pay. And they won't go home."

As he listened, he realized that there was one thing he could say
now, and if he said it, then it might be noted by her. He wondered
whether, if it had been any other day, he might have held back, but
by that time he had already spoken.

"If you ever needed any help at night with troublesome customers, you could give me a shout in the bar. Even if it's late, I'm
usually up. I'd be down right away."

He saw her taking this in. For a second, it seemed as though she
was ready to dismiss it as a casual gesture of goodwill, but then she
joined her hands and lifted them to her mouth. She looked worried.

"I often wish there was someone I could call."

He felt as though he might never get another chance to make
himself clear.

"I often think of you there on your own," he began, and then,
more firmly, said, "I'd be down like a flash if you phoned."

She didn't blush, or smile, or look puzzled.

"I will phone you then," she had said.

He switched on one of the lamps now in the large living room
whose windows faced onto the street. He was glad that he had left
Andy to clean up. As soon as he had seen her on the street, he had
wanted to come up here and be on his own. He was sure it was Eilis
Lacey. If he had spotted her one or two seconds earlier, they could
have locked eyes. He could not think what might have happened
then. Would he have crossed the street and spoken to her?

She had often come into his mind since he had seen her last, and
that was more than twenty years ago. And he wanted to believe
that she must have thought of him, too. Perhaps not every day,
but surely sometimes.

In the weeks after she had left him a note to say that she was going back to Brooklyn and was setting out that very morning, he had expected to hear from her. A longer letter maybe, or a phone call. He had even imagined in the days after her abrupt departure that she might have turned back at some point before embarking, that she was waiting in some hotel in Dublin or Cork or Liverpool and that she would appear in Enniscorthy and say she was sorry about the note, she had panicked, but she was here again and they could be together.

He felt that if only he had guessed she was leaving he would have been able to convince her to stay. He went over the things he might have said. He would try not to be too insistent in case that put her off. But he was sure that he would have been able to convince her that she would be happier with him even if they had to leave the town or even the country. But he never got that chance. He never heard from her again.

And then, about a month after Eilis's departure, Jim's mother, on passing the shop owned by a woman known as Nettles Kelly, found Miss Kelly herself standing at the door. Miss Kelly informed Mrs. Farrell that her cousin Madge Kehoe in Brooklyn knew for a fact that Eilis Lacey was a married woman.

"She is married to an Italian, if you don't mind. I don't know where she met him, but I know where she married him, in some hall in Brooklyn. And then she came home, all rigged out like an American. And I believe that her benighted mother didn't even know she was married. Poor Jim. That is all I have to say. But I hope he has learned his lesson now."

When his mother appeared, Jim thought that something must have happened to his father. Even though he was alone behind the bar, she demanded that he come upstairs with her to hear what she had to say.

"Imagine doing that!" Jim's mother said when she had told him what she had heard from Miss Kelly. "Leading you on, and she a married woman! Well, I'm glad she took herself off."

The idea that Eilis was married made no sense to him. Why did she not say? Why did he know nothing about her life in America? He thought back to an evening on the strand in Curracloe when he had spoken to her about himself in a way that he had never spoken to anyone else. And she had paid attention as though it mattered to her. But it was true, he thought, that she had never told him in any detail what her life was like. Because he had believed that she was going to stay with him, it did not seem important. When she was with him, he was sure, she was not thinking of anyone else. Or was he wrong about that? He could not believe that she had set out to fool him. He wished he could have talked to her, or that she would write to him and he would write back. And then, as the months went by, he realized that she had gone and would not be returning.

In the meantime, rumors spread in the town. Davy Roche, who worked in the bar then, was the first to let him know that he had heard about a big row between Eilis and Jim in the middle of the Market Square one night. Soon his mother came with the same story, to be followed by another in which Eilis had left because her husband had come from America to get her. It was incredible, he thought, that it took time to convince even his mother that there was no truth in any of the stories, except the one in which Eilis had gone back to her husband when Miss Kelly threatened to tell the whole town that she was married. That was all he knew and all he would ever know, he supposed, about what had happened.

It would be difficult to be sure what to say to Eilis if they met. She would have found out from someone that he had never married, that he ran a successful business, that he was still liked and respected in the town. Her mother would have kept her informed if no one else had, or maybe even Martin.

He heard Andy locking up downstairs and went into the kitchen and got a beer from the fridge. Recently, he had decided to stop having a few drinks on his own at the end of the day. It made him morose. But he would have a drink now as he went over in his mind what Eilis had looked like as she passed on the other side of the street.

He hated how the rumors had spread and the relish with which they were recounted to him. Behind the bar, he was a prisoner. Anyone could say what they liked to him. He would never be able to predict when it would come. It could be a lone customer on a bar stool after a few drinks saying in an insinuating tone, "I hear that Lacey one went back to America." On one crowded night, someone he had never seen before, as he was gathering his change from the counter, muttered, "I'd say you're better off without that Eilis Lacey. She was damaged goods to start with."

Eventually, people forgot about it, found other things to gossip about. His parents, by now, were living in Glenbrien in a house his mother had inherited from an old aunt. He had the floors above the pub to himself. His brother Vincent was in Australia and his two sisters were married in Dublin. His mother visited sometimes after Eilis went back to America, but she made matters worse by looking at him sorrowfully and saying that the main rooms over the pub could do with a woman's touch.

"You will find someone else. When I met your father he had been let down like that too. It happens to most people. It is part of life."

He could not take time off from the bar to go to the big dance in Wexford on a Saturday night and he did not like the crowd in the Athenaeum in Enniscorthy. So, the summer after Eilis left, Jim began to drive to Courtown on a Sunday night. It was better not to go with a group. If he wanted to leave, he could slip away. He kept his hair tidy and that summer he wore a good suit and a white shirt and a striped tie. He arrived early and stood at the side watching, knowing that the real crush would not come until the pubs had closed.

He worried that he might look odd standing on his own. He liked some of the women he saw, but they tended to be with a partner, or in company. A few times, he asked a girl to dance, but he did not meet anyone whom he wanted to see again.

He wished he could relax, just enjoy the atmosphere, as others did. He was more than twenty miles away from Enniscorthy. Occasionally he saw someone from home, but most of the time he was a stranger here and that suited him.

Slowly, he got to see that not being with a group really was an impediment to meeting a girl. Crossing the hall at a lull in the music to ask a complete stranger to dance was not as customary as it had been when he had started to go to dances. A few times, a girl turned away as she saw him approaching. A few times also, in exasperation, he left the dance early, drove back to Enniscorthy, happier on his own in the car than standing against a wall in the ballroom in Courtown.

Just as the season was ending, he met Mai Whitney. She was with a group who had come in from the rugby club in Gorey, some of whom he knew. He tried to work out if she was with a boyfriend, but she seemed not to be attached. The problem was how to get her attention. He thought of sidling up in the hope that one of the fellows from the rugby club would introduce him to her, but that would be too forward.

There were only three or four dances left that night. If he didn't make a move soon, the lights would come up and the national anthem would be played and he would still not have met her. She was laughing and talking with two other young women.

"Excuse me," he approached without planning what he was going to say. "I know you're with your friends, but I would like to . . ."

She agreed to dance with him before he could finish. He wondered if she would stay with him for the next set as well, when the lights would go down and the music become slower. In Courtown, as in most places, the last fifteen minutes were devoted to close dancing. It would be easier to talk if the music was quieter.

He wondered what she might say if he offered to drive her home. She lived beyond Coolgreany, she said, and worked in a chemist's shop in Gorey. He got the impression that she did not have her own car. A few times, when he looked, he saw that her friends were watching her. He supposed that she was planning to go home with them. As the evening came to an end, however, he discovered that she presumed he was going to drive her home.

In the car, he liked how she kept the conversation going, asking him about the pub and trying to work out exactly where it was situated in Enniscorthy. Her friends and her two brothers, who had also been at the dance, would definitely know the pub, she said, as they spent time in Enniscorthy, but for the moment she would not tell them anything about him.

"You'll be the mystery man," she said. "It'll drive them mad."

It was arranged that he would collect her at her house the following Sunday and they would go to the dance in Courtown again.

Over the subsequent months, they went to rugby dances in Gorey and Arklow, going as far as Delgany as the winter came in. During the week, when he thought about Mai, he wondered how she might fit in to life running a pub. She would hardly serve behind the counter, but then his mother never did either. On one of the evenings, he told her this as casually as he could so she would know that he would not expect any wife of his to stand behind the counter.

When they were together, he thought of what they would do in the car when the night ended. After a few dates, she agreed that he could pause some distance from the bungalow where she lived with her parents and her brothers so they would have time in the dark.

He suggested that he would collect her some evening and drive her to Enniscorthy to see the pub and the floors above. He watched her taking in the large living room and wondered if he should ask her if she also wanted to see the rooms on the floor above, but since they

97

were bedrooms, he thought he might be moving too quickly. But once they had spent some time together on the sofa, he was on the point of suggesting that she might stay the night and he could drive her to work in the morning. Before he could, however, Mai said that her parents would be worried about her and she would have to go.

Eventually, she did agree to stay over, having taken a Monday morning off work. But in the living room she seemed less friendly than usual. She sat in one of the armchairs while he waited for her to join him on the sofa. He poured more vodka for her.

"Don't think filling up my glass is going to help you," she said.

"Help me?"

"I know what you're thinking."

He was tempted to reply that she was right. But one hour went by and then another. He listened to the story of the family who owned the chemist's shop and their three daughters. She then told him about a cousin of hers brought up on a remote farm near Tinahely. When he patted the space beside him on the sofa to suggest that she might think of moving there to be beside him, she shrugged.

"I don't know what sort of person you think I am."

She slept in the bed beside him wearing her slip. In the morning, when he had to be in the bar to take deliveries, he left her sleeping. Later, when he drove her home, she asked to be let out at a friend's house in Gorey. He realized that she must have told her parents she was staying there.

While he was returning to Enniscorthy, a single moment from the previous evening stayed in his mind. She had come back from the bathroom and said, "I would have that bathroom completely redone." She was not aware how closely he was listening. She did not seem to understand what this sounded like to him. It was its very casualness that made it appear all the more significant. She had let him know that she was imagining this as a place where she would one day live.

Because he worked on Friday and Saturday nights, he could not see her as much as he wanted. It was a pity, he thought, that her parents did not have a phone in their house. Sometimes he called her at work but she was often busy. He asked her if she might agree to come away with him for a week, or even a few days. They could go to Kerry when the days brightened or even think of crossing with the car from Rosslare to Fishguard and going to Cardiff or Bristol, as his parents had once done.

"I'd love a holiday," she said. "But maybe we should think of going to Spain. Somewhere with brilliant nightlife, and everywhere open late. And we could be on the beach in the day. Swims in between cocktails. Maybe we could get a crowd together."

He had no problem with a crowd, as long as he and Mai were sharing a room.

Jim liked the bar at seven or eight o'clock midweek when there were only one or two customers nursing a drink. He would read the newspaper or do nothing at all. If someone wanted to start a conversation, he enjoyed that too, especially with regulars. One evening when the bar was quiet, a young man came in on his own whom Jim had met briefly in Courtown with Mai. He was a friend of her brother's.

"I'm just killing time," he said. "I have to meet someone in a while to get a secondhand television and I'm driving back home so I'd better just have a soda water and lime."

They spoke for a while about the various dance halls.

"We don't see you much anymore," the man said. "How long is it since you and Mai split up?"

Jim stopped himself saying anything in reply. He could easily have told the man that he and Mai had been at a rugby dance in Greystones just a few nights before. And on the way home Mai had responded enthusiastically when he had suggested that she come some Sunday to have tea with his parents.

"She's a right goer, Mai is," the man went on. "She's made us all promise to come with her and the new boyfriend to the dance in Wexford some Saturday. He's from down that way. They go every week. There's a full bar, which is more than you can say for Courtown. I think the days of asking a girl if she'd like a mineral are over. It's gin and tonic or vodka and Britvic. That's the way it's gone now. Did you break it off or did she?"

Jim smiled and shrugged.

"Ah, we both . . ."

He nodded his head in resignation.

"That's the best way," the man said before finishing his soda water and lime and taking his leave.

The following Saturday night, Jim asked Davy Roche if he could look after the bar for the last hour and lock up. Even though the bar was busy, he thought it was best to go early and be in Wexford before half eleven. Someone had told him that it was becoming hard to get into the dance in the old town hall after closing time in the bars.

There was a long line outside. He was the only one who was alone. He looked around, worried that Mai and her boyfriend, whoever he was, and all their friends might appear. She would have a right to ask him what he was doing on a Saturday night in Wexford queueing to get into the dance when he had told her that he could never get away on a Saturday.

Once he was inside, he made for the narrow balcony upstairs. The music was loud; the band was much better than the ones that played Courtown. This band had a brass section as well as a backing chorus. But the main attraction, he saw, was the bar. He smiled as he watched a fellow trying to carry two full pint glasses and two smaller spirit glasses through the crowd.

He was glad that he saw no one he knew. People from Enniscorthy were wary of traveling to Wexford because of the drink-driving laws. On the balcony, he found a stool and moved it to the front. From here, he had a full view of the dance floor below. It was still early enough for all the music to be fast. When it slowed down, as he was sure it would later, the combination of musicians would make a beautiful sound.

But he would not stay that long. He would stay only to see if Mai was here and who she was with. In all their conversations, she had never once mentioned Wexford. It was too far south for her crowd. They seemed more comfortable in Wicklow or Arklow if there was nothing on in Gorey or Courtown.

Nobody except him was sitting alone without a drink, staring at the dancers. Everyone was lively, laughing with their friends, pushing their way to the bar. Even though there were crowds standing at the edges of the hall, the dance floor itself was not packed. He could pick couples out easily and follow them as they moved around. People appeared to know each other. In between dances, there was no stampede of men across the floor looking for partners. The atmosphere was relaxed and good-humored. The band wasn't just belting out versions of recent hits, but playing jazz numbers and then shifting into swing to the delight of some of the dancers.

And then he saw Mai Whitney walking confidently onto the dance floor accompanied by a tall thin man with long sideburns and a brown suede jacket. Jim knew how well she danced and he watched her now with a partner who had the same sense of rhythm. Other dancers made space for them as they began by putting on a display, jiving in perfect harmony, each movement enacted as though they had practiced.

He could see why he had noticed Mai the first night in Courtown. Anyone would have singled her out. Now, in a light blue dress that was held in at the waist by a white plastic belt, she looked radiant. Every time she twirled, she laughed. She could be like this, he knew, when she had one or two drinks, but she could also liven up if she liked a song or a melody.

He waited. He wanted to see if she would, at the next dance, come out onto the floor with someone else. She could be with others and they could be choosing dance partners without it meaning anything much. But the customer in the bar had mentioned a new boyfriend and Jim knew that he was fooling himself if he thought her dance partner was not her boyfriend.

For a slow dance, they came out on the floor again and moved close. He watched them for a while and then he left and drove back to Enniscorthy.

The next evening as they were traveling north towards Wicklow for a rugby club dance he asked Mai what she had done the previous night.

"I needed a night in," she said. "To clean my room, wash my hair and just relax. I managed to wash my hair, but the room is in an even bigger mess. I did go to bed early, though."

He turned and looked at her. He really had believed her when she told him about how little she usually did on Friday and Saturday nights, how happy she was to stay at home.

They danced and chatted and then stayed on the dance floor for the last few slow songs. As usual, he parked the car some distance from her house and they remained there for a while, as they always did, before he drove her to the door, arranging that, in case they did not connect on the phone during the week, he would pick her up at the usual time the following Sunday.

As he turned the car and drove back to the main road, he knew that he would never see her again and felt some satisfaction that he had not bothered to convey to her what he had witnessed the previous evening.

But the satisfaction was short-lived and was replaced by a feeling of shame at how easily he had been led on by her. He was a perfect person to two-time since he was locked behind the bar on Friday and Saturday nights. She had enjoyed going out with him; he still believed that. And in the parked car at the end of each night she had responded to him in ways that were unmistakable. But she must have enjoyed two-timing him, and must have laughed at the thought of him coming back week after week in the hope that they might get to know each other better.

In all the years, he had never seen her again, or even heard anything more about her. Nor had he ever bumped into her brothers or any of her friends. On one occasion, soon after he failed to turn up to collect her, he had answered the phone in the bar and heard her voice and had immediately hung up.

If he were to see Mai now on the opposite side of the street, it would mean nothing to him. With Eilis Lacey, on the other hand, he still wondered if he might have convinced her to stay. If she really was married, they could not have lived together in the town, but they could have gone somewhere else, or he could have followed her back to America.

When Eilis left so suddenly, he felt humiliated that the whole town knew he had been badly fooled. This time no one knew. No rumors about him and Mai started and grew. And there were nights when that almost made it worse. He was alone with his story. He had time to think about it, especially in the mornings when he woke or when the bar was not busy.

Two different women had deceived him. In some way, being fooled by Eilis did not make him feel angry with her. She must have had her reasons for what she did. He was certain that she, too, felt some regret, or even a feeling stronger than that. About Mai, he felt conned. He had believed in her, looked forward to seeing her every week. He had really thought that she appreciated his problem as a man who owned a bar and did not have many nights free. But she was gone now. It was seeing Eilis Lacey on the street that made him remember her.

He looked at his watch and found that it was after three o'clock in the morning. He had drunk several glasses of whiskey on top of a few beers. He knew that he would not sleep. When he stood up and went to the bathroom, he realized that what he was going to do now had actually been in his mind for the past two hours.

If he went out, he was not worried about meeting anyone. The streets of the town would be deserted now. It was one thing that he and Nancy had learned—how easy it was to move unobserved in Enniscorthy in the early hours of the morning.

If he left the house, he promised himself, it would be just this time. He would not make a habit of walking along Rafter Street towards Court Street, passing the top of Friary Hill until he was outside Eilis Lacey's house. He would look up at the unlighted windows, but he promised himself that he would not stop. He would walk as far as the end of John Street and then turn and walk past the house one more time. He thought about Eilis asleep inside. He imagined her breathing, her face in repose, the shape of her body under the blankets. And then he would walk purposefully home, hoping that he might get even a small amount of rest before first light appeared.

PART THREE

I

"Don't just stroll," Laura said. "That won't help. A brisk walk twice a day. That's what they recommend."

"I'll have to get walking shoes," Nancy replied.

"The shoes you have are fine. The thing is, you need to start today."

Nancy insisted that they walk slowly and unobtrusively across the Market Square. And then when they reached the river, she allowed Laura to set the pace.

"What you're doing is not walking," Nancy complained, "and it's not running. It's too fast. That's what it is."

"If you want to lose weight," Laura replied, "that's what you have to do."

Before Laura returned to Dublin it was agreed that her mother would walk the length of the Prom each morning, turning around at the railway tracks.

"And keep up the pace!"

"People will think I've gone mad."

"Everyone wants you to look well."

Nancy began, then, to set the alarm clock for eight, but usually woke in time to turn it off just before it sounded. No matter how determined she was to start the day with a walk, she found herself dozing for a while and then lying in a half sleep, letting her mind wander over the plans for Miriam's wedding.

By this time, Laura, who came down from Dublin every weekend, knew the guest list by heart while Miriam grew more dreamy and vague.

"It's just a day," Miriam said. "Everyone will enjoy it and then forget about it."

"It's your wedding," Laura replied. "It is the most important day of your life."

"All the more reason why I wish it was over."

The decorators had finished their work and even Laura admired the drawing room, as she mockingly called it.

"I worried that the colors would be too pale and I still don't like the fireplace but you'd be proud to invite anyone into the room. Not like before."

When Jim Farrell saw the room, Nancy could tell what was going on in his mind. His own large sitting room had not been touched since his parents lived there.

Although they had not actually discussed where they would live after they were married, Nancy knew that Jim presumed she would move in with him above the pub. She wondered if this might be a good time to show him the plans she had made for the bungalow. But maybe she should tell him first about the site for sale at Lucas Park. And see if he himself might come up with the idea of their building a bungalow there.

She frowned when she heard the cathedral bell ring out ten o'clock. She had already changed twice, realizing that she needed light clothes for her walk and then worrying that she might be too cold if there was a breeze from the river. Normally, she would never appear on the street in the clothes she was wearing now. She would be lucky to get to the top of Castle Hill without meeting someone whom she knew. The prospect of Miriam's wedding would be a perfect reason for anyone at all to detain her in conversation, so she kept her head down as she crossed the Market Square.

Past the handball alley, walking by the river, Nancy saw two women coming towards her, one of whom she immediately recognized as Nora Webster, the other who she soon saw was Nora's sister Catherine, who lived, Nancy thought, somewhere in Kildare. She remembered that Nora had called in to the house after George's funeral. Nancy recalled a moment when they were alone in the living room together and Nora had come close to her and said, "I know what you are going through. Maurice was the same age as George when he died and we were married the same number of years."

The words should have been comforting but they were not. She did not want anyone to presume that they knew what she was going through. It was too easy. But she had nodded and smiled and hoped that someone would come into the room and break the tense silence that had descended. Since then, she had avoided Nora Webster. Now she was about to come face-to-face with Nora and her sister. Both were well dressed, she noticed, and Catherine quite elegant. She wished she were wearing better clothes.

"I hear you have a wedding coming up," Catherine said. "And I hear that all your children are a credit to you."

Since she had opened the chip shop, people tended to treat her less as a widow; they did not put on a sorrowful look tinged with sympathy when they met her. But these two women still looked at her as if she needed kind words.

"I'm working to lose weight for the wedding," she said.

"Have you bought your outfit yet?" Catherine asked.

"I went to Wexford and couldn't find anything. I'll have to go to Dublin this week or next."

Nora watched her silently as Catherine did all the talking. Being confronted with another widow must make Nora sad, Nancy thought. She tried to think of something bright to say, something that might make Nora smile.

She was barely listening to Catherine.

"Now, I can get all her details to you by this afternoon," Catherine said.

It emerged that Catherine knew a saleswoman in Switzers in Grafton Street in Dublin.

"You send her your measurements. You tell her what kind of coat or dress or two-piece you want. You make an appointment and, when you come, she has everything ready for you. Mind you, she doesn't see everybody. But I have a friend who knows her well and that's the only reason I've been able to see her. And if you want, I can phone my friend and we can take it from there. It would save you so much trouble."

It struck Nancy that Nora must have told her sister that the chip shop was making money.

"It's a special day," Nora said. "I think you should do what Catherine suggests."

Nancy would have agreed to anything to get past, and stop them taking her in so carefully.

Later, when she found a note in the hallway, she had forgotten that Catherine had promised to give her the details of the assistant in Switzers and the name of her friend to mention if she were to phone to make an appointment. Since she had time to spare, Nancy decided to phone the number immediately. If it didn't work the first time, she thought, she would not try again.

The call was answered after just one ring. The voice was almost grand.

"Yes, this is Miss Metcalfe."

The second Nancy mentioned Marie Barry, the name that Catherine had told her to invoke, Miss Metcalfe became enthusiastic.

"Any friend of Marie's is a friend of mine. So, what can I do for you?"

When Nancy told her about the wedding, Miss Metcalfe warned her that she would have to move quickly. She asked if Nancy could fetch a measuring tape then and there. Since Nancy was sure she had one in a drawer in the kitchen, Miss Metcalfe said she would hang on, and then when Nancy returned, tape in hand, she slowly took her through the measurements she would need.

"Now, I'll require about a week to get the best selection for you. I have three categories for customers: money no object, a very tight budget, someone in the middle."

"Well, it's my daughter's wedding."

"So, which?"

"The middle."

"Can I see you in the late morning, say at twelve noon, on Thursday of next week?"

As soon as she put down the phone, Nancy determined that she would ask Jim Farrell for a lift to Dublin, where he went most Thursdays. She waited until one night when, having come to see him, she was about to leave.

"Switzers?" he asked and smiled. "I'll make sure you're there on time. You wouldn't want to be late. If you drive as far as the railway station in Gorey, I'll collect you. We can go on from there to Dublin and no one will be any the wiser."

On the day before she was due in Switzers, Nancy went to Cloake's in Main Street and got her hair done, letting Mavis Cloake add the usual dye to her hair that gave it a red tinge. She got her normal perm, though she was worried that it was too tight. But at least her hair would be tidy.

At home, she found herself going through her best clothes. She would not want to look dowdy in Switzers but, as she tried some things on and checked herself in the mirror, she realized that it was Jim she was worried about. Even if their trip to Dublin together was furtive, even if he would not be accompanying her down Grafton Street or going for a walk with her in Stephen's Green, she would be traveling with him. He would watch her getting in and out of the car.

As soon as she had parked at the railway station, Nancy worried that she had arrived too early. She would have to sit here and wait half an hour for Jim. Anyone could notice her and even recognize her and come over for a chat just as Jim Farrell's car was arriving.

When Jim's car finally pulled in beside hers, she smiled at him conspiratorially as though they were in imminent danger of being detected. And then she switched as quickly as she could from her car to his. Without looking at her or speaking, he turned around and they set out towards Dublin.

"I always park in the Montrose Hotel car park," he said, "or I have since the bombs. And I get a bus or a taxi into the city."

"We'll be in plenty of time," Nancy said.

Nancy thought of the two hours and more ahead of them and asked herself what they would talk about. Or maybe Jim would be happier to drive in silence. He hardly wanted her to share what was most on her mind—was the cut of Miriam's wedding dress too low? And what about the extra cost of having flowers on every table at the wedding dinner? And Laura had strong views on the wine, insisting that what the hotel was offering was too cheap.

"I agree that it is a well-known wine," Laura said. "Well known for being cheap."

"Is there one that's less well known?" Miriam asked.

"But cheap too?"

"Well, not expensive."

"Why don't we select a wine that is good but not too expensive?" Nancy asked.

As this conversation went through her mind, Nancy was certain that Jim did not want to hear about it.

"Do people ever order wine?" she asked.

"In the pub?"

"Yes."

"Hardly ever. I'm sure we have a few bottles. Shane would know."

Going through Arklow, Nancy wished she had thought of a more interesting question. She tried to come up with something that might set him talking, but every question that came into her mind sounded banal and every comment seemed as though it would only be uttered to break the silence.

With George, it had never been like this. It was natural for them both to talk. She tried to remember what it was they had spoken about. George loved stories about court cases and accounts of hurling matches and rugby games. Each week he went to the greyhound track and came home with news he had picked up there.

In the car on the way to Dublin with George there would never be silence. She wondered what Jim was thinking about.

For a moment, it occurred to her that she might tell him that she had invited Eilis to the wedding, although maybe this was not the time. But she would have to do it in the next week or so and make it sound casual, mention it when she was telling him about other guests and hope that he would not be offended.

"Do you know who I saw passing last night? I hadn't seen her for years."

She had spoken without thinking. When Jim turned for a second, his gaze was that of a Guard on duty.

"Who?"

"Sarah Kirby."

"She's been home on and off since Christmas," Jim said. "She's run out of money."

"I don't think I know who she married."

"You might have known him to see. He was a big Beatles fan or a mod and rocker or whatever they call it. I think he tried to start a showband. And he took to drink and then they went to England."

"I heard Sarah was very popular."

"She had fellows going mad for her. There was one chap out near Bree who would come into the town every Saturday and leave some kind of letter for her. It was a famous sight. I'll remember his name in a minute."

Jim knew everything about the town, long-forgotten stories, the names of people who had left for Dublin or Liverpool years before. She had heard him talk like this at night sometimes when she came to see him. But he had been more hesitant than he was now even if he still gave the impression that he knew much more than he would ever say.

Because he seemed more relaxed, she felt free to talk about the wedding. He was listening with close attention. He turned regularly to glance at her, and showed no sign that he found the conversation tedious.

"I don't think anyone will complain about the wine or the flowers," he said. "But if you don't do it right, you'll worry. And Miriam might want everything perfect but not want to make demands. So, I'd spend the money. It's a big day."

"My sister Moya," Nancy said, "wants to bring her four daughters and two of their boyfriends. They will take up half a table. Laura suggested I ask the boyfriends just to come later for the dancing."

"I can see her point," Jim said.

As they stopped in front of the Montrose Hotel, he told her that he would ask at reception for a taxi to take her to Grafton Street and he would see her back at the Montrose at four o'clock.

"I always park in the same spot," he said as she got ready to leave the car. "The man keeps it for me if I let him know I'm coming. I'll drop you at the door and I'll see you in a minute."

In the lobby of the hotel, Jim sat with her as they waited for the taxi.

"What would we say," she asked, "if someone from home appeared?"

"I'd think of something," he said, "or even better, I'd leave it to you. But I always get a bus into the city, so you won't have any worries in the taxi. It will be just you."

What stayed in her mind as she traveled into the city was the fondness in Jim's gaze when he had turned to look at her during the journey to Dublin. Mainly, he was serious. Unlike George, he was not a man to be found laughing and joking at the front door of his own premises. George was always watching in case one of his friends from the rugby club passed by. And then he would go to the door and shout out the man's name and some old joke would be retold, or something fresh and funny would be imparted about one of their old associates. And George would be found doubled up with laughter in the Market Square.

In the years after he died, she missed that sound, and his easy good humor. Even thinking about it now made her feel low. He should not have died so young. Of all his group, there was no reason why he should have been singled out. She thought about what it would be like to meet him for tea in some Dublin hotel this afternoon when she had done the fittings in Switzers. She knew how proud he would be to take Miriam up the aisle in the cathedral and how much he would enjoy the company of Gerard now that he was older. They would go for a drink together at the end of the day's business. She sighed at the thought of their both being served by Jim Farrell.

As the taxi made its way past Donnybrook, she saw that, no matter what, she would be disloyal to one of them. In feeling so tenderly towards George, in dreaming how happy she would be with him at the wedding, she was imagining a life without Jim. But if, instead, she thought only of Jim, how lucky she was to be with him, it felt as if she were leaving George behind.

It was too easy to console herself with the thought that George would be glad that she had found someone. That was a soothing idea but it was no use. If anyone had told George that, on a day in the future, his own wife would be driven to Dublin by Jim Farrell in whose bed Nancy often lay at night, George would have known it as a bad dream. It would hardly comfort him to hear that

Nancy was happy. But she was; and she would be even happier, she resolved, if she could put these thoughts out of her mind and live for a while in the present.

As she was early, she drifted down Grafton Street, looking into shop windows, until she came to Brown Thomas. At some stage, she thought, she should buy a proper set of table glasses and cutlery that she could use on Sundays in the new house. Searching for the household goods department, she stopped at various cosmetic stands, trying out a new lipstick that was there for casual customers to sample. As she was looking in the small face mirror, she caught a glimpse of a full-length mirror behind her. She turned and stared into it.

It was not just that she appeared older than she had imagined, but she could not think why she was carrying a white raincoat over her arm. It was a fine day, with no sign of rain. No other woman had a coat over her arm.

She believed she had chosen her best clothes for the day. In her bedroom, they might have been acceptable, but now in the sleek atmosphere that prevailed in Brown Thomas, she was like a woman who did not normally come here. In panic, for one second, she lifted her arm to her nose and smelled her cardigan in case there was even the faintest whiff of fried food or cooking oil there. She detected nothing but maybe someone unaccustomed to the odors that lived in her chip shop might notice. She would have to be brave, she thought, forget the image of herself that had just confronted her and cross Grafton Street to Switzers and ask for Miss Metcalfe.

"The lift will take all day," Miss Metcalfe said. "But we will wait for it if you want."

"I'm happy to walk."

Miss Metcalfe was younger and much less stylish than Nancy had expected. Nothing that she wore was special in any way. Her hair was going gray.

On the top floor, Miss Metcalfe led her to a small staircase.

"We will have privacy up here and there's a skylight which means we can actually see the garments. Something that looks great under bright electric light is awful in daylight."

They went into a long, low room with several full-length mirrors and a rack of clothes on hangers and a dressing table covered in hats and handbags with rows of shoes on the floor.

"You know, it's funny how much you can tell from someone's voice," Miss Metcalfe said. "But I could still be wrong. I thought of a plain dress, not linen because it would wrinkle too much, and then a beautiful rich jacket, maybe with embroidery. Something very brave."

She was inspecting Nancy from head to toe.

"I like understatement," she went on. "That's why I get on so well with Marie Barry. She wants clothes that you don't notice. She is the only woman in Ireland who can wear gray."

Nancy didn't want to admit that she did not actually know Marie Barry.

"I was hoping to lose weight before the wedding," she said.

"That," Miss Metcalfe said, "is the worst idea I have ever heard. First of all, I think you look lovely in your figure as it is. Skinny, you know, is out. Secondly, you don't have enough time, and also you have plenty to worry about already. Diet after a celebration, I always say. Enjoy life before."

Miss Metcalfe began to look through the clothes hanging from the rack.

"I have been generous with the sizes. I don't want anything too tight. Will there be dancing?"

"I am not sure I'll be out on the floor."

"But your husband . . ."

"No, my husband is dead."

"Oh, then you have all the responsibility. How long ago?"

"It's five years now. He died in the summer."

"Well, I'm very sorry to hear that. You are still a young woman and you look great, but you will need to look dignified. Not like a widow, mind you. But the dignified mother of the bride. Can you try on this short-sleeved dress? I know that lime is no one's favorite color. I'm going to leave you on your own with it. And try on all the shoes. And don't let me convince you of anything. I'm sure you know what your best look is."

The dress was wrong. It was too loose and shapeless, intended for a much larger woman, and the color made her seem too pallid when she faced the mirror. She flicked through the garments hanging on the rack and, having picked a few out, was considering trying them on when Miss Metcalfe came back. She had more dresses over her arm.

"Yes, it did strike me that the pale would be too pale. But I don't want you in dark colors. What do you think?"

"I would prefer dark if it was the right cut," Nancy said. She wasn't sure what she meant by the right cut, but she supposed she meant the right size.

Miss Metcalfe showed her a dark blue outfit in wool with thin white stripes; Nancy put it on and walked up and down in front of the mirror.

"The cut is very subtle," Miss Metcalfe said. "Elegant and under-stated."

Nancy nodded.

"I wish I'd lost weight, that's all. But you're right. This is the best. I will feel relaxed in this."

"Not too much, not too little," Miss Metcalfe said. "Are you sure? We have more time."

"I think this is lovely," Nancy said. "So yes, I am sure. I would like to take that."

When they were looking at accessories, Miss Metcalfe asked her if she had driven up from Enniscorthy herself. Nancy found herself hesitating; she worried that she was blushing.

"Someone drove you?" Miss Metcalfe asked, smiling.

Nancy nodded.

"You have someone new in your life! I should have guessed."

"God, I hope you couldn't."

Nancy found herself, then, telling Miss Metcalfe about Jim.

"That is a really beautiful story," she said when Nancy had concluded. "I mean, it's sad too, but still I'm very happy for you."

"We haven't really decided," Nancy went on, "but I thought I would like to get married in Rome."

"I knew someone who did that and she said it was glorious. And you'll be married in the spring?"

"I suppose . . ."

Nancy smiled. She believed she had said too much. No matter how great the temptation, she thought, she should never again share her news with anyone.

"Can you wait for a moment?" Miss Metcalfe asked.

Nancy nodded.

"I had something downstairs, but I was sending it back. Let us hope that it's still here. It wasn't right for a mother of the bride. But it was very special. It would look lovely in Rome. I mean, for your own wedding. And I should warn you that the price is very special as well."

She returned with an ivory-colored dress covered in cellophane over her arm.

"It comes with this jacket. Remember, you wear it with some tinted nylon stockings and I'll have to talk to you about your hair."

The dress and the jacket fitted her. The material felt like silk but it was heavy, or heavier than anything silk she had ever owned.

Nancy moved from one mirror to another.

"It will take time to find the perfect shoes to go with this," Miss Metcalfe said, "and I would advise a very small and discreet bag."

She walked around Nancy.

"Now, the price."

When Miss Metcalfe had told her how much the dress and jacket would cost, Nancy wished she could consult Jim. Surely, he would tell her that she had been trapped! But she could not be certain. He might equally tell her that if she liked it, then she should buy it.

"I'll send you a cheque next week for that," Nancy said coldly.

"Actually, there are two more things," Miss Metcalfe said. "The first is hair. The only dye that works is blond and your perm is too tight."

"Oh, is it? I had it done just now."

"And maybe we can talk about makeup when you come for the final fitting."

"Yes, I'll let you know what day."

When she walked out of Switzers, Nancy turned in to one of the side streets. It was only one o'clock. She did not want to be on her own. She wondered where Jim was. She should have let Laura know that she was going to be in Dublin and arranged to meet her for lunch. But then she realized that it was better like this. She might have been tempted to tell Jim about the wedding dress, and he would think she was mad to choose a dress so long before their wedding. And Laura would want to take her back to Switzers to see what she had chosen to wear at Miriam's wedding. The image of Laura and Miss Metcalfe doing battle over style put her into good humor.

She would find somewhere for lunch, a restaurant where she could take her time. And then she would return to Brown Thomas and look around. She was sure that she would feel different there now, even with her badly dyed hair and a raincoat over her arm. She was sure that when she caught a glimpse in a full-length mirror, she would imagine herself at Miriam's wedding or walking down the grand staircase of a hotel in Rome and people turning to look at her as she adjusted her hat and found Jim waiting for her, with a car to take them to a side chapel of some great old church where they would be married.

II

Eilis had edged past the fridge and the washing machine and the new cooker, all still in their packaging, and was now at the front door. Her mother stood with Martin in the hallway near the kitchen.

"I'll be there for a day or two, that's all," Eilis said.

"And what will I say if people ask me where you are?" her mother asked.

"Is that what you're worried about?"

"Yes, it is. I care what people think about me."

"Tell them I've gone to Martin's house for a day or two by the sea and that you might join me if the weather holds up."

"I wouldn't be caught dead down there."

"No need to tell them that."

Her decision to get away from her mother and Martin was made on the day her mother insisted that she didn't want to hear another word about America.

"It's day and night. Every time I turn on the television, I hear Americans laughing at something that's not even funny. And there was all that Nixon stuff I hated. And now I have you telling me how great America is and how big everything is there—"

"I never said that."

"And their terrible voices. It's the voices I mind most. And their clothes."

"What clothes?"

"Americans! There was a man from the Villas came home after years in Boston or Philadelphia or some place and he went around the town in tartan trousers and a matching cap."

Eilis followed Martin when he went upstairs.

"Is that house of yours in Cush habitable?"

"For me, it is."

"It will be fine for me too," she said.

But the house, when she drove there, had not been cleaned for a long time. The only mattress was stained and the bedclothes were old. And the house itself was closer to the cliff than she imagined, fully exposed to the wind coming in from the sea. It struck her that Martin and her mother would never know if she did not, in fact, stay here. She would, she decided, drive to Wexford and book into one of the hotels and return to her mother's house in a day or two.

In Wexford, she parked her car near the railway station and walked the length of the Main Street until she came to Lowneys furniture shop. Even as she looked at beds and mattresses with a young assistant following her, she really did not have a definite plan. But the prices were low and it occurred to her that all she would need was a bed, a mattress, an easy chair and a deck chair, and some fresh towels and bedclothes.

When she asked the assistant how quickly they could deliver, he went to find the owner.

"I know you from Enniscorthy," the owner said when he appeared. He was wearing a suit and tie. "My brother did a line with your sister. Lacey?"

"That would be a long time ago."

"Ah now, we're all young still."

He asked her when she wanted the delivery.

"Now. I mean today."

She hoped she spoke without a trace of an American accent.

"Every single person from Enniscorthy wants everything today. It must be something in the water up there."

"So could it be today?"

"It could be done this minute."

"I'm in Blackwater, actually, in Cush on the cliff."

"I have no prejudices."

"Will you be able to take the old furniture away?"

"Are you paying hard cash?"

She nodded.

"I'll do anything, then."

He promised to be ready to set out in an hour, when his van would follow her car to Cush. She went back along the Main Street to Shaws, where she bought sheets and blankets and pillows and towels. In the women's section, she tried on the cheapest bathing suit she could find and then bought that too. Once she had packed these purchases in her car, she bought some bread and ingredients for a salad.

When the new bed was in place and the old one taken away, she set about making it, wishing she had also bought a bedside lamp. It was warm, but if she left the door open flies came in. She unfolded the deck chair on the grass in front of the house. Now she could relax; this was what she had come here for, after all.

In the creamy light of the afternoon, it was peaceful and beautiful, the silence broken only by a tractor in a nearby field, by faint birdsong and by the soft, incessant sound of waves breaking on the strand below. Tonight would be the first time she would ever sleep in a house alone, when there would be no one in the bed with her or in the next room. In all her years with Tony, it was something she had often dreamed about, especially at the beginning of their marriage—slipping away, getting a train or even driving to some town and finding an anonymous hotel to spend two nights away from everyone.

What was strange was how close she had lived to Tony's family and how little she thought about them now. She stood up and walked to the edge of the cliff. She hoped there would be fine weather when Rosella and Larry came. Often, there was one stretch of sunny weather in the summer and then it was overcast with rain or drizzle and the vague expectation that the sky might clear towards the end of the day. She wanted them to like the town and think well of her mother and Martin and talk nostalgically when they got home about their time in Ireland, with the idea that this, too, was where they came from, even if it might seem less significant than the Italian world that they had heard about from their grandparents.

Tony's father, over all the years, had never really learned her name. He had a sense of what it sounded like and he often made brave efforts but failed after the first syllable and thereafter made a grumbling sound. Once Larry discovered this, it became another way to make his mother and sister laugh. He would never imitate his grandfather's growl in front of his father, who would not find it funny. But sometimes over dinner if Tony left the room for a moment, Larry would begin to address Eilis as though he were her father-in-law. He would try out several ways to say her name, more preposterous each time, but with his grandfather's voice and his distracted, ponderous expression.

"If they catch you, they'll kill you, that family of your father's," Eilis said. "Don't ever let your cousins see you doing this."

One day, a few weeks before she had left for Ireland, Tony's father appeared at the garage. Eilis saw him and Mr. Dakessian speaking to each other as though they were involved in a conspiracy. It was all gestures and whispers and Tony's father narrowing his eyes and smiling at Mr. Dakessian, who followed what he said with close attention.

"Where is my daughter-in-law?" he asked, coming into the office.

He addressed the question to Mr. Dakessian, who was following him. He managed to ignore Eilis completely as he directed his attention to Erik, who had stood up when the two men came in.

"I drove down to see how my daughter-in-law is doing. I love all three of my daughters-in-law, but the one that works here is the one with the brains and those brains have been passed on to my granddaughter Rosella. I am sure Larry has them too, but Rosella makes us all proud. And that includes her teachers. And it is my view that she got most of her talent from her Irish mother. And that is the truth."

Her father-in-law looked at her with so much warmth and admiration that she was tempted to ask him to say her name, to tell everyone in the room what her name was.

She wondered if his volubility had been caused by drinking, but she had never seen him take more than a few glasses of wine. Quickly, she realized that he had come here deliberately and his performance had been worked out in advance. His visit was a message of support. What she did not know was whether it had been inspired by her mother-in-law as a way of flattering her, embracing her, snaring her further in the great family net, or whether Tony's father was speaking on his own behalf, not having consulted anyone on the content of his most effusive outburst.

"What was that about?" Erik asked when the two older men had left the room.

"He loves me and he admires me," Eilis replied.

"So I can tell, but why?"

"For the reason he explained."

"No, no. He must have another reason."

When Eilis next managed to be alone with her brother-in-law, she told him about the visit and asked if his mother had sent his father to make clear to Eilis that, even though they were not going to listen to her or take her feelings into account, they did not want her to think she was unappreciated.

"No, he did it on his own," Frank said. "But only after he summoned all of his sons and gave us a rambling talk about how he was on our side, and always would be, until he wouldn't be."

"What do you mean?"

"He said that in his country men support their sons, but he and Mr. Dakessian had discussed this and they thought it was right and so he wanted us to know that he supports us. But he and Mr. Dakessian had also agreed that sometimes you would have to put a lot of thought into the matter and it isn't as simple as it sounds and sometimes your support might waver. It took him a while to come up with the word 'waver.' He waved his hands around to give us a sense of what he meant."

"And then?"

"And then he told Enzo he was to stop picking fights with Lena. And Enzo went crazy and asked him if he had anything to say about Tony. My father had not, at any point, even glanced at Tony. He pretended Tony wasn't even in the room."

"And what did your mother say?"

"She doesn't know about it. She was at the chiropodist so she doesn't know the meeting even took place."

"And Tony doesn't know you're telling me all this?"

"That's correct."

"It's hardly helpful."

"I'm doing my best."

Tony was like a ghost in the house, appearing silently in doorways, never settling anywhere. One evening, when Eilis had a suitcase open on the bed and was busy folding what she planned to pack for Ireland, Tony stood and watched her until she was tempted to ask if she could help him in any way.

His mother, using a cheerful tone, had said several times how glad she was that Eilis would be in Ireland for her own mother's eightieth birthday.

"She will be delighted to see you. And Rosella and Larry are looking forward to it. Larry says that he is going to come home with an Irish accent, so I don't know what we will do then."

Her hearty laugh made Eilis more determined not to smile.

As she packed, with Tony still observing her, Eilis was still not smiling. When she lifted her suitcase from the bed, Tony rushed over to assist.

"I can do it on my own, thanks."

"You look like you're packing for a long trip."

"I don't want to forget anything."

"I'll miss you when you're gone."

She looked at him blankly and nodded. She wished she could come up with some remark that would cause him to stop staring at her so sadly. She was about to say that it was only a holiday until she realized that this was not true.

"I can't imagine the house without you," he said.

Eilis remembered now that Larry, on seeing the quantity of clothes she had packed, had asked her whether they did not have washing machines in Ireland.

If only she had known, she would have told him no, that her mother did not have a washing machine and neither she nor Martin had a fridge. When she went inside Martin's house to make herself a sandwich, the butter had melted. All she could do was leave it there, hope that it would solidify when evening came.

Returning to the deck chair, Eilis could feel a heat emanating from the soil, which gave the grass and the clover a pungent smell. Even though she was no longer in direct sunlight, she felt a clamminess in the heat that reminded her of Sundays in the distant past when her father borrowed a car and they would set out for here. It seemed impossible that there could have been five of them in the back of a small car. Rose hated the cold water and could not be induced to join the rest of them when they went for a swim.

The water must be cold now, she thought, but still she went back into the house and changed into her swimsuit and put her dress on again over it. She took a towel and walked across the fields towards the lane where she would find steps down to the strand. Larry would be amused at the idea that she had not even considered the need to lock the door, and she had left the car keys on the table.

The heat coming from the sandy ground brought her back to those Sundays, her father still wearing his suit, her brothers carrying their hurley sticks, hoping to find others who might play with them on the strand. The names of the local families—the Furlongs, the Murphys, the Mangans, the Gallaghers—came to her clearly now as if no time had passed at all.

No matter how carefully they cut the steps into the marly soil of the cliff and firmly added railway sleepers, the last section was just loose sand. She had to run down that stretch without any support.

She decided to walk towards Knocknasillogue and Morriscastle, glad that the strand was now in shade. She left her sandals at the bottom of the cliff and walked along the shore in bare feet.

On one of the days before she left, Larry began following her around the house, observing her suspiciously, until she asked him if he was waiting to say something.

"Carlo says that you and Dad are splitting up. But then Aunt Lena found out and she told Uncle Enzo, who made me promise to forget what Carlo had said."

"Have that branch of the family ever thought of minding their own business?"

"I promised that I wouldn't tell you."

"I am not going to tell anyone that you told me."

"So that's it, then? No more to be said?"

"Are you looking forward to seeing Enniscorthy?"

"You're changing the subject. If I did that, you'd all be against me."

"Who is all?"

"You and Rosella."

"Your father and myself are having a difficult time."

"I know that. But are you splitting up?"

"I don't know."

"I needed to tell you that I like things the way they are. I like how we are all together and maybe I complain sometimes when you or Rosella criticize me, but I don't mean it. I wouldn't want anything to change."

She had no idea how to respond. He was watching her closely. It would not do to remain silent or suggest that she was too busy to talk about this now. Clearly, he had been waiting for a moment to find her when she was not too busy.

"I hope it will be all right," she said.

"Do you mean that there won't be any change?"

"I don't want another woman's baby in my house."

"I get that."

"And your father knows that and your grandmother knows that."

"So what is going to happen?"

"If I knew, I'd tell you. Honestly."

"When will you know?"

She hesitated.

"I think the baby is going to be born when we are away," he said.

She nodded.

"Does that mean that we mightn't ever come back here?"

"You will always come back here."

"But not you?"

She wanted to tell him that he would make a good cop or a good lawyer and they could discuss his future with his uncle Frank, but he was looking at her too earnestly. She would have to take him seriously.

"It would be better if your grandmother did not get involved."

"But what if the man just leaves it here and we're away? How should she react?"

"I didn't cause any of this."

"But you will have to decide what you are going to do."

"I haven't decided."

"I thought I might get you to say—"

"What?"

"Something. One way or the other."

"I don't know. That is the honest truth. But you have to remember that I love you and Rosella and so does your father and that will never change."

She moved to hug him, and he put his arms around her for a moment. But then he turned and, like someone defeated, slowly left the room.

Once she had passed Knocknasillogue, she felt a soft breeze. No matter what she did, she thought, she would not be able simply to think about nothing or just be herself on an ordinary day by the sea. At home, Rosella and Larry came in and out of her presence all day, and Tony did too. It did not strike her until now that even when she was alone they were in the shadows close to her. They were still close to her here.

In the days before she left, she was determined that she would get a car to the airport. She did not want Tony to take her. She did not want to hear his apologies or his excuses, but more than anything she did not want to listen as he suggested that he was unsure what would happen when the baby was born. She knew that he was sure, as his mother was sure. They just didn't think it was worth telling her.

When she asked Mr. Dakessian if he knew a driver, he offered to take her to the airport himself.

"Can Tony not drive you? And the old man would give anything to have you in his car, half broken down as it is, and he would probably drive you to any airport you cared to name. And if they can't take you, then I will."

She was sorry that she had mentioned the possibility of getting a driver to Mr. Dakessian. She looked at the board in the supermarket to see if any local drivers had put up a notice, but there was nothing. Having gone through the phone book, she found a few taxi numbers and wrote them down but did not call.

For a week or more her mother-in-law had kept away, but two days before she was to travel, Francesca came to the kitchen door.

"I'll come in just for one second. I know you're busy."

She put a small package on the kitchen table.

"This is a little gift for your mother. From one mother to another. It's very small. I know that you have a heavy suitcase."

Eilis smiled. She could imagine Larry telling his grandmother about the heavy suitcase he had helped his mother carry down the stairs.

"I'm sure she will be delighted," Eilis said.

"Well, that might be putting it a bit strongly."

Eilis did not ask Francesca to sit down or offer her any refreshment.

"Rosella and Larry are very excited about going. I hope your mother has plenty of help. It will be tough getting the house ready for visitors."

If they remained here for the entire evening, Eilis wondered, would every single thing her mother-in-law said sound patronizing and overbearing?

She wished she had come up with a definite plan about getting to the airport. It occurred to her that it would be easier if Tony drove her and Larry came with them, but then she realized how much

Larry noticed and took in, how he would listen to every remark, seeking out signs of how things were between his parents.

On the night before she was to leave, Tony asked if she needed anything done for her the next day.

"No, I have everything."

"We should leave early so you have plenty of time."

"Are you driving me?"

"Who else would drive you? Or do you not want me to go with you?"

"You're right. We should go early."

As she walked on, she saw on the strand in the slanting sunlight a boulder made of marl that would dissolve when the tide was high. It had rolled down from the cliff above. She sat and rested against it and looked at the sea. This might be a good place to have a swim.

In her early days with Tony, she had learned not to underestimate how easily sometimes he could see what she was thinking. It was often hard to keep a secret from him. But because he seldom asked her questions, he had a way of pretending that he knew nothing except what she had disclosed.

She was sure he was fully aware that she would have counted backwards from the time the baby was due and realized that it had been conceived the previous November or December. This same period was a special time for herself and Tony. For years, when the children were young, they had continued to make love. But then that had stopped. There was a year when they had hardly had sex at all. And suddenly in the last months of the previous year something had happened between them. It was a surprise to her that they had become so passionate. As soon as she woke some days, she would find Tony moving close to her and they would have sex before their day began.

This had continued until Christmas. She saw those months as a happy time. And then, when she found out about the other woman's pregnancy, it occurred to her that the affair between Tony and this woman must have happened during the same period.

In the car to the airport, they did not speak until she asked Tony to make sure that Larry was home by nine any evening he went out and that he should give a detailed account of where he had been.

"He is incapable of telling a lie," she said and then realized that this might sound like an accusation against Tony, who, clearly, was unlike his son in this respect.

"Your mother," he said, "must be looking forward to meeting her grandchildren for the first time."

This was the sort of remark that his own mother might make to reduce the tension, and she saw no reason to respond to it.

What she wanted to say to him, in a voice quiet and firm and controlled, was that if the other woman's baby spent so much as a single night in his mother's house then she, Eilis, would not come back, she would find somewhere else to live and she would take Rosella and Larry with her. She would, effectively, divorce him.

She knew that once it was said, it would change things between them. She had been careful not to say it before. As they edged through traffic, she rehearsed a number of ways of saying it.

She could say, "If you take the baby in, I will leave you and I will take the children," or "I mean it when I say that I don't want your mother to take in the baby. Can you promise me that this will not happen?" She rehearsed in her mind a number of other ways of making herself clear but none of them seemed right.

And then she realized what the problem was. Tony had already worked out what she wanted to say and now, as he stared at the road ahead, he was making it impossible for her. He was doing nothing obvious, nothing she could argue with or seek to undermine. It did not show in his face; she could not detect it in his breathing or his way of driving. And yet she was aware that he was creating around himself an aura of vulnerability, or innocence even, that would prevent her from saying anything hard and irrevocable, from making a threat that she could not take back.

It felt like a battle between them until it occurred to her that she was doing battle with herself as well as with him. Rosella and Larry would barely be bothered by the arrival of a baby in their grandmother's house. They would get used to it. But she would not; she was sure she would not.

She wished she could speak clearly to Tony as he drove, let him know once and for all what the consequences would be if he and his mother did not see sense.

But if she spoke, she would lose him. He had already decided what he would do about the baby. Once more, she saw that if she made the threats, she would mean them. And it was that knowledge that was stopping her from speaking. She was not sure she wanted to lose him, not certain either that she wished to bring Rosella and Larry from adolescence to adulthood without everything they had been used to, including their father. Her uncertainty almost made her nauseous as they began the last stretch towards the airport.

She wanted him to drop her at the curbside, but he insisted that, as they had plenty of time, he would park and accompany her to check-in.

She felt something close to anger now as she stared out to sea, watching a line of birds skim over the water. Since she had not threatened Tony in the car, he would have driven back to Lindenhurst feeling that he had achieved something or that he had managed to contain things. In the airport, as she walked towards her gate, she knew that Tony was standing behind her watching. They had already embraced. And that was enough, she thought. He would now be waiting for her to turn once more and wave at him. But she did not turn; she steeled herself not to.

She stood up and stretched, walking down to the shore to test the water. It was too cold. It would be a few weeks before it was warm enough for swimming. Even then, it would be cold. But she remembered also the glow of warmth that came once she was dressed again after a swim. She would, she resolved, try the water now.

Leaving her dress on the sand, she made her way into the sea. Even if she swam for one minute, it would be enough.

When she was up to her knees in the water, she winced as a wave broke against her and quickly, without further thought, she swam out. Once she surfaced, she felt she had had enough. It was too cold. She could not wait to return to shore and dry herself off and put her dress back on.

She was hungry, and sorry she had not brought more food. She would have to do with sandwiches made from melted butter and lettuce and tinned salmon, with some tomato and cucumber. She was happy, however, that she had bought the new bed and the mattress and the bedclothes. She dreamed of waking to the sun over the sea and going to the edge of the cliff to witness the early morning.

As she headed back along the strand to Cush, she saw a lone figure in the distance walking towards her. It must be after six o'clock, she thought, and this would be one of the locals taking a stroll. Not many others came here, she knew. Martin had told her he could come down here most days and seldom meet anyone at all. Wexford people went to Curracloe, and Enniscorthy people to Keating's or Morriscastle. The cliffs were too high, Martin said, and people could not easily find the steps down to the strand.

Instead of the glow she expected to feel after her time in the water, she felt cold and realized she should have taken a pullover. She had with her a thick woolen cardigan and she would put that on as soon as she made it back. She felt tired and thought that if she lay down on the new bed she would fall asleep, but she must not do that, it had taken her long enough to regulate her sleep after the flight.

She noticed the man coming towards her stepping aside to avoid a wave. He had been walking too close to the shore. He seemed to be looking directly at her. She hoped he was not someone from Enniscorthy who might recognize her and want to know what she was doing on her own down here.

The man glanced towards her as if he was waiting for her. It struck her that, whoever he was, she should pass him as briskly as she could, greeting him if she had to do that, but appear preoccupied or needing to get back to her car quickly.

Then she saw that it was Jim Farrell. He turned towards her and shook his head with a sense of rueful surprise, as if this encounter after all the years could not be happening. And then the expression on his face changed. He appeared serious, almost worried.

She hardly knew what to do. She would try to say as little as possible.

"How did you know I was here?" she asked.

III

When Jim dropped Nancy at her car at the railway station in Gorey after their day in Dublin, he almost hoped that they would be spotted by someone who would spread the news that would have forced them into the open. They could then have announced their engagement. Miriam might be disconcerted at first, but she would get used to it. Jim could explain to her that her mother would need him to accompany her to the wedding and that it would be hard for her to be alone on a day like that. Miriam probably would not mind at all.

His impatience had been prompted by a remark in passing which Nancy had made about a wedding in Rome in the spring.

"Which spring?" he had asked.

"Next spring."

"But that's almost a year away."

"Well, if we get engaged in September, then it would be six months after the engagement."

"Why don't we get engaged now and get married in October?"

"We need to plan."

"Plan what?"

"The wedding. And you know we can't draw attention away from Miriam's."

He wanted to say that he would like to be settled by Christmas but he saw that he would not be able to change her mind. It was best to leave it for the moment.

He had let more than twenty years go by so he wondered why he minded being alone so much now. But once the possibility of being married to Nancy arose, he began to dream about it, the dreams coming in more enticing detail as time went on.

It was the journey to Dublin that confirmed his opinion of her. Before, he had enjoyed driving to Dublin on his own and always hoped that no one would ask him for a lift. He found making conversation awkward and sometimes the silences could be awkward too.

Nancy could also be silent, he noticed, but there was no strain in the car when she didn't talk. When she did begin a conversation, however, what she said was interesting.

Sometimes, when the pub was busy, Jim forgot about the question of when his marriage might take place. He was beginning to enjoy the company of Andy, who took him through local rugby, soccer and hurling matches score by score, with elaborate commentary on the players. On Saturdays and Sundays, Andy arrived fresh from some game or training session. If he had to serve a customer in the middle of a story, he would remember the precise point at which he had been interrupted and resume his description at a moment when they were not busy.

"There was never going to be a goal. Anyone who expected a goal from Mick Scallan knows nothing. But there are eejits everywhere and why should this town be free of them? All he had to do was go for a point and do it again and then one more time over the bar. And then they would be equal. He's sound, Mick. But I don't know what came over him. There is talk that a girl let him down, but I hate that sort of talk. Do you know what happened?"

Jim told him that he did not.

"He hesitated. That's all. And that's fatal. And that's how the Raparees lost the game. There's a fucker called Breen, Mogue Breen, and he took a run at Furlong in that second. Jesus, you should have seen it. And that was Waterloo for the Raparees. There'll be some of them in here later. Don't mention the match to them or they'll go to Billy Stamps and drink there."

"You'd better serve them yourself," Jim said. "I'll avoid them completely."

"Pretend you know nothing about it. It was ignominious. That's all I have to say."

On Mondays, Jim looked forward to the appearance of Shane Nolan, on the dot of four o'clock. Shane, too, might have been at one of the weekend matches with his sons. His views could be more analytical than Andy's. To Andy's annoyance, he always insisted that he only wanted to see a good, fair game and he never minded who lost or won.

Because the bar was never crowded on Mondays or Tuesdays, men often came in alone to talk sport with Shane, who would keep the conversation going while also serving drinks. He argued about scores and tactics but he would never bother Jim with talk about sport. What he really wanted to discuss, and Jim would watch him waiting for his chance, was what his children had done or said over the weekend.

"Geraldine got a star for singing. I don't think she can sing at all, not compared to Maeve, but Colette says she has a great voice, if only she would relax it. The nuns love girls who can sing but they have them singing all sorts of stuff you wouldn't be caught dead listening to. And I'd like Maeve and Geraldine to learn the guitar, but the nuns want them to study piano. I can't afford one and there's no room in the house for all of us, let alone a piano."

Shane, Jim knew, came home every night and gave Colette an account of who had been in the pub and what had been said.

One day, Colette came in, not having visited for a while. As he sat and had tea with her upstairs, she asked him if there was any reason why he was so moody.

"Did Shane say I was moody? Who isn't moody? When it comes near closing time Shane gets moody himself."

"Well, I'm just checking you're all right."

For a second, he was tempted to confide in her. If she knew about the engagement, then he could ask for her advice about how to hasten the date of the actual wedding. But his father had told him as soon as he was old enough to stand behind the bar and serve a customer that if he ever felt an urge to tell anybody anything, he was to stop and say nothing. No one appreciated a barman who talked too much. In his pub, his father added, he would learn much more than he needed to know and his job was to keep it all to himself.

He was sure his father did not have the question of his marriage in mind when he gave him the advice, but it was not his natural inclination, in any case, to share what he thought was private. Even though he trusted Colette, he could not be sure that she would not take her mother or one of her sisters into her confidence. This was how news got spread.

She must, he thought, have her suspicions. Shane had answered the phone a few evenings when Nancy had called. He had merely told Jim the call was for him and handed him the receiver. But Andy, one night near closing time, had come down the bar towards Jim and said, "Your girlfriend's on the phone looking for you." As Jim spoke to Nancy, keeping the conversation as brief as he could, he could not stop himself blushing.

"She sounds in good form anyway," Andy had said when he put down the phone.

"You should clean those tables over there," Jim said, "instead of passing remarks about your betters."

Colette, he guessed, must have heard something from Shane about Nancy's calls. Previously, when she had advised him to think more about Nancy, he had not demurred. She must be curious, but she was, like her husband, more than tactful. Jim was sure that she would say nothing until he did. She would not even ask him if he had put any more thought into what they had discussed in their earlier conversation. All they could do was circle around it.

"I think this room is lovely," she said. "Especially this time of the year when you can have the windows open. I love the high ceilings. But you should get the curtains fixed. Does that curtain not close?"

"I must get it fixed."

"I didn't say this to Shane," she went on, "but I thought you should get Andy to work one extra evening. I know he'd love the money. And you could take things a bit easier. For instance, if it was a Thursday and you were in Dublin, you wouldn't have to rush back."

He thought of what would happen if he told her he had been in Dublin with Nancy just the previous Thursday.

"I think you need to relax more. But you're looking very well. It's just that Shane was a bit worried about you. But don't tell him I said a word."

When Nancy came to visit late the following night, he could see how happy she was. Every detail of Miriam's wedding was now in place. On Saturday, Nancy would drive to Dublin to go into Switzers for the final fitting.

She had begun to behave more casually when she visited him, washing up some cups and saucers that were in the sink, throwing out some milk that was sour and getting a second drink for them both without waiting for him to ask.

He wondered if she might be happier going on like this, more content with the prospect of their living together than the actual life itself that would come after marriage. She spoke about her daughters and their different ways of handling money, Miriam watching every penny and Laura far too extravagant. And, while Jim was listening, he was also wondering what would happen if he asked her directly to give him one good reason why they should delay their wedding until the spring.

In reply, she could ask him why he could not let this matter rest. It would be hard to explain to her how lonely he felt when he came into these rooms after closing time and how that feeling became more intense if he woke in the night or in the morning. He had not felt like this before the possibility of being with her arose. Now that it was there as something that would happen, it made his solitary state almost unbearable, at least some of the time.

When it was still dark outside, Jim lay in bed with his hands behind his head, watching Nancy dressing herself. Soon he would put on some clothes and accompany her to the front door.

"Do you know what I'm looking forward to?" he asked.

"What?"

"Mornings like this when I wake and I can curl up with you beside me and stay in bed until it's breakfast time. It would be great if we could do that now."

He felt a longing again for everything between them to be settled, but she was not listening.

"I'm ready," she said, having checked herself in the mirror.

She held out her hand and he stayed close to her as they walked down the stairs. He kissed her in the hallway before opening the front door and checking there was no one on the street.

The bar was quiet for the first hour after opening. Shane would arrive at four, Andy had the day off, so Jim would be on his own for a while dealing with a few customers.

Usually, when Martin Lacey came in, Shane or Andy served him and Jim avoided him. Martin was always alone, having been in some other pubs, and he was garrulous and in need of company. When he had come home from England first, he would join anyone whom he knew even slightly. But he seemed to have learned not to do that.

When he entered, the bar was empty. Jim served him a bottle of Guinness, then went into the stockroom at the back, pretending he was busy, hoping that Martin would leave when he had finished his drink. When he returned to the bar, however, Martin was still there.

"The sister is back from America," he said. "I suppose someone told you."

"I heard all right."

"You used to do a line with her. It's a pity that didn't work out. I'd have free drink for life."

Jim did not reply.

"Her and the mother aren't getting on at all. They're like a pair of cats. I don't know what's got into the two of them. So Eilis has gone down to Cush, to my little shack, on her own, to get away."

"To Cush?"

Jim knew that Martin had bought the house from Nora Webster after Maurice died.

"Yes, she's down there on her own. I didn't even get the chance to clean the place up before she went there. She'd be a stickler for tidiness. She must be going mad down there. But she has her own car and she can come home if she doesn't like it."

As soon as Martin left, Jim found himself feeling almost as sad about losing Eilis as he had felt twenty years ago. Even when he reassured himself with the thought that he had Nancy now, the sense of loss stayed with him as he sat behind the bar on his own. The sadness that had lingered for six months or so after she left returned at odd times, often on a Saturday night when he went up the stairs after the pub had shut.

The idea that she was now back in the town had been on his mind since he had seen her that night. It seemed so wrong to him that they would not meet, that she would not get in contact. She might depart once more without his catching even another glimpse of her, as though they were strangers.

In the silence, and with nothing to do, Jim decided that he would drive to Cush as soon as Shane arrived. He would tell Eilis, if he managed to see her, that he believed it was a shame they couldn't meet and all he wanted was to speak to her after all the years. But the idea of a firm encounter with her made him stop for a moment. How would he explain his decision to drive down to Cush and find her?

It would be simple, he thought; he would tell her the truth. He would recount to her Martin's visit to the pub. He would not stay long; he would assure her of that. It was really just to see her. Would that explanation be enough?

He could hardly have asked Martin precisely where the house was. All he knew was that it was near the cliff. Years before, he had gone to a party in one of the summerhouses in Cush and was sure he had passed the house belonging to the Websters. And when Martin bought it from Nora, several customers had remarked to him that the price had been low, and that had stayed in his mind. But he still wasn't certain of the precise location.

In Cush, he parked the car at the top of a lane that led down to the sea. He passed a mobile home and a single-decker bus that had been cemented into the ground, and then a few modern huts, all reserved, he thought, for summer use. The smell was of clover and grass, and in the distance he could hear the sound of a tractor. When he turned down the next lane, he found two houses on the left-hand side but no sign of life, no parked car or clothes hanging out to dry. If the tractor sound were not there, this could easily feel like a place abandoned.

At the end of the lane, there was a low ditch, but no set of steps leading to the strand. He stood on the ditch and looked down at the calm sea and the deserted shore. Perhaps Eilis had just driven down here and gone for a walk and was now back in her mother's house. He was almost relieved at the thought that he might not now have to meet her. It would be too much to appear like this, out of nowhere. The stillness, the calm waves, the thin white clouds in the eastern sky, the empty houses, emphasized how settled and hidden this place was, and how inhospitable to an outsider, someone who did not even know what house he was looking for.

As he walked back to the car, a woman standing in the gateway of the second house was studying him closely.

"You look like a man who is lost," she said.

"I was looking for Martin Lacey's house."

"Martin's not there. I heard his car blasting off early this morning and I haven't heard him coming back. He has to do something about the car."

Jim hesitated. He wanted to ask her if Eilis was in Martin's house.

"Now, you are the man that has that pub in Enniscorthy," she said.

He could not think who she was.

"I am Lily Devereux's mother. She used to talk about you. I remembered you because I had seen your name over the pub."

"That's my father's name."

"And I knew him, too, at least to see, and your mother. But that's your name too."

Jim still saw Lily Devereux sometimes in the town. She had been on the board of the Credit Union with him. News would spread that he had been seen in Cush. He would have to be careful what he said.

"Well, I was looking for Martin. But I'll find him in the town."

"His sister is there now in the house, one of the neighbors told me. She has a rented car with a Dublin registration. I don't think I know her at all."

If he did not move away quickly, he thought, she would surely ask him why he was looking for Martin and he would not be able to come up with a credible reply.

"Do you know which house is Martin's?" he asked.

"It's beyond the judge's house," she replied, "below the marl pond."

Jim made clear that he did not know what she was talking about.

"It's the other lane," she said. "I always call it the good lane, although this lane is good too."

Jim nodded.

"And is your wife well?"

"I'm not actually . . ."

"Well, there's plenty of time. And you would be a great catch. A fine-looking man with a nice business. I'd go for you myself if I was a year or two younger."

"I'll tell Lily I met you."

"Don't tell her what I just said. She'd murder me!"

"I'll say nothing."

He had the keys in his hand, ready to open the door of the car, when he stopped. There was another noise in the distance, the sharp, piercing sound of a chain saw. It was coming from over the hill, cutting through the thick silence that seemed to seep up from the strand. He sighed and put the keys in his pocket. He would walk down "the good lane," as Mrs. Devereux had called it. If he saw a car with a Dublin registration, he would know Eilis was there.

The car, parked to the side of a small house that was in need of repair, stood out in the landscape, louder than any noise. A model he had never seen before, it was new in a way that nothing down here was new. He wondered if Eilis might see him from one of the small windows of the house and if she would come to the door without his having to knock. He stood and waited. She would be surprised if she found him on her doorstep. Perhaps she had indeed seen him and decided to retreat into one of the back rooms.

It occurred to him that he might shout her name. He wondered if she would recognize his voice. Maybe he would not recognize hers after all this time.

He would go down to the strand, he thought, and walk by the sea. On his way back, he would stop again, and he might be lucky, she might emerge or appear at a window. He would have to let her know that he was not going to make a nuisance of himself. That would be important, but it might be hard to do that were he to appear without warning at her door.

When he saw her walking towards him on the strand, he realized she would be alarmed at the sight of him, no matter what. He was an intruder on her solitude. But she had seen him; he could not turn. Her hair was wet from the water. She was wearing a blue dress and had a towel under her arm. As he was trying to work out what to say, a wave came rushing in towards him and he had to dart quickly away from it.

He felt for a moment a sense of pure disbelief that this was happening. He looked down at the sand, and when he lifted his head she was there, the expression on her face not angry or fearful but puzzled, almost amused.

"How did you know I was here?"

"Martin was in the bar. He told me."

"And you drove down immediately?"

"I saw you on the street a while ago and I worried we might never get a chance—"

"How are you?"

"Good. I'm glad to see you."

"Will you walk back with me?" she asked.

If anyone were to meet them now, he thought, they might be a local couple taking a walk, but when he stole a glance at her, he saw that this could not be true: she did not look like a local woman.

Her dress could not have been bought in Ireland. And the natural way her hair was cut, accentuated by the wetness, set her apart, as did the smoothness of her skin. But more than anything, it was the ease and confidence she had.

Her face was thinner; he could see some wrinkles at the corners of her mouth. But her eyes were bright and alert and her gaze was focused as she turned to him and spoke decisively.

"I'm told that you are doing a strong line with a woman in Dublin."

"Who told you that?"

"Everyone knows it."

"Except me."

"Is that why you're blushing?"

He could think of nothing to say in reply. He wasn't sure if she had really heard such a thing or if she had made it up in order to break the silence.

"And you?" he asked.

"I'm a married woman and a mother."

"How long are you staying?"

"Four or five weeks more. My children are coming at the beginning of August."

He noticed that she did not say her husband was coming too and was glad. He would not relish seeing Eilis with her American husband in the streets of the town.

"How is your mother?"

"Well. She's well."

He wanted to ask her the reason she was here alone, but every question he thought of seemed wrong. It occurred to him that he really wanted to ask if she had thought about him much over the years and if she had ever regretted not staying with him.

"Do you like it down here?" he asked.

"It's so calm, so empty."

When they came to the steps that led to the cliff, she found her sandals. He helped her climb the loose sand to the first step. As he took her hand, he thought this might have been what he came down here for, to touch her once, to have her smile as she leaned on him. And then to walk slowly behind her up to the edge of the cliff.

"My hair still feels wet," she said. "It takes so long for anything to dry in this air."

In the lane, he saw what she was doing. She was somehow making this encounter natural, uncomplicated. He would get no chance to ask her anything. As the early evening sunlight caught her face, her smile was a mask. But there was no strain in her voice.

"Your accent hasn't changed much," he said.

"Sometimes I try to sound more American but the kids say I just sound even more Irish."

"Have they been to Ireland before?"

"Never."

"Nor you, since you left?"

"This is my first time since then."

Neither of them, he knew, would have any trouble remembering what "then" meant. He wished he had been with her all the years, but there was nothing could be done about it now. For a second, he also wished that she knew about him and Nancy. He did not want her to think that he had no life.

It struck him that since this was probably the last time he would see her, he should say something. But then he thought it would be best to leave it. There was nothing to say, or nothing that was easy or simple, nothing that he could find words for now.

"You look so sad," she said.

"I feel sad seeing you."

"Don't be sad about that. It was the way it had to be."

"And do you ever . . . ?"

"Ever?"

"I don't know. Do you ever think about me?"

As soon as he had said it, he knew how wrong it sounded. It was as if he was looking for pity or needing her to say something comforting to him. He watched her thinking; she had decided, he saw, not to respond. When he had known her, she was softer. She would have made it easier for him. Now, as they stood by her car, it was clear that she wanted him to go. She put out her hand. That was as much as she would do. She did not want to embrace him. He would say nothing more to embarrass her or himself.

"I hope I didn't surprise you too much."

"Not at all," she said.

"I thought we should see each other, and it would be hard to do that in the town."

When she did not answer, he reached out and shook her hand. He walked up the lane to his car, noticing that the noise of the chain saw persisted, cutting through the air with the same sharpness as before. He stood and inspected the horizon before taking out his keys and opening the car and turning it so that he could go back to Enniscorthy.

PART FOUR

PART FOUR

I

"Yes, you do. All we asked was for you to behave like a human being on one day. One single day! So don't bother saying that you don't have a hangover. You do!"

Laura was on the first landing shouting at Gerard.

Nancy remained in the kitchen. Soon she would go upstairs and check herself in the full-length mirror on the inside of the wardrobe door in her room. Both Miriam and Laura had said that they liked her outfit.

When Gerard told Laura that he would be ready in five minutes, Laura withdrew into the living room, joining Miriam, who had been ready for the past hour.

Nancy was glad that she had insisted on Laura driving to the cathedral, even though it was close enough for them to walk. She did not want people stopping her on the way. Once she got to the cathedral she would try to keep out of the limelight. All the attention would be on Miriam in her full-length white dress, her simple veil and plain white high-heeled shoes.

Gerard would walk his sister up the aisle.

As she waited in the doorway for the car driven by Laura to appear, Nancy remembered how she had walked up the aisle of the same cathedral on her own father's arm. She had almost felt sorry for George's mother, who had spoken too freely in the town of her

153

feeling that George might have done better. This had been passed on to Nancy's own mother by some of her neighbors. Nancy had been tempted to have it out with Mrs. Sheridan in the days before the wedding but then she decided to forget about it.

She remembered Eilis Lacey arriving at the cathedral that day with her mother and Jim Farrell and how everyone was sure that theirs would be the next big wedding. But more than Eilis or Jim, it was Mrs. Lacey she recalled, the look of undisguised satisfaction on her face. Her memory of the wedding party itself was a jumble of faces and voices, people trying to be heard over the music and George catching her eyes as often as he could and smiling at her. No one knew that she and George would be spending the first night of their honeymoon in the Strand Hotel in Rosslare. It was customary, then as now, to keep such details secret. But she had recently told Miriam, who had arranged for her own first night to be spent in the same hotel. And Miriam had told no one except her mother. Even Laura did not know.

"I blame Jim Farrell," Laura said as she drove up Main Street.

"For what?" Nancy asked.

"That's where Gerard was until two in the morning. Drinking after hours, if you don't mind."

"Was Jim serving him?"

"Jim went to bed and left that Andy fellow with the keys."

As she and Laura walked through the cathedral gates, Nancy was stopped by the groom's brother to inform her that his mother had also arrived.

Since the Waddings lived closer to New Ross than Enniscorthy, Nancy had met Mrs. Wadding only when she had come to inspect the wedding presents in Nancy's newly decorated living room. Miriam had arranged the visit so that the two women could get to know each other, but Mrs. Wadding's interest in the presents was so overwhelming that she barely even sipped the tea she was offered. She pointed at sets of sheets and towels and cases of cutlery and glass and bedside lamps, asking who precisely had given them. As each name came up, she sought to find out as much as possible about them until Nancy wished she would go.

"Now, which Kirby is that?" she asked when Nancy told her that a set of Pyrex dishes had come from the Kirbys.

"It's from Nurse Kirby," Nancy said.

"Isn't there a Sarah Kirby who went to England?" Mrs. Wadding asked. "Is she one of the same Kirbys? Someone told me she was home. There was a man in Bree, a cousin of my sister-in-law, who was dying about her."

"No, she is a different Kirby," Nancy said.

Mrs. Wadding was now standing outside the cathedral beside two women who were clearly her sisters. Each of the women, Nancy saw, wore a dress made of some shiny material that had been put together by some country dressmaker. Mrs. Wadding's was pale blue, the others wore yellow and pink.

As she turned, Nancy saw Eilis Lacey, who was standing with a group of women but managing to remain apart from them. It was hard to believe that the yellow of her dress was the same color as the dress worn by Mrs. Wadding's sister. It seemed brighter, purer, more glamorous. The jacket Eilis wore was black, as were her handbag and shoes and the small pillbox hat.

"Nancy, it's so lovely to be here," she said.

"How lucky that you were home just now," Nancy replied, refraining, as Eilis did, from smiling or laughing or saying anything inconsequential. Moving away, she felt the encounter with Eilis was too polite and controlled but perhaps this was how she should behave for the rest of the day if anyone approached her. When she looked back, she saw that Eilis had rejoined the group, and was listening intently as one of the other women spoke, nodding her head but not saying anything herself. In the years when she knew Eilis, she thought, and saw her every day, there was nothing special about her. Now she stood out. She seemed like a different person.

Something had happened to her in America, Nancy concluded. She wondered what it was.

Jim, when she saw him, smiled at her warmly and knowingly. He was wearing a sober gray suit and had had a haircut. She must, she knew, stop worrying about how the day would go or how she looked or what Jim thought. She had what she had wanted. Matt, whom Miriam was marrying, was decent and hardworking. The couple gave every sign of being happy. And she, Nancy, had Jim and soon they would be together. She would start her life again, something that had seemed unimaginable a year before.

She and Laura took their places in the front pew. They were early enough to witness the arrival of Matt's family, his father and then his mother with her sisters and then, settling into a row behind, some of his siblings, including two young women who, in their figure and bearing, bore an astonishing resemblance to their mother and their aunts.

Miriam, she knew, had often visited Matt's family but she had said nothing about how old-fashioned they were. Matt's own quietness and shyness, his good manners, could seem like a kind of quaintness. Maybe he would smarten up as time went on. Just now, Nancy concentrated on ignoring the nudges from Laura as more members of Matt's family came to genuflect in front of the altar before finding their places in the front pews on the opposite side of the aisle.

When she looked behind her, Nancy saw that her sister Moya and her husband and daughters were coming up the aisle. They would not take their seats, she knew, before crowding around her and Laura to comment on their clothes and speculate on the type of wedding dress Miriam would be wearing.

"I hear that Gerard was in Jim Farrell's until the dawn," Moya said. "I hope he's in a fit state to walk his sister up the aisle."

"He is perfect," Laura said drily.

"Did you get that in Dublin?" Moya asked, indicating Nancy's dress.

Nancy nodded.

"I think we all look lovely," Moya said.

It was Laura's idea to have no bridesmaids and no best man. She thought the ceremony should be kept simple. Nancy now wondered if this was a sly way of keeping Matt's family from appearing at the altar.

George would have loved this. Because he had worked in a shop all his life, Nancy thought, he could talk to anyone. He would have a way of being friendly with the Waddings, receiving them naturally, that Nancy didn't have, nor Laura indeed, nor Gerard.

Since Jim did a good trade with country people, he would know how to talk to them too. He might not even notice their clothes, Nancy thought. But he would notice Miriam, she was sure, as she walked up the aisle, the congregation turning to look at her.

The mass was simple, the sermon short. As Miriam and Matt made their vows, Nancy concentrated on keeping the tears back, aware of how much Laura would disapprove. She smiled at the thought that she really was afraid of Laura, as they all were. And Laura would have no mercy on her were she to be seen to cry at her own daughter's wedding.

But no matter what she tried to think about, the memory of her own wedding came back to her and then the feeling that George was not watching over them, but he was gone, no part of him was here at all.

Laura nudged her severely as she began to weep, handing her a small white handkerchief.

"Think about something nice."

She thought of George smiling and then she thought of Jim coming from his kitchen with glasses and mixers and ice and pouring drinks for them, no one aware that they were together.

The pride that George would have felt and the image of Jim watching her daughter merged in Nancy's mind as she set out with Laura and Gerard to follow the bride and groom out of the cathedral after the ceremony. As they passed Jim, Nancy took him in openly, letting her gaze linger on him and enjoying how he kept his eyes fixed on her.

They had been right to wait, she thought. If she and Jim had become engaged, then people would be paying too much attention to them and too little to the bride and groom.

She presumed that, by now, Jim had noted the presence of Eilis Lacey. There were a few times when Nancy might have told him that Eilis was coming to the wedding, but she had held off until there was a chance to allude to it in passing, as another small detail, something of little consequence. Such an opportunity had not come, however. She felt now that he did have a right to be warned and she should have found a way to let him know. It must be strange for Jim to see Eilis after all the years. At the wedding dinner, Nancy had remembered to place them so that they had their backs to each other. Jim was at her own table, facing her. Maybe she and Jim could dance with each other at some point in the evening. They had never danced together before.

While the guests began to mill around the tables, checking the name cards, Nancy caught sight of Gerard.

"You look very handsome in your suit," she said.

"Can you call Laura off? She won't leave me alone."

"You were out until what time?"

"I got in the door at twenty past two."

"That's what men do the night before a wedding. You can tell Laura I said that."

It was strange, she thought, how much she was living in Jim's mind. When Matt's father at the end of the meal made a heartfelt speech about the good character of his son and then went on to praise all of his children, Nancy imagined that she was Jim listening and tried to see what he might think. Jim did not like jokes or easy laughter, so he would probably feel respect for Matt's father and his earnestness.

When Gerard spoke for the Sheridan family, reading from a script that his sisters had helped with, he began well. Jim would approve of the way he described his mother and his sisters and his being the only man in the house after his father's death. But when he told a joke about four nuns, Nancy was sure that his sisters could not have seen this beforehand. There were people in the room, she thought, who might not even get the joke. But most of those who understood would not think it was funny. Nancy was almost afraid to look up and catch Jim's eye. His response could be severe. She was relieved, however, when he made a gesture towards her of mock despair, a suggestion that this was how young people behave and there was nothing they could do about it. Then Gerard, as though he realized that the joke was a mistake, began to speak again about his mother and how much effort she had put into holding the family together, how it was her love and her care that had rescued all of them, including Miriam, whose wedding day it was. He had gone back to the script.

Jim was watching Gerard closely as though he might guide him towards ending the speech soon but not before he changed his tone from the solemn to something warm and uplifting and celebratory. Gerard, Nancy observed, was looking towards Jim, getting support from him. And then, when it came to the moment to drink a toast to the bride and groom, Jim raised his glass while focusing all his attention on Nancy.

Later, the dancing started, Laura having engaged a band that could play both classic songs and the latest hits. Nancy danced with Matt's father, who directed her around the floor, she thought, like a man driving a tractor. He neither looked at her nor spoke to her, concentrating fiercely on his steps, with one of his hands gripping her hand tightly and the other hand on her waist.

Once the dance with Miriam's new father-in-law had ended, she saw that Jim was waiting for the right moment to ask her to dance with him.

When they took to the floor, the music was not too loud; they could talk.

"Gerard did well," he said. "I was worried about him. He got into a bit of a state last night. You know, it was a speech that should have been made by his father."

"I thought he just stayed out late drinking."

"He did that too. I left him with Andy and a few others and they made sure he was all right."

"I didn't like the joke."

"It's one of Andy's. He was telling it to everyone in the bar until Shane put a stop to his gallop. His big mistake was telling the story to Colette, who has an aunt a nun."

"What did she say?"

"She threatened Andy that she would tell his mother. He's afraid of his mother."

The band played a slow Elvis song. They stopped talking. Nancy shut her eyes and felt Jim's hand on hers and enjoyed how close to her he was. She would remember this. It was fate, she thought, that had brought them together. If Eilis Lacey had not gone back to America, Jim would be married to her. And if George had not died, Nancy would be dancing with him. She wondered, since Jim would always have been invited to this wedding, if she and Jim might still have noticed each other, perhaps even danced together.

She looked around her and saw Eilis Lacey deep in conversation with one of the Waddings, who was, like nearly everyone else, constantly glancing about and smiling and laughing. But Eilis was not doing that. She was listening and nodding.

Nancy welcomed the two boyfriends of Moya's daughters who had come in time for the dancing. One of them was, she realized, a habitué of her chip shop at the weekend and never too sober. And then she was glad to be joined by Lily Devereux, with whom she had worked before she was married. Lily, no matter what her real opinion, would reassure her.

"The Waddings seem very nice," she said.

"Yes," Nancy replied.

They looked at each other, making clear that there was much more they could say.

Jim brought them over drinks and then turned away to talk to a group of men.

"My mother met Jim recently," Lily said.

Nancy was barely listening, too busy studying everyone on the dance floor, until Lily said that her mother had a long talk with Jim down in Cush when he was walking past her house.

"With Jim?" Nancy asked. "Are you sure it was Jim?"

"Oh, it was Jim all right. Mammy never gets anything like that wrong. And he was half-lost, she said. She didn't know what he was doing down there."

"What day was that?" Nancy asked before realizing that she should not seem so interested.

"Oh, I don't know that. It must have been last week."

Jim was now standing at the bar talking to Gerard and one of Gerard's cousins. More and more, he let her know the smallest changes in his routine. If Andy arrived late, or one of Shane's daughters got a good mark in school, Jim told Nancy about it. How strange that he would not tell her about a trip to Cush and a meeting with Lily's mother. What could he have been doing there? As she thought about it, Nancy became sure that Lily's mother must have mixed him up with someone else.

The band stopped and left the stage for a break. Voices rose in the high room and it was hard for Nancy to make out what Lily was saying. Although she heard tapping on the microphone, she paid no attention until someone began to shout. When she looked, she saw that it was one of Matt's brothers.

"It is a long Wadding family tradition," he said, "going back into the old days, that my mother and her two sisters, the great Statia and the legendary Josephine, will sing 'The Old Bog Road.' So can I have a round of applause for the three of them and can they come to the stage without delay."

"He must be joking," Lily said.

The three sisters ascended the stage and began their song. And it was as if they sang with one voice. None of them moved higher or lower than the others. They looked neither happy nor sad, nervous nor excited. They simply remained placid as they sang. At the second verse, Nancy hoped she would never have to hear this again, no matter who the singer was. Even the radio had stopped playing it because it was too doleful.

As they intoned, "My mother died last springtime," Lily whispered, "Imagine singing this at a wedding!"

Nancy glanced towards the bar. Jim Farrell, Gerard and Gerard's cousin had been silenced by the performance. Jim was gazing with great seriousness at the singers. Moya, Nancy thought, would never stop describing this event and soon the whole town would be talking about it. Miriam had her eyes cast down. Nancy did not dare to look at Laura. And she felt a sudden pang of remorse that she had even considered inviting Eilis Lacey to witness this.

"We'll put it down to experience, Nancy, that's what we'll do," Lily said. "We'll have a great laugh about it in the months ahead."

Once the song had ended, Matt's brother was back at the microphone.

"No wedding this side of the Tramp's Heartbreak," he said, "is ever complete without a rendition from Miss Suzanne Wadding of a song we have all come to love. It is the Wadding family national anthem."

"It would be great if it was something to cheer us all up," Nancy whispered.

Suzanne, who had changed into a leather miniskirt, called for silence and then, placing her mouth up against the microphone, let out a roar. She repeated the word "I," the emphasis more dramatic each time until she embarked on the song itself.

"Lord," Lily said, "she is singing 'Delilah.'"

She sang it in a rough, raspy voice, as if she were, in fact, the man in question, a man in a state of uncontrollable passion. She grimaced fiercely as she belted out each line. When she came to the chorus, Nancy noticed that some of Suzanne's brothers and their friends had gathered behind her and, after each mention of Delilah, they shouted in unison, "Get them off you."

"Did you hear that?" Lily asked.

"Do they mean what I think they mean?" Nancy replied.

Nancy decided that it was time she went to a room Laura had reserved for them to refresh themselves. She invited Lily Devereux to accompany her and also Moya, who came over to deplore the rendition of "Delilah" they had just heard.

While Nancy sat on the sofa in the room, Laura told her aunt and Lily about the house in Wexford town that Matt and Miriam were restoring. They were adding a room that would open right out onto the garden. As she spoke, a waiter came to the door with a bottle of champagne in a bucket of ice and some glasses.

"Who ordered this?" Nancy asked. For a second she thought that it might have been Jim who had sent it to the room.

"I did," Laura said. "This is what I was trying to do when I saw you. I could tell you were going to get away from all that racket. It was enough to make you want to emigrate."

The waiter opened the bottle ceremoniously and poured the champagne. They were soon joined by others and had to order another bottle and more glasses. When the room got too crowded and the second bottle had been finished, Laura insisted they should go back to the hall as surely the dancing would have resumed.

"I'm in the mood to dance the night away," she said.

On her return, Nancy was waylaid by Mrs. Wadding.

"Now, sit down for a minute with me," Mrs. Wadding said. "I have to make a big apology. We've been singing that old song since we were little girls. I mean, someone should have told us to think of some more suitable song now that times have changed. And this is a wedding. What were we thinking of?"

As Mrs. Wadding sipped her drink, Nancy felt very tired.

"And then Suzanne with that song and then her brothers and their friends. We'll all have to learn new songs. And I have issued strict instructions that there is to be no further display from our side of the family, just nice dancing."

It occurred to Nancy that she, in turn, should apologize for Gerard's joke, but she decided not to.

"I'm sure the rest of the evening will be lovely," Nancy said.

Mrs. Wadding was looking at her closely.

"And someone just told me that you were a Byrne from Court Street before you were married. I think one of your aunts married one of the Gethings of Oulart and my mother knew her well."

Nancy thought she would love another glass of champagne. When she took in the room, looking to see where Jim was, she could not find him. Instead, she caught Gerard's eye and signaled to him.

"I think Mrs. Wadding and myself would like a drink, Gerard, and we know that you will be kind enough to get one for us."

When Miriam and Matt were saying their farewells with much cheering, Jim Farrell came and stood beside Nancy. For anyone watching, she thought, they could have seemed like a couple. She considered for a second asking him for a lift back to Enniscorthy, but Laura was waiting for her and too many people would notice.

For a second, having said good night to Moya and her family, she saw Jim Farrell speaking to Eilis Lacey. But then Lily Devereux approached her. When she looked again, there was no sign of either of them.

Once ready to go, however, she regretted not having taken the risk. Surely no one would notice or care! Gerard was staying in Wexford. Laura could easily drive home on her own. She decided to find Jim and tell him that she wanted to travel with him. They could even go back to his house and have a quiet nightcap.

The staff were clearing away chairs and tables but the area around the bar was still crowded. She stood back to check where Jim was but she could not see him. Then she saw Gerard talking to someone whom she did not know. She pushed her way through the drinkers to ask him where Jim was. He told her that Jim had left. He was sure about that.

"When did he go?"

"A few minutes ago. Do you need him for anything?"

"No, nothing. I just wondered if he was still here."

They walked towards the side street where Laura had left her car. Nancy stopped for a moment when she saw Jim's Morris Oxford parked on the other side of the street. She was tempted to ask Laura if they could wait by the car for a few moments and even thought of going back into the hotel to see if Jim had returned to the bar. But she could not think how she might explain this to her daughter, so she resigned herself to traveling back to Enniscorthy in Laura's car.

Even as Laura started the engine, even as she nosed the car out into the street, Nancy was looking back in case Jim appeared. But he did not appear. Nancy knew that Laura would be eager to discuss the wedding and she gave in to this as they made their way home.

II

"It's not right," Eilis's mother said.

"What don't you like about it?" Eilis asked.

"Blue is not your color."

"What is my color?"

"I don't know. I'd have to see you wearing it."

"I have that other yellow dress."

"The whole town will be looking at you. And they will all have an opinion."

"And do we care?"

"I care. I certainly do."

"And none of the hats suit me?"

"Only the pillbox one but it's too black."

When she appeared in the yellow dress, her mother walked around her.

"I think you could wear anything and look marvelous. You always do."

This was, Eilis thought, the first kind thing her mother had said since her return.

"And I have an idea," her mother continued. "If you put your black jacket over the dress, it will be glamorous. And then the black hat won't stand out so much."

167

Once she was ready to set out for the cathedral, her mother stood in the hallway.

"I wish you were getting a lift. Is it normal in America for a woman to drive on her own to a wedding?"

The instant she walked through the gates of the cathedral grounds, Eilis saw people she knew. A woman who had been in school with her shouted out her name in surprise.

"It must be great to see your mother so well," one of them said, to be interrupted immediately by another, someone whose name Eilis could not remember.

When Nancy appeared with her daughter, Eilis waited for a while before approaching her.

"Nancy, it's so lovely to be here," she said.

Nancy seemed to look at her for a second as if she was not quite sure who she was. She appeared to be thinking about something else. And then she focused on Eilis.

"How lucky that you were home just now," she said, but it sounded like an afterthought.

Soon Eilis was approached by a woman who had known her sister, Rose.

"Elegant. That's how I always describe her. Elegant. Your mother was elegant too in her day and, of course, you are elegant. But Rose beat the band for elegance. She was elegant out."

Eilis nodded. It was hard to think what to say.

"And are you home for long?" the woman asked.

Just as she was about to reply, Eilis saw Jim Farrell and, for a moment, was tempted to move towards him. But she realized how closely they would be watched. Everyone here must know some version of what had happened between them.

When word came that the bride was on her way, they all entered the cathedral. Eilis went up a side aisle, aware that Jim Farrell was somewhere behind her. He too, she presumed, would be cautious. He would not sit in the same row as she did, nor even, she imagined, in the row behind.

He had come into the cathedral grounds alone. She had noticed that he was the only man who was by himself. Perhaps she was also the only woman on her own. She was sure that Nancy could not have planned this and hoped that no one else had taken note of it.

As the bride was accompanied up the aisle by her brother, Eilis, who had never seen them before, was amazed at how much they both looked like their father. The same dark eyes, the same short chin. When she had heard from her mother of George Sheridan's death, she had written to Nancy to say how shocked she was. But now his death seemed starkly present in this image of his son standing in for him and his daughter going up the aisle without her father. Nancy, she imagined, must feel the loss on a day like this, with everyone watching. George was so good-humored, so solid and decent. Nancy and he were lucky to find each other. And now he was absent. Perhaps most people in the congregation had become used to that, but for Eilis his death felt sudden and immediate, something that she had not taken in before.

The mass began. She found her mind wandering as the first prayers were said. For days now, the image of Jim walking away from her on the lane in Cush had stayed with her. If he had glanced behind, even for one second, he would have seen her standing on the lane, looking after him, wondering why he did not turn.

She went over in her mind what she would have wanted then. She imagined them both sitting in front of Martin's house in the shade, neither of them knowing what to say. And then him asking her quietly what it had been like, being away all the years. No one else had asked her this, not her mother or Nancy or anyone.

Tony's relief that she had come back to him in Brooklyn was so great that he never inquired if she had met someone else in Ireland.

Her being away that summer was simply never mentioned again. And that had made life easy between them.

She had believed that when Rosella and Larry were older they would want to know how she came to America. And she often planned the story she would tell, how she never wanted to go any-where, how those around her arranged everything for her. How no one ever asked her if she wanted to go to Brooklyn. And how that made her even lonelier in those first months away. And how she was happy when Tony came into her life. No one else had arranged that. It was what she had wanted.

But in recent years, Tony's brothers, as a way of entertaining the table, had invented another version of the story. Tony, they said, had gone to an Irish dance. As soon as he saw Eilis, even before he spoke to her, Enzo said, Tony knew the Irish girl was for him. He asked her to marry him a week later.

"He knew she was the one for him," Mauro said. "And the rest is history."

"It was a whirlwind," Enzo added. "Tony was a miserable bach-elor one day and the next was a happy married man."

Eilis knew that it would be futile to ask Tony to tell his brothers to give this up.

She knelt down and stood up with the rest of the congregation. As the sermon began, she continued thinking about home, going over her efforts to let Rosella know that what Tony's brothers were saying was not true.

She remembered telling Rosella one Sunday as they were walk-ing back from lunch that she was not just picked out on a dance floor and led to marriage by Tony, that it was her choice as much as his, but Rosella did not ask her any questions and she did not say anything more.

She did not go to the altar to receive communion, nor, it seemed, did Jim Farrell.

Tony did not even know that Jim existed. And Jim knew nothing about how she lived in America. No one really knew anything about her. In this pew in the cathedral, and the ones behind and in front, sat people who had lived in the town all of their lives. They did not have to explain themselves. Everyone knew who they had married, the names of their children. They did not have different accents which they used when they met different people. They did not live in a place where their children often tried to speak before they did at a ticket office or in a shop so that their mother's accent might not become a subject of inquiry.

On the strand in Cush, Jim had shown himself as someone who might listen. What she had liked most about him was that he could leave silence. In the time they had walked along together, he had said almost nothing. But she wished he had not asked her if she ever thought about him. What did he want her to say?

Now they would have to spend this whole wedding avoiding each other. She would have to pretend that she was not thinking about him.

When the time came for the marriage vows, suddenly Eilis imagined Tony, like a ghost, walking up the side aisle searching for her, then seeing her. Tony would know no one. Even if she introduced him to people, he would be an outsider, a stranger. And he might get a sense of how she had felt in all her years away from home.

She had learned not to dwell on these feelings that seemed more intense now as the bride and groom kissed and then walked down the aisle. She had made her own life, she thought. She should not feel sorry for herself on a day like this. The rooms in the house in Lindenhurst belonged to her as much as to Tony and Rosella and Larry, and the leafy streets around, the salt air coming in from the ocean, the light shivering with expectancy on the days when the weather on Long Island was about to change, all this had become her life.

As she followed the wedding party down the aisle, Eilis caught Jim's eye for a moment, but he bowed his head.

Before the meal, Eilis was, a number of times, on the point of approaching Nancy to chat with her, but when Nancy saw her she seemed to move away.

Eilis was glad that she was at a table with her back to Jim, with Nancy's brother-in-law on one side and an aunt of Matt Wadding's on the other. The Wadding aunt thought that she had a cousin somewhere in America.

"She used to send dollars in envelopes, but my mother didn't know what to do with them until someone told her that she could change them in the bank, but by that time she couldn't remember where she'd put them."

Once her neighbors had begun animated conversations with people on the other side of them, Eilis concentrated on passing dishes around and trying to hear what the woman opposite her was saying.

She'd noticed, when they were having drinks before the meal, that Jim seemed very alone. Surely if Jim did have a girlfriend in Dublin this would be a good moment to produce her. Eilis wondered how he had lived in the years since she had seen him. She would love to ask him, even if she might have to hear how badly he had felt after her departure.

Once Rosella and Larry came from Long Island the following week it would be even harder, she realized, to find a time and a place where she and Jim could meet again. It wouldn't be possible to talk here at the wedding when everyone would notice.

She wished she could have had one more conversation with Nancy when she might have been able to raise the subject of Jim again and get more information on how things stood with him.

Rosella and Larry would bring with them from Lindenhurst whatever news there was. She had not heard from Tony. It would be difficult, in any case, for him to know what to say. Years ago, when she came here after Rose's death, she had received regular letters from him. She remembered with a sigh that she had not been in a rush to open them. She had other things on her mind then. But when she finally did read them, she noted that they were well written and loving, and she was ashamed that she had not replied to them.

It took her a while, having returned to Brooklyn, to discover that the letters had, in fact, been penned by Frank because Tony's own handwriting was not good, nor his spelling, nor his ability to produce a clear sentence. It was something that no one in his family mentioned and no one made a joke about. Over the years, Tony had asked her for help if he needed to write something and she would do it for him.

Now, she thought, Tony could hardly ask Frank to write to his wife for him, knowing that she would not be misled by the good handwriting and clear sentences as she had been before.

She had been watching the dancing, having assured two of Matt's brothers that she would dance later, but not now. She worried that she had been brooding too much and should move among the guests, talk to people she remembered and enjoy the day.

When the three women sang "The Old Bog Road," Eilis could see Jim clearly from where she stood. Since most people were focusing on the stage, she felt free to glance over at him as much as she wanted. Maybe her interest in him was too open, she thought. She looked at the floor; she studied the singers. And when she looked back, she saw that Jim's eyes were on her. He smiled, but she did not return the smile. She was tempted to move away but then it came to her that she did actually want to see him.

One of the groom's sisters, to much whooping and laughter and catcalls, began a raucous song. Eilis did not glance over again to see what Jim was doing. Instead, she edged towards him until she was standing close by.

Before the song ended, she noticed Nancy and another woman leaving their table and making their way out of the room.

Jim was near enough to lean over and squeeze her hand. He then indicated that she should follow him. She allowed him to move a good distance ahead, not letting him out of her sight, and was sure that no one had observed her as she joined him at the doorway to the side. Everyone was too involved with the stage and the song.

The stairs they descended belonged to the old part of the hotel. On one of the landings there were boxes piled up, and the next flight of stairs looked as though it had not been used for some time. It was dimly lit and opened onto a coffee shop, now closed. Jim sat down at one of the tables near the door.

"It's nice to find somewhere quiet," he said.

She sat opposite him.

"I think my dancing days are over," he added. "How about you?"

She smiled and left silence for a moment before saying, "I felt sorry that you left so quickly the other day."

He shook his head and laughed.

"I thought you couldn't wait to get rid of me."

"I didn't know what to say. It was a surprise seeing you."

"I'd like to see you again."

"My children are coming next week. It might be hard to find a moment."

"We should try. How could I get in touch with you?"

"I don't know. My mother watches everything. And my brother."

"My phone number is in the book, both the bar number and the upstairs one."

"You want me to call you? My mother doesn't have a phone."

"I want us not to lose touch. Maybe you could use a phone box?"

She considered this, and then, abruptly, stood up.

"Perhaps we should go back upstairs. Someone will miss us. I'll go first."

Back in the hall, having found Nancy's sister, Eilis set out to detain her in conversation for as long as she could. She would like to leave, but since no one else was going, then she would wait.

Very quickly, Moya let her know that she planned merely to stop for a moment and exchange pleasantries. She said that her husband was waiting for her at a table across the room.

Since Eilis was driving, she did not want the drink which Gerard offered to bring her. She would just have a glass of water.

What she discerned now, over the music, was a loudness in the room, voices raised in darting conversation and easy laughter. She walked around with the glass of water in her hand, desperate for a group to join. When she was approached again by Matt's brother asking her to dance, she accepted. It would get her through the next ten minutes. Nancy, she saw, was deep in conversation with Matt's mother. Soon, she determined, she would slip away.

As she was preparing to depart, she saw Nancy and Laura standing up. Perhaps, now that the bride and groom had gone, they too thought it was time to leave. Eilis had been careful not to look around for Jim but she sensed that he must be alert to where she was.

When he appeared behind her, she was not surprised.

"I'm over the limit," he said. "I'll have to leave my car where it is. Is anyone else traveling with you?"

"I can take you home, if that's what you mean."

"There's a small car park opposite the Talbot Hotel. Do you know it?"

"I'm sure I can find it."

"Why don't you drive there and I'll meet you there in a while?"

She was about to say that her car was just outside but she realized they should agree quickly on how to proceed.

"I'll be waiting there," she said and turned away from him.

There were a few cars in the Talbot Hotel car park, but otherwise it was desolate. As she waited, she shivered and almost wished she could start the engine to go home. However, no matter what, she was going to stay here until Jim arrived. She would work out what to say when she saw him.

He had not seemed drunk to her. His assertion that he was over the limit was probably a ruse. It was a clever way of getting to see her again. When he appeared, she was glad that he had thought of this way of going home together.

As she drove along the quays, he kept his head down.

"Can you turn right at the bridge?" he asked.

"That would take us to Curracloe."

"We can turn at Castlellis and go to Enniscorthy that way."

But when they saw the sign for Curracloe, he told her to turn right.

"Are you in a hurry home?" he asked.

"My mother will be awake."

"Waiting for you?"

"I imagine so."

"You can always say that the wedding went on late."

In Curracloe village, she indicated right without waiting for him to suggest that she drive to the car park at the sand dunes.

"You know your way."

"Some things I have not forgotten. My father drove us here on Sundays in a car he used to borrow. Sometimes it was Cush, sometimes here. This is where I learned to swim."

She drove down the hill to the dunes, closing the window against the wind and turning on the wipers as a light drizzle had begun. In the car park when they opened their doors, it was obvious immediately that this was not a night for walking by the sea.

"It was such a mild day," he said. "I thought it would be calm down here. Sorry for taking you out of your way."

In the car, she waited for a moment before starting the engine again.

"Is there something you wanted to say to me?" she asked.

"I wanted to talk to you. That's all. But I feel like a fool for taking us here."

"It could have been perfect."

She should watch every word she said, she felt, in case she gave him a false impression. But at the same time she did not want to drop him in the town and spend time trying to pluck up the courage to phone him and trying just as hard to keep the idea out of her mind.

"Could you drive into the town?" he asked. "I'll get out on the quays and you can park where you usually do and then walk down to the pub. The door to the house will be on the latch. I'll be waiting for you in the hall."

She drove slowly on the narrow roads between Curracloe and Enniscorthy. Now they were alone, she thought, they had every chance to talk but neither of them broke a silence that seemed to her relaxed, almost natural. Perhaps it made no sense to begin a conversation as they both faced outwards into the headlights and the night.

If her mother could see her now, or Nancy, or if Tony had any idea, none of them would understand. She did not understand either. It occurred to her that she could drop Jim on the quays in Enniscorthy, letting him know that she had no plans to visit him secretly that night. She could easily tell him that she was going home to bed. All it would need was for him to say the wrong thing or to insist too much.

After Glenbrien, she broke the silence.

"These roads are very lonely."

"We're not far now," he replied. "Your driving is steady."

When they drove down the steep hill from Drumgoold into the town, she pulled in on the quays at Kehoe's pub. It was past closing time. The quays were empty. No one would see Jim getting out of her car.

III

In the hallway waiting for Eilis, with the door on the latch, Jim realized that this might easily be a night when Nancy would call. If she did, he decided, he would let the phone ring out and pretend the next day he had not heard it.

It suddenly struck him that it would be easier somehow if Eilis did not come. He would know what to do then. He could go through the conversations they might have had, imagine what drink she would have asked for, dream of moving towards her in lamplight in the room upstairs.

She must have parked the car. He pictured her walking along Court Street. He listened, but there was no sound. If she did not come tonight, and since it was unlikely that they would see each other once her children came, then the car journey just now was a lost opportunity. He had liked being quiet with her, giving her a chance to concentrate on the road. But if it were to be their last time together, then he should have started a conversation.

And it occurred to him again that, after all the excitement, Nancy would surely want to see him. This could be a night when she would feel less cautious and decide to come to visit him without any warning. He shivered at the idea that Nancy and Eilis might, in fact, meet at his door, each wondering what the other was doing here.

When the door was pushed open, he had to stop himself from moving backwards in fright.

"I hope I'm in the right house," Eilis whispered.

She gently closed the door behind her.

"I was worried you'd changed your mind," Jim said.

He was safe now, he thought, as he accompanied her up the stairs.

In the living room, once he had got drinks for them, Jim sat opposite her by the fireplace. This was the room that she might have come to know well had things been different. But he should not mention that. He should not sound as though he wished to remonstrate with her.

He thanked her for coming. She nodded and sipped her drink. He asked about her children.

"My daughter," she said, "is studious and serious. I don't know where she got it from."

"Aren't you serious?"

"I suppose I am. But she has better chances than I did."

"And your son?"

"Larry? He's very excited about coming here."

"More than his sister?"

"Rosella starts college in September, so she has other things to look forward to."

What Jim noticed was that Eilis had not mentioned her husband.

"What's strange," she said, "is how American they are. Not just their accents, but everything about them. I'm meeting them at the airport on Tuesday morning. I'll see it as soon as they appear."

He looked at her and tried to listen as carefully as he could, aware that he might never get another chance to be with her like this. A few times he felt an urge to go to the kitchen on the pretext of needing more ice or another drink, so that he could be alone, so that he could have time to convince himself that she really had come here, that he really was hearing about her life.

Soon she would leave. He was sure she had not come here to spend the night with him. He kept hoping that she wouldn't go yet. It was clear that she wanted to talk. He would ask questions, but not too many. All the time he was watching out for any reference to her husband. She spoke about Lindenhurst, her job at the garage, her Armenian boss, but she said nothing about who was there when she went home in the evenings besides her children.

It was important not to ask. In one second, in one statement, his sense that her husband was absent could be deflated. Also, a question about him could appear too direct; Jim did not want to seem too interested. In a while, he thought, she would be bound to say something that would let him know. But she wasn't doing so yet. He had the impression that she was being careful.

If she were to indicate that she was happily married and would soon be returning to her husband, that would, it now occurred to him, make things simple. He would not have to make any decisions. He would feel a dull disappointment. But he was used to that. It was what he carried upstairs to this room most nights.

Since he and Nancy had agreed to marry, he had often returned to this chair once the pub had closed with thoughts of what she had said the last time they had met and dreams of when he would see her next. He slept easier knowing that she was not far away. What would Nancy say now if she came into the room?

When he did eventually go to the kitchen, he found it barely credible that Eilis Lacey was still in his sitting room, sipping a drink, describing the boardinghouse where she first stayed in Brooklyn.

Over the years, he had imagined many things, but not this. He wanted to return to the room and ask her why she had come—was it merely to tell him about her life since they had last seen each other?

"Are you still living with your husband?" he asked suddenly when he was back in the armchair. He had not intended to speak and realized that he had interrupted her as she resumed telling him about her first job in America.

"Tony?" she asked, as though he might have been referring to someone else.

He nodded and then examined her carefully as she hesitated. If she were living with her husband, she would surely say so immediately.

"He drove me to the airport, so I suppose that says something."

He wondered what she could possibly mean.

"But I'm not sure what to say about it," she added.

She was letting him know there was a problem at home. She had, he thought, said enough to make that plain.

"Why did you never marry?" she asked.

He smiled at the idea that she, too, could ask questions that sounded abrupt. He decided to spare her an account of how he had felt when she had left. And if he did begin to tell her what his life was like, he would need to pretend that Nancy had not recently sat in the very armchair where Eilis was now. He would have to pretend that he was seeing no one at all.

On the other hand, Eilis might be the one person he could confide in. She was an outsider. He could tell her how he was engaged to Nancy. She would, most likely, keep the secret. He saw her as a most trustworthy person. She would congratulate him, say how pleased she was. And he would have no more reason for wondering about her husband. Perhaps she would call one more time before she left. But she would leave soon and all the excitement he felt in her presence would follow her.

He knew what he should do, but he wanted to keep this going, whatever it was. He did not reply to her question.

She agreed to have another drink. As he got more ice and mixers, he felt that he should say more. But he would still have to be careful.

"Are there things that you regret?" he asked her when he returned.

She smiled and sipped her drink.

"If I had been stronger, I would never have left here. I had no big dreams about leaving. I would have stayed. But then I wouldn't have had my children."

When she looked at him sharply, he could not tell if she meant that she would have stayed with him.

"And after that, do you regret other things?"

"I would like to have studied more, but that was never going to be possible."

What could she say that would satisfy him? He was, he saw, hoping for too much. She could hardly have said that she regretted not being with him.

When she asked him what he regretted most, he was at a loss. He regretted the years going by; he regretted that he taken so long to find someone he could be happy with.

"I'm sorry that I didn't follow you that time. As soon as I got the note from you that morning to say you were going back to Brooklyn, I should have gone to the train station to find you, or failing that I should have gone to the boat. I used to think about it, what might have happened had I followed you."

"Is there anything else?"

He sat back, closed his eyes and shook his head.

"There is something else," he said. "But I'm not sure I could tell you."

"I'll have to go soon," she said. "If you don't tell me, that could be another regret."

He shook his head again. "Some things are private."

"Is it about me?"

Maybe, he thought, she wanted him to say something about being in the room with her now and how that made him feel bad about all the years without her. But he wanted to tell her something that would make her respond.

"Times have changed," he said. "I see that in the pub. Things were different when we were young. But I've often regretted that we never spent a night together. I wish we'd done that."

For a second, he thought she was going to stand up and leave. But instead, she laughed.

"I wasn't expecting that."

"It is the truest thing I've said tonight."

She smiled.

"Have you ever felt that?" he asked.

She looked directly at him but did not reply.

"I mean—" he began and stopped.

"What were you going to say?" she asked.

"You have to be in Dublin on Tuesday for the airport. If you went up on Monday I could meet you and we could stay in Dublin."

"Stay?"

"In a hotel. There's a hotel I stop at sometimes on my way home. It's called the Montrose. It's in Stillorgan. You wouldn't know it. It's a modern hotel, sort of anonymous. We could meet there."

She stood up and asked him where the bathroom was. He noticed how calm she seemed.

"You have it all planned," she said when she appeared again. "You really do."

"I just thought of it a second ago. I had nothing planned. But I could meet you there at two o'clock on Monday or a bit later if it suited you."

"You used to be so shy."

"I need to find some way of meeting you again."

"Yes, I can see that."

"Maybe I shouldn't have asked. But it's what I want. Honestly, it came into my head just now."

"Let me be clear. You would go to Dublin in your car. I would go in mine. We would meet in the hotel. Just one room. For the night. Is that right?"

"Yes."

"And I would go to the airport in the morning to collect my children?"

"That's right. But, listen, forget it if I have gone too far."

"Hold on, I'm thinking. What would my mother say?"

"Is that what you're thinking?"

"No."

He was waiting for her to mention her husband.

"So what are you thinking, then?" he asked.

"That I have exhausted your hospitality and should go home now."

"Maybe I went too far."

"Not at all. Just give me time to consider it."

She stood up to go.

In the hall, he turned on both lights and was careful not to try to embrace her or kiss her.

"I'll think about it," she said. "I promise—"

"You mean there's a chance?"

"It would be great just now if you said nothing more."

He unbolted the front door and glanced up and down the empty street.

"I'll think about it," she said again. "And I'll leave you a note to let you know. I'll do that tomorrow."

"Do you remember the name of the hotel? It's just beyond Stillorgan and before Donnybrook."

"I must go home now. And no more questions! Do you hear me?"

He put a finger to his lips.

"Not a word," he said and closed the door.

PART FIVE

I

"Now, I have good news for you," Father Walsh said as soon as he came into the reception room at the Manse.

"I really appreciate you seeing me," Nancy said.

"I love hearing good news," Father Walsh said. "And we're all delighted that you're getting married again."

"You know, we haven't told anyone yet, no one except you."

"It will be time enough to tell them. Now, the priests here have no problem at all about you getting married in Rome. We have an old friend in Rome, Father Seán Anglim. He will find the right chapel. He suggests you stay a week, if not more. And he says the weather will be perfect, not too hot."

"Does he know where we might stay? A small hotel?"

"I can ask him. We have plenty of time."

When they were sitting on facing armchairs with tea and biscuits on the low table between them, he asked her if she thought one week in Italy would not be too short.

"I know you both have businesses to take care of but every couple needs time to get to know each other. I'd stay for two weeks if I were you."

Nancy noticed the priest rubbing his hands together slowly. She nodded. She wondered how he would respond if she told him that she had been visiting Jim late at night and did really feel that she

knew him well enough. Before going to Rome, she thought, she
would drive to Wexford and queue for confession in the Franciscan
Friary and hope that the friar who was known for his sympathy and
understanding was on duty.

"Are you kind?" this friar had asked her on her last visit to the
confessional.

"Yes, I hope I am."

"Are you a good, conscientious mother?"

"Yes, I am."

"Then say an act of contrition and go in peace."

Suddenly, she found that Father Walsh was looking at her curi-
ously as she smiled to herself at the memory.

"Do we need to fill in forms?" she asked him.

"All the church side of things will be done for you," he replied.
"We are glad to be of service and the cause is good."

"The cause?"

"Holy matrimony," he replied and quietly bowed his head and
then looked at her, smiling.

"You know, I saw Jim Farrell," Father Walsh continued, "on the
street yesterday. Of course, I said nothing to him about anything.
But he seemed happy. I hear so much bad news that it lifted my
spirits to see him in such good form. Your children must know
him already?"

"Oh yes, they do."

"I'm sure the news, when they hear it, will bring them great joy."

He sounded for a moment as he did when he was preaching to
a large congregation.

"But it must be hard to keep a secret like that," he said.

"My policy," Nancy said, "and Jim's, is to tell no one. So the
only others who know are you and your colleague in Rome. And
perhaps some of the other priests as well?"

"And we keep secrets. It's our job, if you can call it that."

He pointed to his collar.

*   *   *

At the top of Cathedral Street, Nancy did not feel like going home. Gerard had still been in bed as she was leaving. If he were up now, she would have to discuss further what had happened on Saturday night.

Brudge Foley, who normally came to help in the chip shop at the weekend, had called off sick on Saturday afternoon. It really was impossible for anyone to run the shop alone on a Saturday night, so Nancy had suggested to Gerard that he cancel his plan to go to the dance in Whites Barn. And he had bluntly refused, even though he understood perfectly that his mother could not manage on her own.

"We agreed that I don't have to do Saturday," he said. "If I do all three weekend nights, I'll have no life at all."

"What about me?" she asked. "Should I have no life either?"

"You can take Friday or Sunday off," he replied. "There's no one stopping you."

"I can't do tonight on my own. You know that better than anyone."

"I have arranged to go to Whites. All my friends are going."

"Next week, I'll have help. You can go then. If Brudge can't do it, I'll get someone else."

He turned away from her.

"Ger, I need you here tonight."

An hour later, as she was cleaning behind the counter, he appeared again.

"I'm really sorry that I can't do tonight. You'll have to try and get someone else."

"Have you any suggestions?"

He shrugged.

Close to midnight, a man whom she did not recognize joined the crowd waiting to be served and then began to vomit over several customers before vomiting further on the counter itself and the floor. Nancy immediately thought of phoning Jim, but then she realized that he would want to know where Gerard was. Also, she did not think she could ask him to help her clean up the vomit. She would have to do it herself, having told the customers to wait outside.

On the way to get a bucket of hot water and a brush, she realized that she had forgotten to lower the heat of the cooking oil. The chip shop was soon full of acrid smoke so that she had to open the door to the street, telling those waiting outside that they still could not come in.

Since the pubs were closed, more people gathered in front of the shop. Even so, she did not feel she could call Jim and have him witness the scene. As soon as the shop was cleared of the smoke, she would shut for the night. There were too many people outside. She would never be able to heat the oil again and start to get the fish and burgers and chips and onion rings ready.

Maybe it was a lesson she needed to learn. She could never manage the shop on her own at the weekend. And maybe it was a lesson for Gerard also. He was not entitled to go to Wexford with his friends when she had no one to help her. He would have to take more responsibility for the business.

She cleaned as much as she could. When she finally closed the door, a few people began banging on the window. She responded by turning off the lights and going upstairs, where she sat at the kitchen table, afraid to switch on the lights in the front room, whose windows gave onto the square. She found that she was shaking. Even if she decided to phone Jim, she was afraid that he would find her in a state in which she did not want him to see her.

It was George that she found herself thinking about. If only he could come into the room now. If only he came, in his absent-minded way, to fetch some water or wonder where he had left his glasses, and if she could glance up at him from the newspaper she had spread out on the table. And Gerard could come in, spruced up for the dance, looking for the keys of the car or some money from his father.

If only George had not died, there would not be a belligerent crowd outside her chip shop in the Market Square. Even when she knew she was going to lose him, she had never once imagined that she would find herself worried that the shouting outside would cause the neighbors to come in the morning to remonstrate with her, and worried also that the smell of vomit might linger in the shop if she did not go back down now and wash the floor one more time.

What would it be like when she was married again, when Jim would have finished by one o'clock on a Sunday morning? He would have to wait until she, exhausted, finished cleaning up. What would that be like for him and for her?

Now, on Cathedral Street, she dreaded having to face Gerard. He had already mentioned to her that he had met several people, including their immediate neighbors on the Square, who had given him a description of the scenes outside the chip shop in the early hours of Sunday morning. He had made what happened seem like a failure on her part.

She had walked out of the room before he could go any further and had been careful to avoid him for the rest of the day.

As she walked by the Green, it struck her that she should go to visit Eilis Lacey. At the wedding itself, Nancy recalled, she had not spoken to Eilis much. Maybe Eilis would be going back to America soon. She went along the Back Road and then, when she had passed the Technical School, she turned down Hospital Lane.

The front door of the Laceys' house was wide open and there were workmen in the hall. Nancy was almost relieved at the possibility that this was the very wrong moment to call. She stood outside and waited. If Eilis did not appear soon, she would move on. Instead, Eilis's mother emerged from the kitchen.

"I never wanted a fridge," she was saying to one of the workmen, "and I never wanted a washing machine, and the cooker I had did me nicely. But what can I do?"

"Go on out of that," the workman said, "you'll be made up when we have it all connected."

Mrs. Lacey noticed Nancy at the door.

"Who is that?" she asked. "Is it Nancy?"

"I think I picked the wrong moment," Nancy said. "Is Eilis here?"

"She is in Dublin," Mrs. Lacey said.

"I hope I haven't missed her altogether."

"No, you have not. She'll be back tomorrow with her two children. And I'm using the day to get overdue work on the house done. I have these nice men to help."

Nancy could hear the sound of hammering from the kitchen.

"No," Mrs. Lacey continued, as though Nancy had asked her a question. "I don't know why Eilis went up to Dublin this morning. She said she had shopping to do. But she'll be back in good time tomorrow."

When Nancy said that she would call again soon, Mrs. Lacey insisted that she should come in now.

"We can have tea in the back room."

In the kitchen, a plumber was installing a washing machine. The new fridge and oven looked strange among the old cupboards and the chipped tiles and the faded paintwork.

"This will be a big surprise for Eilis," Mrs. Lacey said. "She won't know the kitchen. What I wanted was to get a modern kitchen so the children wouldn't feel they were visiting outer space. And haven't I done well? Doesn't it look great?"

"They'll be delighted," Nancy said.

"And I heard all about the wedding," Mrs. Lacey said when they were settled in the back room. "Eilis is a good person to send anywhere. She comes home with all the news. She said the Waddings were lively, one and all. And your rig-out was, she said, most beautifully chosen and really suited you. And there was singing!"

"Well, I didn't sing," Nancy said.

"I think widows at weddings are best to let others do the singing," Mrs. Lacey said. "How long is George dead?"

"Five years last month."

"You don't get over it at all," Mrs. Lacey said. "Or at least I didn't. All we can do is thank God for the small mercies and take each day as it comes."

"That's the truth," Nancy said. She tried to finish her tea so that she could go.

"And Eilis said that Jim Farrell was at the wedding."

Nancy nodded.

"I always thought it was strange he never married."

Nancy sipped her tea.

"I asked Eilis if she spoke to him at the wedding, or did she even have a dance with him for old times' sake but she nearly bit my head off."

Nancy looked at the floor and said nothing.

"Jim is always very nice to me when I meet him," Mrs. Lacey continued. "I often think it's not good that he's there on his own in that big house over the pub."

Surely, Nancy thought, the old woman must notice that she was not responding.

"But everyone to themselves, that's what I always say. Amn't I right, Nancy?"

"You certainly are, Mrs. Lacey."

"Now, you'll have to excuse me as I must oversee the lifting of a bed into the attic room so that Larry, my American grandson, can have a place to sleep."

*   *   *

Gerard was in the kitchen when Nancy got home.

"It occurred to me that you might be better off getting a job," she said.

"I have a job."

"You have a job you don't do. I didn't see you on Saturday night. Unless swanning around Whites Barn is a job."

"We talked about that yesterday."

Gerard stood up from the kitchen table and moved towards the door.

"Most of our business," Nancy said, blocking his way, "is at the weekend. You cannot take Saturday night off."

"I won't work Saturday nights. I'll do every other night."

"Even when I'm left on my own?"

"Brudge will be here in future."

"She gave us two hours' notice that she couldn't come. That could happen anytime again. Actually, on Saturdays all three of us should be there anyway."

"I won't do Saturdays."

"And that's why I think you should get a job. It's a pity you didn't study when you had a chance. Your sisters . . ."

"Don't give me that stuff about my sisters."

Eventually, she got out of his way and sat at the table. As soon as she heard the front door closing, something occurred to her and she went into the main room and stood looking over the Market Square.

Once she married Jim, she realized, she wouldn't go on running the chip shop. If Gerard were not involved, then she might consider selling the entire building. At nineteen, he was too young to handle the business on his own. But when she was married, she would not want to spend the weekend doling out fish and burgers and bags of chips to people and come away smelling of oil and fried food. Jim must have considered this. Maybe it would be enough for her to keep house for him, especially if they were to move to a bungalow with a garden.

The more she thought about the chip shop, the more she under-stood that the idea of her giving up work there would have to come from Jim. He knew that the business was lucrative. He had a better idea of her income than she did of his. But surely Jim made enough from the pub for them both to live.

If Jim said that she should stop working in the chip shop, she would pretend not to have considered it until now. She would express surprise. She wondered if it would help Gerard if Jim had some role in the business. Perhaps he could guide Gerard, even control him. She could pretend to be involved too but slowly she would leave the decisions to Jim. She would have to be careful, especially at the beginning, not to look as if she was angling to retire completely. Somehow, she would appear busy, but she would not join the golf club or take up bridge.

Since it was half past two and most of the lunchtime customers would have dispersed, she believed that it would be a good time to call in to the pub and have a talk with Jim. She had been tempted to do this several times before but had stopped herself. She would do it just one time. Shane would not be there until four and Andy did not start until much later. Jim had told her how peaceful it could become. It was the time he liked best, he said.

If she phoned, she imagined, Jim would suggest that they meet much later when he had finished work. But she could pretend that she needed to share the news about Rome with him. She foresaw how they would move down the far end of the bar so she could explain in hushed tones what Father Walsh had said. She hoped that Jim had not heard too much about Saturday night. He might wonder why she had not called on him to help. She would have to pretend it was all nothing.

If she saw that Jim was busy, she would go as soon as possible. But her hope was that, at some stage in their conversation, she would be able to give the impression that she was exhausted. She would let Jim know that managing the chip shop was running her down. And then, if they met later, she would encourage Jim to feel that the chip shop was not something she should do forever, and soon, over a few meetings, Jim would understand that, once they were married, he would not like her to continue working in the chip shop.

Days like this, warm and windless in the town, could be stifling in houses like hers and his. She imagined a bungalow with double doors from the kitchen into the garden with a patio where she would have a table and chairs. She would position the house so that the patio space would bask in the morning sun.

She was sure about this plan. No matter what time of the day it was, or what mood she was in, she never wavered in her desire to live away from the town center. But she found herself uncertain about smaller things, such as her suggestion to Gerard that he should go and get a job.

Gerard had been fourteen when his father died. While Miriam and Laura had never left each other's side in the days around the funeral, and had cried openly, Gerard had remained alone. He said nothing, showed no signs of any grief. He was frozen. No one could get through to him. And then when he went back to school the complaints began about his attitude towards the teachers. Nothing Nancy said or did made any difference to him. He stopped going to the tennis club and, when winter came, he got dropped from the rugby team because he did not come to practice.

As soon as she stepped inside the pub, she was greeted by Shane Nolan, who was behind the bar.

"The boss is away," Shane said.

"What time will he be back?"

"He didn't say but he told me to lock up later so it won't be soon."

"Do you know where he is?"

Nancy realized as soon as she had asked this that it sounded as though it might matter to her where Jim was.

"He's in Dublin. He has business in Dublin."

Nancy could not think what this business might be. Jim's accountant and his solicitor were both local, and she didn't understand why he hadn't told her he was going to Dublin.

"Do you want to leave a message?" Shane asked.

"No, no, I was just dropping in."

Even that, she knew, sounded untrue.

"Well, I'll tell him you were looking for him."

"Don't worry at all."

How strange, she thought, that both Jim and Eilis were in Dublin. Jim normally traveled to the city on a Thursday and this was Monday. And Eilis's mother had wondered why she had gone to Dublin so early. And why would Jim need to stay in Dublin until late?

Nancy imagined them meeting each other by accident in Grafton Street. What would happen? Would they stop and talk? For a second, an image from Miriam's wedding came into her mind. She had seen Eilis and Jim talking to each other in a way that appeared casual, relaxed, almost familiar. It was odd because she had presumed that any encounter between them would be strained and uneasy. But then someone distracted her, someone demanded her full attention, and she did not think about that scene again.

But now it became more solid. Perhaps Jim and Eilis had had a conversation earlier during the wedding and all the tension between them had worn away. And that meant they could seem to be talking like two old friends.

But there was something else. There was something in Shane's expression just now, in his tone, and it was also in Mrs. Lacey's when she spoke of Eilis's being in Dublin—a sense of uncertainty, a feeling that there was something that could not be explained. "He has business in Dublin," Shane had said. No one talked like that in Enniscorthy. Shane had sounded too formal. But still, it was not impossible that Jim really did have things to do there that he did not want her to know about. Perhaps it was something to do with money. And it wasn't impossible that Eilis had gone to Dublin early simply to get away from her mother.

As she passed the monument in the center of the Market Square, Nancy saw Gerard walking towards the house, his head down, his hands by his sides. She suddenly felt sorry for him and wondered if she should tell him, once they were both inside the house, that he could go to Whites Barn any Saturday night he wanted. But that would be a mistake. She wished Jim had been in the pub just now. Even telling him the story might have been a relief.

She felt helpless. She had built herself up to have a talk with Jim not only about Gerard but about how they both might live after they married. Jim had a way of reassuring her. He liked Gerard. Jim himself might want to consider living somewhere outside the town. It was such a pity he hadn't been there just now.

After what happened on Saturday night, and after her conversation with Father Walsh about Rome, she wasn't sure she could easily spend a dull afternoon alone. Something would have to change; something would have to happen. It struck Nancy as she waited for a car to pass so that she could cross the street, that she should tell Gerard of her plan to marry Jim, and tell him now, this minute. For a second, she felt almost excited. She walked briskly towards the house so that she could find him before she changed her mind.

II

"That's not what I said," Larry interrupted. "I said that you guys used to eat each other."

"But when?" Eilis asked.

"I told you. In the Famine. In the Great Hunger."

As soon as they set out from the airport, Larry, in the back seat, told Eilis about the book that Mr. Dakessian had given him.

"He gave Rosella a book too but she didn't bring it with her."

"It was too heavy. I'll read it when I get back. But Uncle Frank gave me another book and I read that on the plane."

"It's by this woman," Larry said.

"Larry, I can tell my mother about the book myself."

Rosella rummaged in her bag.

"It's called *The Price of My Soul* by Bernadette Devlin," she said, producing a paperback.

"Mine is called *The Great Hunger*," Larry said. "And it says that you guys ate anything you could find at that time, including each other."

"What do you mean, 'you guys'?" Eilis asked. "Honestly, Larry!"

"That's what it says. Don't shoot me, I'm just reading the book."

"He read the worst bits out in a loud voice so the whole plane could hear."

"And what is your book like?" Eilis asked.

"It's really sad at the start and then I really wanted to meet Bernadette Devlin. I admire her. If she came to Enniscorthy while we were there it would be amazing."

Beyond Ashford, Eilis found a safe place to pull in.

"There's something I need to say to you both. Your Enniscorthy grandmother knows nothing about what is going on at home. Nothing! She's old and it would upset her too much. So, not a word! Not a single word! And her house has not been decorated for years. I'm not sure what rooms we will all be sleeping in. But no complaining. Your grandmother is very proud and very sensitive."

"How did she get that house?" Rosella asked as they were on the road again.

"What do you mean?"

"Bernadette Devlin says it was impossible for Catholics to get houses."

"That's in the North."

"But not in the South?"

"No. There's nothing like that."

By the time Eilis had driven through Arklow, Rosella and Larry were both asleep. They had been careful not to mention their father or their grandmother. Eilis wondered if they knew that Tony had not written to her.

As she ran her tongue along her teeth, she could still taste Jim Farrell's mouth. That morning, in the hotel room, she had promised him that she would soon call him, using the phone box at the bottom of Parnell Avenue, even though she had explained how hard it might be to find an excuse to leave her mother's house.

At the reception desk of the Montrose Hotel, the day before, when Eilis had asked for Mr. Farrell, Mr. Jim Farrell, the young receptionist had immediately directed her to a room on the top floor.

The day was bright and warm; it would make sense for them to go for a walk, but she imagined that they would stay in their room until she left in the morning. Jim came awkwardly to the door in his shirtsleeves and socks.

"I was having a little lie-down," he said.

"Don't let me . . ." she began.

She saw that there was a double bed. She smiled at how easy it had been.

"I hope the room is all right," he said. "It might be a bit small compared to American hotels."

She did not want to say to him that she had never stayed in an American hotel.

She took off her shoes and, after a while, lay on the bed with him. She kissed him. As he fumbled with the buttons on her blouse, Eilis was tempted to whisper to him that there was no rush, she would be with him until the morning.

In the early evening, Jim dialed a number from the phone beside the bed. She heard him booking a table for two at eight.

"Are we going out to a restaurant?" she asked.

"It's a quiet place. Italian. It'll be all right. I often go there when I am up on Thursdays."

In the city, Jim seemed confident with the flow of traffic and found a parking space in a side street. In the restaurant, he asked for a table at the back that was free.

Since the place was lit only by table lamps, no one would ever notice them, Eilis realized, once they were sitting down.

Jim left her to order for both of them.

"Nothing too fancy, but surprise me. I always order the same things. But now that I am with an expert . . ."

"That's a good name for me."

"I still don't know if you're an American now," he asked when the wine and the first course came.

"I think I became one when I got to vote against Nixon. I felt like an American then."

"I had a group of old-timers in the pub. They were all clued-in to politics, English politics, the North, American politics. So I heard a lot about Nixon."

"What did you think of him?" Eilis asked.

"I was surprised by one thing," Jim said. "I was surprised that they got him on something small. I mean, considering all the other things he did—"

"You mean they got him on Watergate?"

"It mightn't seem small, but it looked small from my perspective. Maybe if you were in America, it was different. And Ireland must look different from the American side."

"I don't understand how little I see and hear just now about Derry and Belfast," Eilis said. "I thought there would be flags and marches down here too. In America, it's what everyone wants to talk to you about if you are Irish."

"At the beginning," Jim said, "the subject of the North was very heated. There was a shouting match one night in the pub with fellows demanding we should invade the North. And then later people who were burned out of their houses in Belfast, Catholic people, came to the town. Everyone bought drinks for them and they had terrible stories. But not long after, they were huddled in a group together with no one paying any attention to them. And then we never saw them again. They must have gone back to the North."

When the bill was paid and Jim went to the bathroom, Eilis had a moment where she felt surprised at herself. She realized that she was actually looking forward to the rest of the evening, to being in the car with Jim, to returning to the room with him, to resuming this conversation, and then to spending the night in bed with him.

*　　　*　　　*

Rosella and Larry were still asleep in the car. By now, Jim would be home, she thought as she drove towards Enniscorthy. She had asked him not to contact her but to wait, let her be the one to get in touch.

"When?" he had asked her.

"Soon," she had replied.

"What kind of soon?"

"I don't know yet."

"I want to know if you're free."

"We can talk about that."

"But you must know. You yourself must know!"

She did know. In that second, she was convinced that, if she could, she wanted to be with him. But she needed to be certain that she would feel the same that night or in the morning.

"Don't press me too hard," she said.

"If you're free, then I—"

"Don't say it just yet."

"I would like to be with you, no matter what, even if I had to—"

"You've said enough!"

"This time, I would follow you to New York. That is what I want to do. That is what I am asking you if I can do."

She had to hold herself back from saying that she would like that too. Instead, she smiled and left silence and held his gaze.

"Not a word," Eilis said when she had parked the car in Court Street. "And no complaining. Be nice to her. Put up with things you mightn't put up with at home."

"You make her sound very difficult," Rosella said.

"She is difficult," Eilis said. "Or she has been since I arrived."

Once the front door was opened by her mother, Eilis noticed that the fridge and washing machine and cooker were no longer blocking the hallway.

"Well," her mother said, with her grandchildren standing on the pavement outside her house, "you don't take after our side at all. You are a pair of Italians. Come in, come in, the whole town'll be talking about how I left you standing on the street."

In the kitchen, their grandmother put them sitting at the table. Ignoring Eilis's surprise at the installation of the fridge and washing machine and cooker, she opened the fridge, which was empty except for a bottle of milk and a pound of butter.

"In a minute we'll have the dinner," she said. "It will all be a bit rough and ready. But let you first get settled."

They followed her up the stairs. She showed Larry the way to his bedroom in the attic and then explained that she had made the front room downstairs into a bedroom and that could be used by Rosella.

"Why don't you take my room," Eilis said to Rosella, "and I'll sleep downstairs."

"Why would I take your room?" Rosella asked.

"Because it's beside your grandmother's room and she would like to have you close to her."

"It would be a lovely change," Eilis's mother said.

When Martin arrived and questioned them about their journey, Eilis went to the hallway and opened the front door and closed it again as quietly as she could. It would be easy to slip in and out of the house without being noticed while everyone was sleeping.

Martin and her mother were telling the children about Eilis's efforts, as soon as she arrived, to make the house more modern.

"All the things were wrong," her mother said. "Too big, too small, the wrong color, the wrong make. I had to send them all back."

Eilis decided not to point out that the fridge, washing machine and cooker were precisely the ones she had bought. They had not been sent back.

Larry had a way of becoming instantly friendly with most people, but there were others of whom he was wary. It had taken him a year or more, for example, to warm to Mr. Dakessian, and he could even be distant with his uncle Frank if he had not seen him for a while. Eilis now watched him taking the measure of Martin, who was offering to accompany him on a tour of the pubs of the town.

"They don't mind fellows your age coming in and having a mineral. They don't mind them at all."

"What's a mineral?"

"You don't have minerals in America?"

"It's a soft drink," his grandmother said.

"So, anytime you're ready," Martin said, "let's hit the pubs. Look out, pubs of Enniscorthy!"

"I think I'll stick around for a bit," Larry said. "I haven't seen my Irish grandmother for a while."

"You've never seen her before," Rosella said.

"That's what I mean."

Once they had eaten and Martin had disappeared, Eilis went into the sitting room and wrote a short note on aerogram paper to Tony to let him know that Rosella and Larry had arrived safely and were now in Enniscorthy in her mother's house.

She did not know what to put at the end of the letter. It could not be anything as formal as "yours sincerely" or as clear as "love." Instead, she wrote, "Will be in touch again soon" and added her name. She went with the aerogram to the post office.

In the first week, Eilis took her mother, who had no problem at all getting in and out of the car, and Rosella for a drive each afternoon, leaving Larry to explore the town. They went to Wexford and walked along the quays and they drove to Rosslare, where they had tea in Kelly's Hotel. They went as far as Waterford and even to Kilkenny.

After the first day, her mother asked if Eilis would mind if she and Rosella sat in the back of the car as she wanted to hear everything her granddaughter said.

"You have her all the time," her mother said. "Now Rosella and myself have to make up for what we've missed out on."

Later, Rosella explained to Eilis that she thought this arrangement strange.

"I'm perfectly happy for her to sit in the front and I'll shout if she can't hear what I'm saying."

"Best give her what she wants."

In the mornings, as soon as breakfast was over, Rosella and her grandmother went to the shops, Mrs. Lacey pausing to introduce her granddaughter to anyone she knew. Rosella was tall and suntanned. While she had brought a few pairs of jeans, she did not wear them since her grandmother had expressed her disapproval of young women in jeans. She had also packed some simple dresses that her grandmother thought were stylish.

"You are the most elegant girl to set foot in this town," her grandmother said, "since your mother came back from America a quarter of a century ago."

"Was she that elegant?"

"She broke many hearts before she ever went to America."

There was nothing about Rosella's life that her grandmother did not want to know. Rosella explained the American education system to her and went through her own grades, appearing not to grow weary of the constant questioning. At times, Eilis found herself listening to her daughter, noting the reticence about Tony or indeed about Rosella's other grandmother. Rosella was being cautious, Eilis saw, and realized that her mother would see this too and it would not satisfy her.

Within two days, Larry had been in most of the pubs in the town.

"They don't ask my age or anything. And you never told me about cheese-and-onion crisps or salt and vinegar. I order one soda and one packet of crisps and then I look around. And I can go on to another pub if anyone asks me too many questions. But most people are nice. They all want to know where I'm from."

"And what is your favorite bar?" his grandmother asked.

"I like Stamps," Larry said. "I like the Antique Tavern. I like the Club and I like Jimmy Farrell's."

"Jimmy Farrell's?" his grandmother asked.

"Andy who works there is going to take me to a hurling match. Aidans are playing the Starlights."

"It's Jim Farrell, not Jimmy," his grandmother said.

"Andy calls him Jimmy."

"Not to his face, I'm sure."

On the Saturday, they came home early from a drive to Curracloe to find Martin in the kitchen.

"Did you know that Larry has been in every pub in the town?"

"We did," Mrs. Lacey said.

"He's telling our business to everyone," Martin said.

"What kind of business?"

"All about your eightieth birthday."

"What about it?"

"How that's what they're here for."

"But that's true," Eilis said.

"And there are all sorts of other things that are none of anyone's business."

"Like what?"

"There are a lot of people curious about how you could have a rented car for so long. So some busybody asked Larry in Larkin's pub and he told them that his uncle Frank gave you money so you could rent a car."

"How did he know that?" Eilis asked. "Who told him that?"

"My other grandmother," Rosella said.

"But why would he give you money?" Mrs. Lacey asked.

"He has plenty of it," Rosella said.

"It's a pity he didn't come with you, so," Mrs. Lacey said. "Plenty of money! That's a good one."

All of them could see, Eilis knew, how embarrassed she was.

"Now, the minute Larry comes in," Mrs. Lacey said, "I'll talk to him and I'll let him know how nosey the whole town is."

Larry appeared in time for his tea.

"Now, where have you been, you little imp," Mrs. Lacey said, "with your grandmother expecting you to take her down the Prom for a walk. I've been sitting here waiting for you."

"I didn't know . . ." he began.

"Well, you know now. So I have my walking stick ready. We can go down by the Folly but, mind you, we have to go very slowly. If I fall, they'll blame you and we wouldn't want that."

"I'll make sure you don't fall."

"You see," Mrs. Lacey said, "he is a perfect American gentleman."

Once they disappeared, Martin went out again, leaving Eilis and Rosella alone together.

"I wish your grandmother hadn't told you about the money," Eilis said. "In fact, I wish Frank hadn't shared the news with his mother."

"She was trying to reassure us that everything would be nice in Ireland."

"Were you worried about that?"

"I think you know what we're worried about."

"They make things very difficult, your father and your grandmother."

"Aren't you going back to him?"

"I wish I could tell you that it's all going to be fine."

"So it isn't?"

"I don't want . . . you know what I don't want."

"So what should happen?"

"It's not my business. I told your father and your grandmother my views and it's up to them. If they want to pretend that I don't matter, then—"

210

She broke off.

"Then what?"

"Then I don't know."

"My father asked me to tell you that he wants you to come home."

"He's using you to pass on messages?"

"Shouldn't I have told you?"

"I need to keep in mind what you and Larry want."

"What Larry wants is simple. He doesn't want any change."

"And you?"

"I don't want you to be unhappy. And I am going to college. From next month I will be away most of the time. But I'd like to come home and find you and Dad and Larry there. Of course I would!"

At night, Eilis considered sneaking out of the house and walking to the phone box and calling Jim.

Both Rosella and Larry complained about not sleeping. All it would take would be for one of them to hear a sound and come downstairs to find that her bed was empty.

She was worrying too much, she thought, about being discovered. It might be simple: she could go to the phone box at Parnell Avenue and call Jim. He would answer the phone. And they could arrange to meet. She could go to his door, as she had done on the night of the wedding, and join him in the upstairs room.

In the morning at breakfast, her mother asked Larry to lift one of the large cardboard boxes that were in the corner of the living room onto a side table. She busied herself for a while rummaging through the box and then called on Rosella to come and help her. When Larry went out, Eilis could hear her mother and her daughter talking quietly. It struck her that if she told them she was going out to get a newspaper, she could get as far as the Market Square without being missed.

She would walk by Jim's pub, which would not yet be open. He would probably be still upstairs but it was not impossible that he, too, would go out and get a newspaper or some groceries.

She headed towards Rafter Street, watching out for him.

Having bought a newspaper in Godfrey's, she crossed the Market Square again. She could linger at one or two shopfronts but not for long. If he looked from his upstairs windows, Jim would see her now.

In the house, Rosella met her in the hallway.

"She's gone upstairs. Come and look."

On the side table and spread out on the floor, Eilis saw piles of photographs, some black and white, some color, all small in size.

"She has them all in order. I've never seen any of them before."

In all the years, Eilis thought, her mother had never acknowledged that she had received these photographs sent month by month as the children grew up.

"She has everything dated," Rosella said.

Eilis picked up a group of photographs and flicked through them. In one, Larry was a baby in his father's arms on Jones Beach. Tony was wearing a bathing suit that she thought she recognized. In another, Eilis herself was holding Rosella by the hand, Rosella squinting at the camera. Eilis supposed that Tony must have taken this and she must have taken the one of Tony throwing Larry in the air. The next photograph puzzled her. It was Tony on his own, bare-chested, smiling, the ocean behind him. Why would she have sent this to her mother?

When her mother came back, she pointed at other boxes in the corner.

"I thought Rosella would like to see those photos but maybe she has them at home."

"I don't," Rosella said. She lifted one of the other boxes onto the seat of an armchair and began to take out the small folders that held each set of photos.

"I usually sent ten or twelve at a time," Eilis said, "but I never knew you were keeping them."

"Would I throw them out?"

As she looked through the folders, Eilis saw that she had, in the early years of her marriage, included some of Tony's family in photos she took.

"I got to know them all," her mother said, "the uncles and the two wives and the grandmother and grandfather. And I watched you all growing up."

The next afternoon, because the weather was overcast, they decided to stay at home and go through another box of photographs while Martin was in Cush and Larry was at a hurling match.

Eilis noticed, as they found photographs of Rosella as a young teenager, how self-conscious she was and how much she posed for the camera. Larry was more natural. He laughed or made funny faces if he knew she was taking a picture.

She made to put aside a few photos for Larry when he came home, but her mother stopped her.

"I've always kept them in order. If you do that, I'll never be able to find them again."

When Larry came in, Eilis tried to interest him in the photographs.

"Andy took me to this hurling match where the two teams started to beat the shite out of each other."

Her son's own accent, Eilis noticed, was merging with the accent of the town.

"Larry, you can't use bad language in front of your grandmother."

Larry was breathless with excitement.

"And there was a man standing beside me. He was a big Starlights supporter and one of the Aidans players had his back to him, so he went right up behind him and gave him an almighty kick up the arse."

"Larry!"

"And Andy says there's going to be an inquiry so I should pretend I didn't see it at all. But I did see it and the weirdest part was the man just walked quickly back to where he'd been and stood there like he'd done nothing wrong. The player he kicked was on the ground moaning. Your man's boot went right up his arse."

"Larry!"

Eilis made Larry look at photographs she had taken at Christmas when he was six or seven.

"Dad has long hair."

"Everyone did then," Eilis said. "Enzo and Mauro did too."

"I often meant to write and say that their hair was far too long," her mother said. "One brother, I don't know which of them, looked like the Beatles."

"That would be Enzo," Eilis said.

Larry found photographs of his tenth birthday party.

"Look, there's the bicycle I got."

"The one you fell off?" Rosella asked.

"I just fell off it once."

Later, in the evening, when they came to the last box, Eilis's mother asked, "Did you stop having parties?"

"What do you mean?"

"All the photographs in this box are of Rosella and Larry and there are some of you. Did all of the others become camera shy?"

"I suppose I wanted to show you the kids growing up. But, to be honest, I didn't even know you ever looked at these photographs."

"I suppose they tell their own story," her mother said.

"What do you mean by that?"

Her mother shrugged and looked into the distance.

When Larry had gone out to a pub to discuss the match and her mother had gone to bed, Eilis noticed that Rosella was starting to say something and then stopping, interrupting herself by finding another photograph to comment on.

"There's something I was trying to tell you yesterday when you came back in, but I didn't know whether I should or not. Do you remember when Larry took Granny for a walk? She was meant to warn him not to speak so freely in the pubs. Instead, she forced him to reveal what was wrong at home. She promised to tell no one. But she told me while you were out getting the newspaper yesterday. She knows everything."

"Everything?"

"She knows that there's a baby coming."

"Does she know that your Italian grandmother is planning to take the baby in?"

"I don't think he told her that."

Over the following days, Eilis waited for her mother to say something. Her mother, she thought, must want to know what her plans were. Now, of course, it would make sense why Tony had not traveled with them and why she had so little to say about him when she arrived.

Her mother would blame her, she thought, for not confiding in her, as she, in turn, blamed her mother for taking advantage of Larry, who had trouble keeping secrets. Her mother, perhaps, was waiting for her to discuss the problem, but there was nothing she could say. She could hardly tell her that she had spent a night the previous week in a room in the Montrose Hotel in Dublin with Jim Farrell. Nor could she tell her what she intended to do about Tony since she did not know herself.

She began to piece together how she and Jim might live. She imagined a small bedroom in a bungalow in one of the towns near Lindenhurst. She dreamed of waking to find him beside her.

But what she could not envisage, as she surveyed this house they might rent, was where Larry would sleep or a room for Rosella. Tony's family would do everything to lure both Rosella and Larry to their Sunday gatherings. Larry would not want to move in with his mother and Jim. If Jim came, she believed, she would lose Larry, and Rosella too.

She came to see that there were too many uncertainties. She could not make her mind up now. She would have to tell Jim that she needed more time.

One night, when the house was quiet and they were all, she hoped, asleep, Eilis dressed and then slipped out of the house. She moved along John Street and went into the phone box at Parnell Avenue. She had Jim's house number with her. But then she saw that a coin was stuck in the slot so she could not make a call.

Since there was, she remembered, another phone box at the top of Cathedral Street, she walked quickly across the Back Road. It was almost one o'clock in the morning.

She put her coin in and dialed the number, but when she heard Jim's voice she could not bring herself to press button A and get through to him. She heard him saying hello a number of times and saying "Press button A." And then she put down the receiver. She stood in the booth trying to think of reasons why she should and why she shouldn't call again, but the reasons she thought of made no difference.

She left the booth and went by the Green towards Weafer Street. If she walked down to the Square and then turned into Rafter Street, she might cross the street and knock on Jim's door. She imagined herself frozen on the pavement opposite his house, looking up at the lights in the main room. She would not cross the street. It would be best, she decided, not to go down to Rafter Street. She made up her mind to return home and try to get some sleep so that the next day she and Rosella and her mother could go on another drive.

III

Gerard sat in the armchair opposite Jim. It was the hour after four in the afternoon when Shane could manage the bar downstairs on his own.

"I don't know how much your mother has told you," Jim said.

"The bare minimum."

"She might have mentioned that it makes no sense for her to go on running the chip shop. If things were different, we would think of selling the whole building but obviously your mother doesn't want to do that, and I don't either. The next question is: do you want to run the chip shop?"

"There isn't really much else I can do. I suppose I thought the business would be passed on to me at some stage."

"That is still the case. But it's a bit early, that's all. What your mother suggested is this. You use the same accountant and the same bank as I do. You pay your mother rent at half the market price. We meet once a week and we go over accounts and any other queries and problems. I will have full access to your accounts. We do this for the next few years and then we talk about the next move."

"The next move?"

"Well, maybe hand the place over to you in its entirety. But that's for the future. Does that make sense to you? It's a big responsibility. Having to work nights at the weekend is not for everyone."

COLM TÓIBÍN

"I'll do my best."

As Gerard was standing up, Jim thought of one more thing he wanted to say.

"It's important that you leave the announcement of the engagement to your mother and myself. I know it might be tempting to tell someone, even your sisters. But it would be great if you didn't. In a while, we'll be letting everyone know. I think she feels a bit guilty for telling you before the others, but it's done now."

When Gerard had gone, Jim sat back and closed his eyes. He wanted Eilis to get in touch with him and he wanted her to say that he could follow her to New York. If she agreed, then he would speak to Shane and Colette about renting the pub from him. He had some money saved, but the income from renting would make his life easier in New York, especially at the beginning.

If Eilis came and said she wanted to be with him, then he would find Nancy as soon as he could and tell her that he no longer wanted to marry her. It would be better if she had not told Gerard about their engagement, but she had, he was sure, told no one else. If he went to America, Nancy would not have to deal with all the gossip in the town.

He still believed that Eilis might say yes. After all, she had agreed to meet him in the Montrose Hotel. It had not taken much persuasion. When he had tried to begin a conversation about how they might live, she had told him he would have to wait. So he would have to do that. But he could not wait for too much longer.

He imagined a scene in which he crossed the Market Square to see if he could find Nancy alone, or in which he phoned her to ask if she could come to his house that night. She would be full of arrangements, forms to fill in, dates for travel, hopes that he would spend Christmas in Miriam's house with Laura and Gerard. It would be so natural once their engagement was announced. Also, she had spoken about moving out of the town completely and building a bungalow and having a garden.

218

She would be careful about this, he knew, as he had not expressed any great enthusiasm for the idea. He liked being able to take a short break in the rooms above the pub. He liked being able to climb the stairs at night and put his feet up instead of getting into a car and driving out into the countryside. He looked forward to Nancy being there at the end of the day, having a drink with her when all his customers had gone home and everything was cleaned up. And then he realized that there was no point in looking forward to this—it was precisely what he was ready to walk away from.

He tried to picture Nancy's face when he told her that he no longer wished to go through with what they had arranged. What reason would he give? What would she say? If he told her that he was leaving the town but did not state why, what would she conclude?

She would not believe him. It would surely take time to make her understand that he meant what he said. How long would this meeting between them take?

Since only Nancy herself and Gerard and Father Walsh were aware of their engagement, then there was no reason why Eilis should ever know that he had had any relationship at all with Nancy. Even in the future, he thought, it was something he would never share with her.

He went down to the bar to tell Shane that he had some business to do and he wouldn't be joining him behind the counter for an hour or two. And then he returned to his armchair and put his head back once more and closed his eyes.

He understood something about people, he thought, because he owned a pub. Each night from behind the counter he studied customers who were fully aware that they should go home or that they should not even consider having another drink. He watched them doing what made no sense, unwilling to listen to argument or reason.

He had become so used to this that normally he hardly put a thought into it. He and Shane, and even Andy, prided themselves on being able to manage these men and were proud also that they themselves never touched a drink when they were working.

Now, however, in the plans he was making, Jim realized that he himself was like one of his own worst customers, someone who knew what he should not do but was driven to do it regardless, no matter how much trouble it would cause.

He was also accustomed to hearing men boast, talking like big fellows about all the money they had or some girl they would soon get engaged to, or a son who had made a fortune in England. He knew to smile and nod his head. Most of what they said was fantasy. Jim wondered if he also, under the spell not of alcohol but of the heady plans he and Nancy were making, had been indulging in fantasy when he thought Eilis might want him to follow her to New York and be with her there.

What evidence did he have for that? What evidence did he have that she had not met him in the Montrose Hotel on a whim or as a way of completing something that had begun years before? But as soon as the thought came into his head that it might have meant nothing to her, he convinced himself that it was not true. He believed from what had happened between them in the hotel that she would not disappear on him as she had done before.

But still, if the moment came when she had to decide between the father of her children and a man who was already engaged and was prepared to destroy the life of another woman, an old friend of hers, what would she do? It was essential, he saw, that Eilis never guessed about Nancy.

He was still dreaming and he resolved that he must stop. He loved Nancy and she loved him. When he looked around the room, it was easy to imagine the life they had planned. Why would he destroy that? And Eilis had not been in touch. She could have no idea how urgent it was that she give him a sign.

In all his life, he had never imagined himself capable of going through that scene with Gerard, who trusted him so fundamentally, while knowing that he was preparing to walk away from Nancy, never to see her or Gerard again. What was most strange was that he had meant every word he had said to Gerard, or had meant every word at the time.

Often, when a customer was really drunk, he could seem sober for a few moments, could stand up straight and no longer slur his words before reverting even more intensely to his drunken state. Jim felt as though, in talking to Nancy and Gerard, he was acting the part of a sober man. But soon he would begin to sway again and slur his words and call out for another drink.

What if Eilis and he did not manage their life in America? After a silence of almost twenty-five years, they had seen each other only three times. What if her children didn't like him? How could they like him if he was the one who would change their lives by coming to America to be with their mother?

And how would he live knowing that he had betrayed Nancy? How could he coldly inform her that he did not want to be with her? That was on one side of the scales. On the other was a question that was starker and more pressing: how could he let this chance to be with Eilis slip by? If she gave him any intimation that she wanted to be with him, he would be like the man standing at the bar knowing he should not have another drink but utterly determined at the same time to forge ahead, his last pound note face up on the counter.

"Gerard's been different since you spoke to him," Nancy said. "He's agreed to work on Saturday night even though his friends are going to Whites."

They were having a late-night drink in Jim's living room.

"Gerard should take one night of the weekend off," Jim said. "It wouldn't do to have him miss everything that's going on."

"Well, he can't take Saturday night off. It isn't just the busiest night, but the night when you need someone in control."

221

Jim was almost tempted to tell her about his own Saturday nights running the bar, nights when most of his friends were at dances.

"What are you thinking about?" she asked.

"It's hard, working Saturday nights. I always found it hard."

"I never heard you complain."

He shrugged.

"Maybe we should arrange for you to have a Saturday night free now and then," she said.

He poured another drink for both of them.

"Did you see this week's *Echo*?"

"I never have to open it. If there's any local news, a customer is bound to tell me."

"There's another site for sale at Lucas Park. It has outline planning permission."

"You mean for a house?"

"Yes."

"You mentioned that before."

"No, that one was different. It was in a hollow. I thought it would be damp. This one is on higher ground."

"Have you actually seen it?"

"I drove by it."

He realized that Nancy had put more thought into this than she was ready to let him know. She had done this before when she had raised the possibility of them marrying in Rome. If he wanted to stop her making plans to buy a site, he should do so now. But there was something so certain and passionate about Nancy when she spoke about their future together. She could have no inkling, not the slightest, that Jim's mind was drifting back again and again to Eilis, to where she was and what she was thinking now.

"You know," she said, "I've drawn up plans for the kind of bungalow we might build. I've been working on them for some time."

She, he saw, was living in the future. Her life was made up of plans. Her good humor depended on what life would be like a year from now, two years from now. He was in the future too. He dreamed of coming home from work in some American suburb, pushing the gate and opening the front door to find Eilis there. Maybe if the weather was right, they could take a walk together. He saw her as he had seen her when she came home from America the first time and appeared with her mother at mass. He saw her then as she was coming towards him on the strand at Cush. He saw her in the lamplight in their room in the Montrose Hotel.

"Are you tired?" Nancy asked him.

He nodded and smiled.

Gerard, it seemed, began to soak in every word that Jim said. And he did not seem to have any problem with the news that Jim was going to marry his mother and that she would move out of the house on the Market Square. But more than that: after the rows with his mother, Gerard appeared to want guidance. If Jim had told him he had to work every single night of the week, Gerard might quietly assent. This, he supposed, was what went on in most houses in the town every day. This was what Shane did when he went home. He spoke to his children; he paid attention to what they needed. And they listened to what he said.

But Shane had been looking after his children since they were born. Jim could advise Gerard all he liked, but he would never be his father. He never had to get up in the night when Gerard cried; he wasn't there when Gerard took his first steps. He found himself, some days, feeling sorry about this.

Gerard behaved differently now that he had been told he was taking over his mother's business. His way of nodding to Jim and Shane before he took his place on a stool at the bar was gruff and serious, as if he were someone arriving from a hard day's work in a bank or an office. He seemed to be carrying weight on his shoulders. When Shane asked Jim what the matter with Gerard was,

Jim found himself tempted to share the news with Shane. But he was careful to stop himself.

On one of these nights, and it would not be far away, Nancy would tell him it was time they finally announced their engagement. She would have a plan. She would tell her daughters first and then her sister, then Jim would tell Shane and Colette and get in touch with his siblings. And they would go to Kerr's or Dermot Rock's, where Jim would buy her a ring. And from that moment, it would be public.

When Nancy was ready for the announcement, Jim would be able to think of no excuse to postpone it. Sometimes he was able to tell himself that the matter was in Eilis's hands. If she said yes, he would follow her. If she said no, he would do what he already had planned. His worry was that she would prevaricate. She had no reason to believe that he was in a desperate hurry to find out what she wanted. She could easily tell him that they should wait and see, that they might keep in touch once she returned to America. But that would not be good enough.

One Saturday in the bar, Jim asked Shane, "Who is that tall, dark-haired young fellow? He's been in here a few times."

"That's the American. He's called Larry. He's Eilis Lacey's son."

Jim caught the fellow's eye for a second. He moved away from the group around Andy and approached to shake Jim's hand.

"Hi, Jimmy," he said, smiling. "I'm Mrs. Lacey's grandson. I'm here from Long Island. Mrs. Lacey of Court Street."

Jim smiled as best he could. When he turned, he saw that Shane had noticed that he was upset. He was annoyed for letting that happen. But he could not stop himself. The boy had his mother's smile. Without saying anything to Shane, Jim made his way quickly to the door that led to his own hallway and he went upstairs.

This was proof, in case he needed it, that Eilis had another life, that she was married to another man, that, no matter what they decided, Jim and she would have no children together, that the time for all that with Eilis or with Nancy was over. He had let his life pass him by in a way that Eilis had not, Nancy had not.

He went into the bathroom and looked at his own face in the mirror. He wished Larry had gone to some other pub. It was easier just to have Eilis describe him. He imagined Eilis driving this boy and his sister from the airport to Enniscorthy after being with him in the hotel. He was glad to have had that time with her. At least he would have the memory of that, if nothing else.

When Colette appeared the next evening he was certain that Shane had sent her. He heard her voice in the hallway.

"Do you mind if I come up for a minute?"

If she had found him in the bar he would have told her he was too busy to have a chat. But that was probably why she had not come earlier.

She and Shane missed nothing. His absence on the day when he met Eilis at the Montrose Hotel would not have gone unnoticed, nor would Nancy's calling in to the pub looking for him that same afternoon. But he was sure, despite their ability to draw conclusions, that they had not pieced together what was happening.

As Colette came into the room, he was glad she and Shane did not know anything. They would see things more clearly than he did. He did not want advice from Colette.

"There's something going on, Jim," Colette said.

"Did Shane say that?"

"If there's anything you want to tell me and you don't want me to repeat it to Shane, then you can trust me completely."

"I know that."

"All we want is for you not to be upset."

225

"I know, but it's not simple, is it?"

"It could be."

He would have to be careful, he thought. It was important that no one at all knew about Eilis. If he were to marry Nancy and settle down with her, then he did not want Colette or anyone else to know how ready he had been to go with Eilis.

"Can we talk in a week or so?" he asked.

"Will you have news then?"

"I might."

She smiled.

"Is it who I think it is?"

"Go away now! I know you. You're looking for too much information."

That night, as he was about to go to bed, the phone rang. He picked up the receiver and, hearing silence on the line, he guessed that the caller in a phone box was not pressing button A.

"Press button A," he said.

But there was no sound on the other end. He waited, listening closely. Whoever was calling waited too. And then the call ended. It was one o'clock in the morning. Nancy would never call from a pay phone.

But Eilis could have sneaked out of her mother's house. It could be Eilis trying to speak to him. Perhaps she was having trouble with the button. Perhaps the phone was broken. Or maybe she had hesitated when she heard his voice. All he had said was "Hello" and "Press button A." He was sure his voice had not been unfriendly. Still, if the phone rang again, he would try to put more warmth into the way he spoke.

He sat by the phone willing it to ring again. He closed his eyes and concentrated hard and clenched his fists. But nothing happened. He imagined her standing in the box wondering if she might try again, have more courage this time. He would give anything for her to call and agree to come to him.

When he had waited for long enough, he fetched his jacket, making sure the keys were in the pocket, and set out to walk to the phone box at Parnell Avenue. He knew how unlikely it would be to find her there but at least he would see the box, at least he would not regret that he had failed to come out to look for her.

There was no one on Court Street. He moved quietly past her house, sure now that she was in there sleeping, that the call had been a wrong number. When he got to the end of John Street he hesitated. If he took a few more steps, he would see the phone box. No, it was not possible she could be there. And when he looked, he was right. It was empty.

PART SIX

I

"This must be a quiet month for you," Nancy said.

"It's funny, if you're selling sites, August is busy."

Oliver Rossiter had driven up from Wexford to collect Nancy and take her to see the site at Lucas Park.

"Sites look better in the sunshine," he continued. "It's a pity it's so cloudy today."

Beyond St. John's Manor, they stopped at a For Sale sign posted beside a rusting farm gate. Since the road was narrow, Nancy wondered if it was safe for Oliver to park.

"We'll hope for the best," he said. "And we won't be long. There's really not that much to see. Just the site. It's more a field now, but it has outline planning permission for a bungalow."

Perhaps if the sun were shining, Nancy thought, it would look more appealing. But now it was merely a small field enclosed by low ditches under a gray sky. It would not take much to create a drive for easy access to the road. Jim might know whether gravel or tarmacadam would be best.

She imagined the bungalow in place, its tiled roof, its horizontal windows, and the places where the fresh white paint would soon be tarnished by damp. As she walked around the site, it seemed the wrong place to build anything.

"You should really talk to a landscape gardener," Oliver said. "There's a good German woman in Bunclody. Someone like that could transform the site."

Nancy had an idea what Jim would say were he to be shown this site. In all the plans she was making, she thought, she should do nothing that might seem impulsive or ill-advised.

"I'll need to think about it."

"Is it the price? I could talk to them about that."

"Maybe it's too near the road."

"Do you want something away from the road?"

"I thought I wanted something near the road, but now I'm not so sure."

"On the other hand," Oliver said, as they made their way back to the gate, "no one likes going up a long lane. I have a site near here that's been on the market for a while. And that's up a lane. We're thinking of handing it back. I hate not selling a property, but that's the way it's going to be."

"Where is it?"

"Just down the river, near Ballyhogue."

"Can I see it?"

Back in the car, Nancy worried that Oliver might start to believe that she was wasting his time. She had contacted him because he was based in Wexford town and she didn't want to approach any of the estate agents in Enniscorthy, who would be too curious about her plans. He had shown her several sites by now, agreeing that he would not disclose her identity to the owners. At the beginning, she had been certain about what she wanted. She felt that he must be wondering about her.

"I said I would show this site to a prospective client one last time, so this is the last time. And I did warn you, didn't I? It's up a lane."

He turned and smiled.

Even as the business had begun to fail, Nancy had, after George's death, continued to make deliveries in the countryside around

Enniscorthy on Friday evenings. That was, she remembered, when she was at her lowest, when she had to face the possibility that her suppliers could no longer be paid, when Miriam and Laura had come to see that she had nothing in reserve, no money, no energy, no plan. At times when she returned, she would find that her daughters had been involved in some dispute with Gerard that had left him in tears.

Oliver turned up a steep and narrow lane on the river side of the road.

"I know this lane," she said. "I made deliveries here. A woman called Mags O'Connor lives up here with her sheepdogs."

"She's in the County Home now. She's the one selling the site. A right bag of tricks, she is."

"I always found Mags to be very nice. I'm sorry I had to stop the deliveries."

"One of her nieces got full planning permission to build a bungalow up here and then she changed her mind."

The lane had become more rutted and overgrown since Nancy used to drive up here.

The field was large, with a view of the river. After the narrowness of the lane, it felt open and bright.

"But how would you build?" she asked. "It's on a slope."

"I suppose they had plans to flatten it. If you could get an excavator up here, that could be done in a day. The soil is soft. No big stones or anything like that."

"You're a good salesman."

"No, I'm serious. The thing is if you could clear that brush on the other side of the ditch, you'd have a better view of the river. Mags says there used to be a pathway down. It would still be a right of way."

"How much does Mags want for this?"

"Fifteen thousand."

"What?" she said. "Is she mad?"

"'Mad' is one of the words. But, if you didn't mind the lane, it's a great site. It really is."

"Can you imagine the wind from the river in the winter?" she asked. "There's no wind like the one that blows towards you from a river. I can't remember who used to say that."

"It's a lonely place enough," he said.

"Is Mags in her right mind?" Nancy asked.

"Unfortunately, she is."

"Can you tell her the price is double what it should be?"

"She knows that."

"Can you tell her you have someone who would like to buy it, but the price would have to be right?"

"The first thing she'll want to know is your name."

"You can tell her my name. Every time I delivered groceries to her, she told me how nice the Sheridans were. So here I am, tell her, as nice as ever."

"I have to warn you that she likes a fuss and wants to have visitors. Having a site for sale keeps her going."

"You mean she doesn't want the selling part to end."

"I think she wore out the patience of the Enniscorthy agents. And she wore out mine too, I have to say."

A few days later, Oliver phoned her.

"I could have predicted it, but here it is. She wants to see you."

"What exactly did she say?"

"She said tell you to come and see her before the end of today or she will sell it to someone else."

"Did she recognize my name?"

"She knows who everyone is."

At four o'clock, as arranged, Nancy found herself at the gates of the County Home, noticing the prominent sign that said

"Mortuary" as though that might be the building most people would need to find.

In the hall, she encountered a nun and told her that she was looking for Miss Mags O'Connor.

"Mags O'Connor, Mags O'Connor," the nun said. "That is all I ever hear."

Mags O'Connor, who seemed to have grown larger, was seated in an old armchair in the day room near the door.

"There you are, Nancy," she said. "Like a bad penny. I told Oliver that it couldn't be Nancy Sheridan. Sure, what would she want a site up a lane for? And where would she get the money?"

"We all have our secrets, Mags."

"You know, I remember when you married George and old Mrs. Sheridan told someone that she believed he could have done better. But everyone knew that, Nancy. Everyone knew you were lucky."

"Or maybe George was the lucky one."

"There's that too. Now, why do you want a site?"

"I'm telling no one that."

"Where are you getting the money? From the chip shop? I hear your daughter married one of the Waddings from beyond Clonroche. Is the site for them?"

"You look very well, Mags, and comfortable."

"I am tired one minute and I forget what I was asking. Tell me, Nancy, why do you want the site?"

"I'd need it at a much keener price."

"So I heard. So Oliver told me. Funny you went to him in Wexford and not one of the local people. So who is it for? Are you buying it for someone else?"

"No."

"Well, if you don't tell me, I'll never know. And I can't guess. That's old age."

"The site is too expensive."

"Who is buying it?"

"I am."

"There's someone else behind this."

"I am marrying Jim Farrell from Rafter Street and that's where we are going to live."

Nancy could not believe she had spelled it out. She watched Mags taking it in.

"And is that a secret?"

"It is."

"Well, it's safe with me. Didn't Jim do a line years ago with that girl who went to America? Eilis Lacey?"

"He did."

"I hear she's back."

"She is."

"You'd better marry him quick, so."

Mags looked around the room and then fumbled in her bag for a moment.

"I often forget where I am."

"The site is too expensive."

"Does that man you mentioned have plenty of money?"

"No, he doesn't."

"Well, the whole town drinks in the pub. Now, the best thing is if he comes to see me himself instead of sending you."

"You'll have to deal with me, Mags."

"Does he not know about the site?"

"He'll hear about it when I get the price right."

"You learned business the hard way. Dunnes took all your customers away, one by one. I hear you're a sight to behold in the chip shop late at night, every amadán in the town waiting for their bag of chips. How much do you charge for a bag of chips?"

"I'm here to make a reasonable offer for the site."

"Oh, Oliver will deal with all that. Tell him to come and see me."

*   *   *

When Nancy phoned Oliver a few days later, the price of the site had been halved.

"You obviously charmed her."

"She could not have been nosier."

"That's what the other buyers said too, but she wouldn't lower the price for them."

Nancy was tempted to go immediately and find Jim at the bar. And then she thought it might be better to telephone him, but he was often brusque and businesslike on the phone during the day. She called him later when the pub was closed and he was upstairs. She told him about the site.

"Hold on. It's near Ballyhogue?"

"Not as far as there. Beyond Edermine."

"And beyond Macmine?"

"Not as far as there."

"And up a lane?"

"Yes, up a lane."

"Why would we live there?"

She could imagine him sipping his drink. His tone was calm; he seemed almost amused.

"When you see it, you will know what I mean."

She gave him precise directions so they could meet at the site the following afternoon.

Nancy made sure she was there before him. She smiled at the memory of waking that morning and being ready to pray, to go to the cathedral if necessary and get down on her knees, to ask for good weather, pure sunshine, even just for the first five minutes when Jim was at the site.

All morning there had been a summer haze over the river that was slowly burning off. Even as she waited, the air became clearer.

She imagined a long room with a window that might have a view of the river; it would be a kitchen and a dining space. She would like their bedroom to face east so the morning light could come into the room. Maybe put heavy curtains on the windows so the sun would not wake them too early. And before she did any more planning, she would get in touch with that German woman in Bunclody who could advise her on the garden. She would also need Laura's help with the interior decor, but would have to be careful not to allow Laura to boss her around too much.

She wondered if there was a moment when Jim would say no. As his car pulled up and he got out and looked around him warily, she asked herself if this very moment had not now arrived.

"I drove up to a sort of ruined farmhouse," he said. "I thought I was lost."

"Yes, you can miss the turn."

She followed him closely as he walked the site, deciding to say nothing. A pale sun had broken through the haze.

"This is a part of the country no one knows," he said. "It's very isolated."

"That's what I thought when I delivered groceries here."

"And they think there's a right of way down to the river?"

She noticed that he was not saying he did not want the site.

She wondered how she had ever tolerated the town, the semi-detached house in Aidan's Villas where she was born, the narrow house in John Street they had moved to, and then George's house in the Market Square. Enclosed, watched-over places.

"Are you all right?" Jim asked her.

"I was thinking about the view of the river."

"It's strange that the river doesn't make a sound," he said.

She listened. There was nothing at all, not even any birdsong. She wanted to ask Jim if he liked it here, but he had already moved away, walking towards the farthest ditch, rapt, it seemed, in his own thoughts.

*   *   *

In the days that followed, she drove out alone to the site each afternoon. The air was sultry, with a hint of thunder. The growth in the ditches was sumptuous and dense.

All she did was walk from one end of the site to the other. On paper, she had measured out the long room: it would be twenty-five feet by fifteen. She sought the perfect place where it could be positioned. The house, she imagined, would be built around this room. If she could get the long room right, then the rest of it would fall into place.

On the nights when she saw Jim, he said very little when she spoke about rooms and views and measurements. A few times, she found him looking away into the distance, as though he had not been listening. So she tried not to go into too much detail about these plans. It would all happen in its own time. She would let him know bit by bit what she had in mind. But she was impatient to get out of the town.

She would not miss the house in the Market Square. Although the rooms over the shop were big enough and bright enough, and there was no damp and the roof was good, she recalled with no pleasure trying to dry nappies in a house without a garden, or attempting to keep children amused on a hot summer's afternoon.

And then there was grief that would forever be associated with that house in her mind. She remembered when Miriam and Laura found her in the hallway with a pile of George's clothes, ready to take them to a shop in Wexford. They had accused her of throwing out his clothes behind their backs and, even when she told them that this was precisely what she was doing as a way of sparing their feelings, they remained angry with her.

"Why don't the two of you do it, then?" she had asked. "There's half a wardrobe left and all his shoes. You two do it!"

As she looked towards the river, she thought of all the cement and stone that made up the town, the hard surfaces and sharp angles. That was all she had known. She smiled at the idea that she would put the same energy into making a garden as she had into opening a fish-and-chip shop. And then she turned and looked at the western sky, realizing that she should put another large window on this side of the house from where she could witness the light at the end of the day.

II

"I don't mind where anyone goes tonight or what anyone does," Mrs. Lacey said, "as long as everyone is ready by twelve o'clock mass tomorrow. We will leave here in a body at twenty-five minutes past eleven."

"Would it not be better if one of us drove you?" Jack asked.

"I have these lovely grandsons here, two from England and one from America, and a lovely granddaughter. I will lean on them if I need to."

Eilis looked around the table, whose leaves had been pulled out to accommodate the new arrivals—Jack and Pat, who had crossed from Fishguard in Jack's car with Jack's son Dominick and Pat's son Aidan.

Her two brothers who lived in England were close in age. They had once looked alike, but the difference between them now was, she noticed, extraordinary. Jack was in an expensive suit. He looked around the table, smiling. He was perfectly shaved, his silver hair neat. Pat, on the other hand, needed a haircut and a shave. He smiled nervously. He seemed to be in pain as he stood up from the table. His shoelaces were torn and frayed.

Eilis knew that Pat worked in a warehouse. He had five children. Aidan was the eldest. It had been agreed, Martin told her, that both brothers would bring their eldest sons for their mother's eightieth birthday.

"And how did Jack make so much money?" she had asked Martin.

"He saw something that no one else saw," Martin said. "He saw the value of reliable union labor. If you wanted a stretch of motorway built by a certain time, Jack was one of the people you went to. It cost more, but he could deliver by the date agreed. He had the union bosses on his side. Some people said it was an Irish thing but it wasn't really."

Eilis had never heard Martin talk for so long and make so much sense. She noted how animated he became in his brothers' presence, but she saw also how Jack turned away from him if Martin tried to get his attention. Pat hardly spoke at all.

Larry complained to her about his cousins.

"They keep talking about football. But they mean English football. I've never heard of any of their clubs. They've never even been at a hurling match."

"Maybe you could introduce them to some of your friends," Eilis said.

"I thought they were going to be Irish, but they're not."

"And what do you talk to them about?"

"I don't get a chance to talk."

He did an imitation of their English accents that made Eilis laugh.

Jack and Pat and their sons were staying at Murphy Flood's Hotel at the bottom of Main Street. Eilis watched Martin trying to find out in what pub they intended to spend the evening.

"I hate all that 'Are you home for long?' business," Jack said. "And I don't want to meet any old-timers."

"But there will be fellows looking forward to meeting you," Martin said.

"How do they know I'm home?"

"Sure, everyone knows everything."

"Well, that's what I'm going to avoid."

"We'll be in Larkin's maybe," Pat said, "and we could go to Stamps and we'll look in to Jim Farrell's and then we'll end in the bar of Murphy Flood's."

"I'm glad their wives didn't come," Mrs. Lacey said when her sons and grandsons had gone out. "At least we have that to thank God for."

"Why, Granny?" Rosella asked.

"Because they'd leave them here while they went to the pub and we'd have to talk to them for the whole evening. I don't mind Betty so much, she's English, but it's Eileen who adds years to me. She has put on an English accent, if you don't mind, and she's from the west of Ireland. Jack met her at a dance."

"Is there something wrong with that?" Eilis asked.

"Well, in my day, you could meet someone at a dance who you already knew. But you wouldn't meet a stranger at a dance, or at least I wouldn't. You might have one dance with him and then you'd go back to your own group."

"That's how I met Tony, at a dance," Eilis said.

"Yes, but that was in America."

In the morning, having gathered in Court Street, they set out for the cathedral.

"No straggling and no smoking," Mrs. Lacey ordered as she made sure that the front door of the house was closed. "I want Rosella on one side of me and Dominick on the other. The rest of you can walk behind. Larry, would you fasten the top button of your shirt and straighten your tie, like a good man."

They had been up late, the men, and they were, Eilis saw, subdued. Her efforts to discover whom they had met and what pubs they had visited were met with shrugs and sighs.

Her mother proceeded slowly. She was wearing a light green outfit with a silk blouse. She had on her good black shoes and a stylish gray hat.

At the corner of Weafer Street, a man appeared who had been drinking with Jack and Pat and Martin the previous night.

"Well, missus," he said to Mrs. Lacey, "you should have witnessed the scene in Jim Farrell's last night, the three wise men and their three wise sons, all home for your birthday."

Larry looked at Eilis, as if she should set the man straight that he was not Martin's son.

They arrived in the cathedral early enough to find good places close to the pulpit. While the others fidgeted and looked around them, and while Pat went outside to smoke, her mother and Rosella stared straight ahead, dignified and distant.

Eilis did not know whether Jim usually went to eleven or twelve o'clock mass. As they had made slow progress up Main Street, it had struck her that they could easily meet him. Or he could come into the church, finding a place towards the back, as men on their own usually did. When time for communion came, he would see them, as he had seen the brothers and the boys in his pub the previous evening.

Eilis knew she should phone Jim as she had promised to do, but there were too many questions she could not answer. If Jim were really to come to America, when would he come? And when she herself went back, as she would do soon, where would she live? If she arrived at the airport with the children, what would she say to Tony? If she arrived a few days later, where would she go? Would she let Tony collect her? Take her home? Encourage life to go back to normal except for the arrival of a baby and the possible appearance of Jim Farrell?

She could, on returning, with the rest of the money Frank had given her, find lodgings somewhere for a while. But when would she see the children? And under what circumstances?

They should never have lived so close to Tony's family. That was the first mistake. If they had their own house away from the others, she could ask Tony to leave. Perhaps she could still do that, though he would simply move in with his parents and she would have to see him every day. But Rosella and Larry would see him too and that would be an advantage.

How would she break the news to Rosella and Larry that Jim Farrell might be following her to America, that, despite the years that had passed, she wanted to be with him?

Pat came back just before the priest appeared at the altar.

"Granny says it's Father Walsh," Rosella whispered. "And he's her favorite."

Her mother, Eilis thought, must have come here every Sunday on her own, one of the many widows who liked to sit in the same pew each time, or who always went early to communion, or who stayed behind to avoid the crush of mass-goers eager to get out into the air.

Rosella, she thought as the mass began, would need help settling into Fordham. She would also need new clothes. Eilis would accompany her to her accommodation. Tony would want to come as well and Rosella would need him there. And Eilis would have to keep in contact with her over the first few weeks and be there if she returned home for a weekend. And Larry was drifting at school. If Eilis didn't pay attention, he would, she was sure, in Rosella's absence, find excuses to do even less work.

She had promised herself that she would help Larry with his maths and his English and perhaps some of his other subjects, sit with him each evening doing the same homework as he did. Mr. Dakessian had, he told her, done that with Erik.

"Did Erik not mind?" she had asked.

"Mind? He went crazy. But I didn't give up. And he enjoyed it when I knew less than he did, although I was just putting on a show. He thought I was an idiot. And our relationship has been perfect ever since. I only wish that my own dad had done this!"

She would have to make amends to Mr. Dakessian for being away so long. There would be a backlog of work.

It occurred to Eilis that if she stopped thinking about herself and what she wanted, then everything would fall into place, at least over the next few months. She would consider Rosella and her needs and then Larry, and then her job at Mr. Dakessian's. And she would concentrate on these three things. As long as the baby was not physically carried into her house, then she would not think about it. And she would be polite to Tony and do her best with him because that was what the children would want.

The thought of herself as suddenly altruistic and concerned only with the welfare of others, the same person who, not long before, had spent a night in a hotel with Jim Farrell, made her smile.

What would she say to Jim? It would be easy to tell him that she needed more time. How would he respond to that? In the hotel, he had told her that he had to know, as if it was somehow urgent. The idea that he would come to New York, or even to Long Island, was fraught with difficulty. Perhaps in some months' time she would have a better idea what they could do.

She would have to ask him to wait. She thought of coming back to Enniscorthy next summer, but she would hardly have the money for the trip. And perhaps the same uncertainties would be there.

She would have to be decisive. Since she did not want Jim to come to America now and join her, then she would have to tell him. She would arrange one meeting with him. It would be difficult. And then she would change her ticket, if she could, and travel back on the same flight as Rosella and Larry.

When the lines formed for communion, Eilis looked to her mother, who signaled that she wanted to wait. Just as the line was shortening, she noticed her mother making a sign to Jack at the end of the pew. He stood up and the entire family walked up the aisle to the altar, Eilis's mother flanked by Rosella and Dominick. It was not the waiting that mattered, Eilis saw, or the kneeling at the altar rails to take the host. It was the turning and the walking back, the large congregation all watching them—Mrs. Lacey, her sons, her daughter, her grandchildren all home for her eightieth birthday. Eilis realized that her mother had planned this moment, knowing the right time to step out into the aisle and how to walk back to her place as though no one was looking at her.

Later, as the others were in the back room, the men preparing to go out again, Rosella found her in the kitchen and suggested they go upstairs.

"Larry says that Jack owns this house, he owns Martin's house in Cush as well and he owns Pat's house in Bolton."

"How does Larry know?"

"Jack told him."

"Did Larry tell Jack anything in return?"

"I'm not responsible for what Larry says."

The next morning, the day before her mother's birthday, Jack found Eilis alone. He closed the door solemnly. Eilis presumed he wanted to discuss their mother's welfare in a house with too many stairs.

"I'm a bit worried about you," he said, "and wanted to talk it through."

"You've been going around the pubs with Larry."

"I thought your husband and his brothers had a big business and I thought it was all good in Long Island."

"Enough for you to visit? I was always hoping you'd come."

"I'd like to sometime. I often wonder what would have happened had I gone to the States instead of Birmingham. I might own a corner shop."

"I expect you'd be even richer than you are now."

"Larry says you are going to leave his father."

"I'm sure that's not what he said."

"If you would accept, I could help you. I could buy you a house of your own, for example. It would make you independent."

"Like you did for the others?"

"I still own Pat's house and Martin's house only because I don't want to give them the chance to sell. I'm offering you something with no strings attached."

"You are offering to buy me a house? Are you serious?"

"I don't make idle offers."

"You sound like a businessman!"

"Why don't you just say yes?"

"It's very generous of you."

"Are you saying yes?"

"I am a bit surprised. But it would make a difference if I had my own house."

"Good. I'm glad there's someone decisive in the family. It took a while to get Mammy to come around to the plan to buy the house from her. But you probably know all that."

"I know very little. She barely replied to my letters."

"You didn't write much though, did you?"

"I wrote once a month. I never failed."

"Maybe she didn't get the letters?"

"Of course she got them! She has all the photographs I sent."

"It's hard to know what to make of her sometimes. But anyway, the offer is there. Just say when and it will all be put in train. Larry told me about prices and property so I know what I need to know."

"Larry is sixteen."

"He's smart. I can't think where he got it from. Maybe from all those Italians."

"I don't," Mrs. Lacey said, "want every so-and-so coming to this house to view me like it was my wake."

"I will look after the door," Jack said.

In the morning, some of the neighbors came to wish Mrs. Lacey a happy birthday. They talked about the town and how the summer had been so far. As Eilis stood in the doorway, she listened as they tried to find out from her mother how much longer she was staying.

"I thought she was just coming for a week or two," one of them said.

"The whole summer," another commented, "isn't she lucky she can get away?"

"And to keep that car for so long. It must cost the earth."

"That's America for you. I heard someone saying it on the radio. The dollar is king."

When more people came in the afternoon, Jack said it might be best to begin turning well-wishers away, but his mother demurred.

"You could end up turning away my best friend."

"Who is your best friend, Granny?" Larry asked.

"Oh now, Larry, that's a tale not for telling."

Towards six, Nancy Sheridan came to wish Mrs. Lacey a happy birthday. She was, Eilis thought, at her most friendly.

"Is that your car outside?" she asked. "I'd say renting a car like that cost a pretty penny."

Eilis regretted that she had not moved the car to another parking spot.

"I got a good deal on it," she said.

Since the back room was crowded, Nancy followed Eilis into the kitchen so they could talk.

"It's a happy day for everyone," Nancy said. "Larry has been telling me about all the preparations. It's great that himself and Gerard have become friends. I saw you all in the cathedral on Sunday and what a fine sight you were. It's lovely seeing the next generation. But it's sad that they will never have known your father and Rose. I feel the same about Miriam's husband. I would love for him to have known George."

For a second, Eilis wished she were back in her own sitting room in Lindenhurst, reading the newspaper, the house empty.

"It must be marvelous, America," Nancy said. "Maybe not all of it, but New York, and Laura worked two summers ago in Maine. I was so worried about all the crime but she said there was no crime at all in Maine."

"Yes," Eilis said, "Maine can be quiet."

"It's funny, she'd never laid eyes on an oyster before she went there. We just don't eat them here. She spent the summer cutting open the shells. But she was well paid for it. Especially the tips."

"Laura looked lovely at the wedding."

"It would be great to go to America sometime. We might be able to go on a trip next year or the year after."

"You and Laura?"

Nancy hesitated for a moment.

"I don't know who I would go with."

"Well, you would be very welcome. We'd love to see you."

Once the birthday was over and Jack and Pat and their sons had returned home, the others went back to their routines, Rosella going to the shops each morning with her grandmother, Larry seeing his friends and going to the pubs, Eilis driving her mother and her daughter to nearby towns and villages each afternoon.

Rosella, she felt, was watching her, looking for some sign, but Eilis was waiting, planning to contact Jim to say that she was going back with the children, but still postponing it each day.

In the mornings early, a sliver of sunlight came into the room where Eilis slept and slid across the bed where she lay awake. She knew it was eight o'clock when she heard the postman.

One day, when she heard post coming through the door, she got up and went to see what it was. It was a large envelope with many stamps, with "airmail" written several times in big letters. It was addressed to Rosella, sent by Francesca.

Eilis took it with her into the room and closed the door. She examined the tape and saw that if she opened the envelope carefully, using a thin knife on the lip that was glued, she would be able to close it up again without leaving any evidence that the envelope had been tampered with.

She went quietly to the kitchen and found the type of knife she was looking for. Back in her room, she managed to open the envelope without making a tear.

Inside was a letter and something held by tape between two pieces of cardboard. When she pulled back the tape and saw the photograph, she put it aside immediately. She unfolded the letter.

Darling Rosella, it began.

> *I have great news and I am sure you will be delighted. Your little sister was born two days ago. She is healthy and happy and beautiful. Just now, I have to send all your cousins away because they want to spend time holding her, as we all do. She will be called Helen Frances, Frances after her grandmother, yours truly, and Helen after your grandfather's mother. Your father is besotted with her and your grandfather has not stopped smiling since little Helen came into the house. He is already talking to her in Italian. I got the film developed extra fast because I knew you would want to see her. How lucky she is, I told her, to have a sister like you! (And you'll be glad to know I said this in English!) I hope you are having a great time in Ireland. And we are longing to see you when you are back, and that, of course, includes little Helen Frances.*

The handwriting was not Francesca's. It was Frank's. The image of them both working together to lure Rosella towards them made Eilis want to tear the letter in two.

She looked at the photograph. The baby was alert, having been put sitting on someone's lap. When Eilis examined the picture more closely, she saw that the hand on the baby's stomach holding her in place was Tony's. If the photograph extended to a fuller frame, it would show Tony too and no doubt he would be smiling, as the photographer would be smiling, as his mother and Frank must have smiled as they wrote the letter. She studied Tony's hand again. How delicate his hands were! His position in the photograph was one she knew because that was precisely how he had often held Rosella and Larry. If she went into the back room, she would find photographs that showed him sitting just like that, with the baby held in the same way.

She winced at the thought that in all the years married to him she had woken in the morning, or often in the night, and reached out for Tony's hand, finding comfort from touching it.

She put the photograph and the envelope and letter into her suitcase.

Martin was in the kitchen.

"Are you going back to Cush today?" she asked him.

"No. I have things to do here. There's a friendly match in Belle-field that Larry and me are going to go to."

"Can I have the key to your house?"

"It's under the mat."

The stuck coin, she discovered, had been removed from the slot in the phone box at Parnell Avenue. She had to call a few times before Jim answered the phone. He must have been asleep, but when she asked him if he could meet her in one hour at Martin's house in Cush, he sounded wide awake. He said that he would see her there.

III

Eilis lay asleep beside Jim in the narrow single bed. If he moved at all, he would wake her, so he stayed still. It must be coming towards eleven in the morning, he supposed. Normally, he would be dressed by now, taking his time, getting ready to open the bar.

He had, since the Montrose Hotel, been imagining their next encounter, when he could ask Eilis, plainly, if she wanted to be with him.

There would be time to discuss these things once she was awake.

Two hours ago, when she had opened the door of Martin's house to him, Jim had been afraid to ask her if she had made a decision, even when she had whispered how happy she was to see him.

They had gone together to the cliff's edge and looked down at the strand and the calm sea. Asking a direct question about plans would have broken the ease between them. He let the moment pass. And then they had returned to the house together.

Eilis woke up and smiled.

"Why did you let me fall asleep?"

He touched her face with his hand and then he sat up and reached for his shirt and his trousers and underpants.

"Those underpants will have to go," she said.

"What's wrong with them?"

"How long have you had them?"

"Go on with your American fads!"

The morning had been overcast when he parked his car behind hers on the lane. Now the clouds had blown away and the sun was seeping through and felt warm on his skin.

He heard her in the bathroom. Saying that his underpants would have to go suggested that she had plans to see him in the future. But maybe it was just a joke.

Something would have to be said in the next hour or two that would let him know precisely how things stood. Any day now, Nancy would decide it was time to let the town understand that she and Jim were engaged. Even though they had decided to wait until the beginning of September, she could easily suggest bringing the date forward.

"I stopped in The Ballagh," Eilis said, "and bought something I might cook, a sort of breakfast."

"Like what?"

"Scrambled eggs, tomatoes, toast."

"I sit here and look out at the sea and you cook my breakfast?"

"That's what's on offer."

Once they had eaten, they went towards the steps that led to the strand, Eilis carrying a towel.

"The water used to be beautiful at the end of summer," she said, "but maybe that's something I imagined."

"Which way should we go?" he asked.

If they went south, he knew, they could find people on the strand at Keating's, holidaymakers but also day-trippers from Enniscorthy, especially now that the sun was out.

"What are you thinking about?"

"If we go towards Knocknasillogue, we'll see no one," he said.

They took off their shoes and left them near a pile of stones. Eilis went to test the water.

"It's not warm," she said. "Maybe it's too early in the morning."

There were a few seabirds flying low over the waves.

"But if we can just brace ourselves and get down quickly in the water it will feel great," she said.

"I haven't been in the sea since that time with you, that time with Nancy and George," Jim said.

"That's not possible."

"I just never went into the water again. No big reason."

"Not even in Curracloe?"

"I'm not even sure I know how to swim anymore."

She was briskly taking off her clothes, having put her bathing suit on in the house.

"You did this all those years ago. We thought it was so modern, not changing on the strand with everyone looking."

Eilis seemed to flinch at the coldness of the water. He watched her as she jumped to avoid being splashed by a wave. And then she began to swim. He stood with the towel at the ready so she could dry herself quickly when she came out.

On their last night home, Jack and Pat had come into the pub with their sons and Martin and Larry. Jack appeared to Jim drunker than his two brothers. He came to the bar when Jim was alone near the sink washing some glasses.

"I don't know if you know that Eilis is home as well," Jack said.

"I saw you all at mass on Sunday," Jim said. "Your mother is looking very well."

Jack moved in closer.

"I always thought it was a pity that it didn't work out between the two of you that time."

Jim shrugged.

"Ah, now. That's years and years ago."

"I'm sure you haven't forgotten it and I'd say she hasn't either."

"Water under the bridge, Jack. Water under the bridge."

"You know, if you were ever going to have another try, I could help out."

Jim knew immediately to do nothing, say nothing.

"Just so I've marked your cards," Jack said. "Do I need to say more?"

Jim smiled at him as though he had not spoken at all.

"She is a young-enough woman and has her whole life ahead of her," Jack added.

Jim went down the bar to find Shane.

"Can you serve that Jack Lacey and his company for the rest of the evening and keep him away from me?"

"It's a done deal."

As Eilis dried herself, Jim checked that there was no one watching from the edge of the cliff.

They walked north towards Knocknasillogue and Morriscastle.

"Are you going to ask me?" she began.

"What?"

"Why I phoned you this morning and not some other morning."

"I'm asking you now."

"I got news from home and it made me realize that I don't want to stay married to Tony. But there are complications and I need to let you know about them."

They walked silently for a while close to the water, Jim feeling that he might find out more the fewer questions he asked.

"I'm going back next week on the same flight as the children if I can change my ticket. I need to get them both settled, Rosella at university and Larry back at his high school. I also have to return to work and get everything back to normal as soon as possible."

Jim refrained from asking where her husband would be during all of this.

"My brother has offered to help me buy my own house. It will be in Lindenhurst, where we live, or in one of the towns close by. It will take me time to find the right house."

"How much time?"

"Maybe six months."

They walked on until the cliffs were higher and there were no easy ways down to the strand. Ahead were miles of empty beach. When Jim looked behind, he saw no sign of anyone. Even the birdlife was scarce, despite the pocket-size tunnels in the cliff made by the sand martins.

"All those years ago," he asked, "when we danced together and saw each other, were you thinking about, you know, the fellow in America, the one you are married to, and were you looking forward to seeing him?"

"That's the longest question you've ever asked me."

"What's the answer?"

"I was confused," she said.

"Are you confused now?" He deliberately kept his voice soft and low.

"No."

While there were some stray clouds banked on the horizon, the sky was mostly blue and the sun was becoming hot. Jim knew that the skin on his face and neck would turn red very quickly, but there was nothing he could do about it.

Just before Morriscastle, a small stream cut through the sand, enough for a flock of seabirds to have gathered. The light had a dreamy edge to it. At first, the birds did not fly up in alarm at the intruders as quickly as he expected. They waited. And it seemed for a moment that they might even remain where they were. But then, as one flew upwards, the rest followed, letting out small shrill cries, the last few flapping their wings noisily as though in protest about being disturbed.

Eilis stood for a moment looking out to sea.

"I don't want to be responsible for you uprooting yourself and then maybe coming to regret it," she said. "You would be away from all your friends, from everything."

He presumed that she meant he would be living with her in the house she would buy.

"I'd rent the pub out to Shane and Colette," he said. "Obviously, I haven't asked them but I believe they'd be happy to take it on."

"What would you do in America?"

"I don't know. Who would give me a job? And I don't know about visas or how I would get legal over there."

"My brother-in-law is a lawyer and I'd enjoy asking him to recommend someone to help with that."

"When should I come?" he asked.

"I can send you word."

"You mean you want me to wait but you won't know until when."

She did not reply.

"I couldn't do that," he said. "I'm sorry. I would worry so much about never hearing from you at all."

"What do you want, then?"

"I want to go to New York as soon as I possibly can."

"I won't be able to be with you, though."

"But we can see each other. And then eventually . . ."

She moved close to the water's edge.

"Where I am on Long Island," she said, "it's very quiet, it's a neighborhood. It's not a town or even a village like we have villages."

"I could live somewhere else and see you when you're free."

They heard a noise on the cliff face and looked up to see some crows squabbling.

"I need to concentrate on getting the children settled and being really diligent at work."

"In the beginning," he said. "I could see you once a week. Say on Sundays."

She sighed.

"I live in a sort of enclosure with four houses. Tony's two brothers and their families have a house each and my parents-in-law have the fourth. It sounded like a great plan. And it has been very good for the children. It's very safe. But it hasn't been good for me."

"Is that why you are—?"

"No, there are other reasons. But what's vital for me now is that, if I leave, I do not want to be blamed for anything. Everything that happened, they did. Or Tony did."

"You are the innocent one?"

"I am the innocent one."

"And coming back to America with me would not help that?"

"So you understand it? Also, it might matter in a divorce settlement."

"Eilis, I can't stay here and wait for some sign from you. I need a decision now. I really do."

"And you know that you will have to spend months, and it will be the winter, on your own, and I won't be able to meet you much or even talk to you on the phone very much. It will be really hard."

"It would be harder here when I would worry all the time that you would never get in touch."

"And we tell everyone that you just happened to be in New York and we happened to meet up and I was single and you were single and we began to see each other. That's my story. What's yours?"

259

"That I always wanted to go to New York and spend a while there. Though I'm not sure who'll believe that. But when I'm gone six months people will have forgotten all about me anyway."

"Maybe if I gave you the address and phone number of the garage. And I will write to you from there. But my boss misses nothing and he's a friend of Tony's father. Maybe I could come in early some days and we could talk on the phone then."

Jim thought for a while. She was going into too much detail while still not telling him when she thought he should come. He decided to change the subject.

"What did Tony . . . what did your husband do? I mean, what went wrong?"

"He had a baby with a woman. He was working in her house."

"So he's still seeing her?"

"No, but he has decided to take care of the baby and he's moved it in with his mother."

"But not the woman as well?"

"No, just the baby. Is that not bad enough?"

They had passed Knocknasillogue and were coming towards Cush.

"So this time next year," he asked, "or even earlier, we will be living together in some place on Long Island and we will be planning to get married?"

"That could be our plan," she said.

He kissed her and then looked around, almost making fun of the worry that someone might be watching them, and then he kissed her again.

"Can I ask if you love me?" he inquired.

"That's why I am here."

"Can you say it?"

"Yes, I can."

They stood together at the edge of the water. When he looked at his watch, he found it was half past one.

"I told Shane I'd be back by two. He's manning the fort for me."

"Why don't you go ahead, then," she said. "Don't forget your shoes."

"Can I see you before you leave?"

"Yes, I'll phone you. I've learned how to press button A."

"Was that you? I guessed it was you."

"I got cold feet."

"Could you get cold feet again? You won't leave me a note to say you've changed your mind?"

"I won't do that. I promise I won't do that."

PART SEVEN

I

"I'm in Ferns, which means I am nearly in Enniscorthy," the man's voice said. "I will see you in half an hour."

Nancy had met Birdseye first when he had convinced George to put a freezer into his supermarket and begin to stock frozen food. He loved arriving with new products, insisting that frozen peas and frozen fish fingers would soon be outselling fresh bread.

"People want something new, something that is being advertised on television."

Once Dunnes Stores opened in Rafter Street, Birdseye had been the first to warn her.

"You can't compete with them."

"So, what do I do?" she asked. "Just close up?"

"Yes, you are going to have to close up sooner or later. I'm sorry to be the one to tell you."

"And what will I do?"

"There are always options, missus, there are always options."

"I don't see any."

Two weeks later, Birdseye came to her with a plan.

"We will help you install a chip shop if you sign up to using our products, which are, in any case, the best. Everything comes packaged and ready—the fish, the chips, the burgers. They'll be frozen. And I can guarantee you that you won't lose money."

"So why doesn't everyone open a chip shop?"

"Because not everyone owns a premises on the main square of a small town."

Nancy consulted no one. Even when she was borrowing money from the Credit Union, she told them it was for work on the supermarket and the floors above. She did not mention a chip shop.

Once it was opened, Birdseye came every two weeks to take her order. She made him tea and a sandwich in the kitchen upstairs. He knew from the size of her order how well she was doing.

"You were the bravest. Anyone else would have let the supermarket sink before making a decision. All over the country grocers and small supermarkets are going to the wall slowly, ending up in debt. People are being ruined."

This morning, Birdseye, sitting at her kitchen table, seemed more formal than usual. As soon as the tea was ready, he took out the order sheet for her to sign and indicated the amount that was due to be paid.

"You're all business today," she said.

"I'm a man on a mission."

"I haven't seen you like this since the day you came with the first batch of chicken nuggets."

"This is bigger," he said. "In the longer term, this is bigger."

"Tell me."

"It might seem like nothing. But if pubs began to serve toasted cheese sandwiches and toasted ham-and-cheese sandwiches, it would be a whole new ball game. They'd buy them frozen from us. They'd be delicious. That is the main thing, missus, they'd be delicious. There's no one in Ireland wouldn't want one."

"Is that what has you fired up?"

"In each town, we are looking for a pub to start off with. It has to have young people, rugby people. That sort of bar. And I thought you would know what pub in Enniscorthy we should start with."

"I most certainly do."

"The next step then is for the owner to fill in this form. And just a signature expressing interest. And then we'll set the ball rolling. We want to reach a stage when ten lads will order not only ten pints but ten toasted cheese sandwiches as well."

She looked at the form.

"I could get this signed for you this morning," she said.

"It would be great if you could. What if I call back at two when I'm on my way home? Make sure you tell the bar owner that this doesn't commit him to anything. But if he has a brain in his head, he'll jump at this chance."

Nancy thought that she would walk over to Jim's pub once twelve struck and Jim, having just opened the bar, would, she hoped, be on his own there. It occurred to her that she might even offer to take responsibility for the sandwiches. It could be her way of helping out. She would have to be careful, however, not to appear to be making decisions for him. But he knew about Birdseye, and he would surely want to serve toasted sandwiches if it was made easy, even though he would have to buy plates and cutlery.

When she pushed open the front door of the pub, she was met with silence. There was no one behind the long counter. The first customers had not arrived yet. Jim must be outside in the store. She sat on one of the bar stools to wait for him. But it was Shane rather than Jim who appeared in the doorway that led to the backyard. When, at first, Shane didn't notice her, she called out his name.

"The boss's not here," he said.

"Will he be back soon?"

"I can't tell you that."

She wondered if Shane was being deliberately dismissive and casual. She hardly knew how to reply. Shane did not move from the doorway.

"I'll give him a shout later," she said and turned to go.

"Right you be," he said.

It reminded her of the other time she had dropped by in the morning, that day when Shane had told her that Jim was in Dublin. Even afterwards, when she had questioned Jim about the trip, Jim had brushed her off, given no satisfactory reason for going to Dublin.

The way Shane had said "I can't tell you that" irritated her. It was as if she were a nosey person coming in from the street.

Back home, she put the form on the hall table and went upstairs, finding Gerard and Larry, Eilis Lacey's son, in the kitchen.

"How is your mother enjoying her stay?" Nancy asked him. "Your grandmother must be delighted to have her home."

"I think my grandmother is delighted to have my sister here," Larry said. "They're inseparable. They drink their tea from the same cup."

"Do they really?"

"Well, not actually, but it feels like that."

"And your mother is well?"

"Yeah, she's good. She's gone to Cush, where my uncle has a house. She went this morning."

"I hope the weather lifts a bit. Did the others go with her?"

"No, she went on her own. My uncle Martin is in the town because he is coming to the match with us."

"She's on her own down there?"

"Yes, just for the day, I think."

Nancy moved towards the sink and pretended to be washing a cup and saucer. At the wedding, Lily Devereux had told her about Jim appearing on a lane in Cush. It had seemed puzzling at the time and she wondered if Lily's mother hadn't mixed him up with someone else. But it occurred to her also that the day Jim was in Dublin, Eilis was, by coincidence, in Dublin as well. And now Eilis was in Cush and Jim was not where he usually was. And

Shane had used the same offhand tone with her just now as he did on that other day.

It added up for a second and then, when she considered it further, it didn't add up. It was not possible that Jim and Eilis Lacey were together at this moment in Cush, or somewhere else. But if Jim needed to see Eilis, how would he do so? He could hardly call to the house in Court Street. And Eilis could hardly come into the pub or be seen knocking at his door.

Just before the end of the wedding party the two had spoken. Nancy was sure of this. She had caught a glimpse of them, but she thought nothing of it. Yes, surely Jim might want to see Eilis before she went home. Nancy remembered Eilis asking about him when she visited her that first day. It seemed that she genuinely didn't know whether Jim was married or not. Now that he was about to get married and she was soon to return to America, Jim would want to talk to her. Perhaps he would hint to her, or even tell her, that his life was going to change.

But if they had, indeed, arranged to meet that day in Dublin, and if Jim were in Cush at this very moment, and had also been there before when he was spotted by Mrs. Devereux, and since they had met at the wedding, this morning's meeting was clearly more than a valedictory occasion.

But maybe all of this surmising was nonsense. Maybe Jim was at the bank or seeing an accountant.

It was too much of a coincidence or it was nothing. Whatever it was, she knew, it would go through her mind all day. How ludicrous it might appear were Jim even to discover that she, Nancy, believed he was seeing Eilis Lacey, that they had sneaked off to be together!

It would be easy, she thought, to drive to Cush. It wasn't yet half past twelve. The drive there would take only half an hour. She had plenty of time and no one would ever know she had done this. But it would be wrong not to trust Jim. It was tempting fate. She put the idea out of her mind. She could easily relax for a few hours or even go for a walk by the river. But then she would not be able to stop herself going over every possibility, analyzing every clue.

She found the car keys and walked down the stairs. As she reached the car, another image came to her. It was the sight of Jim's Morris Oxford parked on the street in Wexford on the night of the wedding when she had been told that he had already gone back to Enniscorthy.

As she drove out of the town, she tried to piece together, once and for all, the evidence that she had. Yes, Eilis would want to see Jim, of course she would! Nancy should have understood that the very first day Eilis came home. And, since she knew how madly in love Jim had been with Eilis all the years before, why did she not imagine that he, in turn, would want to see her?

But had they really met? And how many times? Was it actually possible they were together now?

As she passed through The Ballagh and then Blackwater, Nancy was glad she had made the decision to go to Cush. She was nervous. In the run-up to the announcement of their engagement, she still often wondered if it was all real. Today, she determined, once she got home, she would give up being nervous, give up worrying. It would be all right. In April, she would be married.

On the road between Blackwater and Ballyconnigar Strand, Nancy turned left at the ball alley. She parked her car at the top of the first lane that led to the strand. If she saw someone, she would ask where Martin Lacey's house was. She could even knock on the door of the first farmhouse and inquire. But then she saw that she would not have to. As she made her way down the lane, she saw Jim's car parked straight ahead. And the car parked in front of it was Eilis Lacey's rented car.

Farther along, she could see a gate into a field where a small house stood. She walked past the cars to the gate, which was open, and headed towards the house. The morning had brightened. There was not a sound.

She looked in through the windows of the house and saw a single bed with blankets and sheets all tossed and some women's clothes on a chair. If anyone came, she decided, she would simply say that she was down here for a walk and thought she would call in on Eilis, since Larry had told her that Eilis was here. But then it struck her that the person most likely to appear was Jim and she had no idea how they would face each other, what they would say. She felt as though she would be somehow in the wrong.

When she went to the edge of the cliff, she saw Jim and Eilis on the strand below and she realized that if she did not crouch down, they would easily be able to see her. Over to the right, nearer the gate, there was a mound of earth half covered in grass. She moved back from the cliff and approached the mound on all fours, finding that the only way she could get a view of the strand below without running the risk of being spotted was to lie on her stomach and look down.

Jim and Eilis were having an intense conversation. Both, she saw, were in bare feet. Eilis was carrying a towel. When Jim said something, Eilis moved away from him, closer to the waves. And when she came back, he embraced her and they began to kiss.

Nancy noticed Jim glancing at his watch, and then, after another embrace, edging away from Eilis. He was going to walk up the steps in the cliff. She would have to get back fast to her car. She did not want Jim to see her; she did not want a confrontation. She made her way as quickly as she could to the lane and walked to her car without looking behind.

When she finally did turn, she saw with satisfaction that Jim had not yet come to the top of the cliff. He would have no idea that she had been here.

On the journey back to the town, her mind did not waver for a single instant from a plan that she had begun to formulate even as she lay on the clifftop looking down.

*   *   *

She went to her bedroom and looked through the jewelry box on her dressing table. If her old engagement ring was too tight for her finger, she would go straight to Kerr's and buy a new one. Were it another day, she might worry about how to explain the purchase to the Kerrs. But today she would simply find an engagement ring that fitted her and write a cheque for the amount it cost. She had no interest in what anyone might think.

Nor did it detain her for a moment when she found her old engagement ring and knew that she would be using the ring that George had bought for her.

At first, she could not get the old ring on. It had always been a struggle, she remembered, but she liked that George had chosen it and, at the time, didn't want to go back to the jeweler's with it. It was years since she had worn it. With time and with all the working in the chip shop, her fingers had become thicker.

Years before, there was a way to get the ring on. Since her mother-in-law owned a lot of rings, it was old Mrs. Sheridan who taught her to apply Windolene, the pinkish liquid used to clean windows. Nancy remembered that you wet the finger with it and then you could slide the ring on.

She put the ring beside the sink and began to massage her finger with the Windolene, pressing hard against the bone. And then she remembered her mother-in-law lifting her hand high in the air for a moment before the liquid dried and then slipping the ring on in one try.

She winced with pain as she felt the ring cutting the knuckle. But it was on her finger. She washed the Windolene away. She was wearing an engagement ring.

All she needed now was to change her clothes, brush her hair and put on good shoes.

She kept her left hand to her side as she walked across the Market Square and then along Rafter Street and Court Street until she came to Mrs. Lacey's house.

The door was answered by Eilis's dark-eyed daughter.

"Is your mother in?" Nancy asked.

"No, she isn't."

"Who is that?" a voice came from the kitchen. "Rosella, who is that?"

"It's Mrs. Sheridan, Granny."

"Tell her to come in."

Rosella ushered her into the back room, where Mrs. Lacey, moving laboriously, soon joined them.

"You're looking very well, Mrs. Lacey."

"Rosella picks out the clothes for me every morning and she has the best taste."

"And will Eilis be back soon?"

"I'm sure she will. She went off early. We are waiting for her too."

"There was something I wanted to tell her. You know, she's one of my oldest friends. Can you say I called in specially?"

"Well, I can get her to drop down to you."

Nancy lifted up her left hand.

"I wanted to share the news with her that I got engaged."

"Congratulations, Mrs. Sheridan," Rosella said.

"Oh now, engaged! Congratulations!" said Mrs. Lacey. "And who, might I ask, is the lucky man?"

"Well, it was a secret but it's not anymore. And can you tell Eilis that I walked up here specially to tell her. I'm engaged to Jim Farrell. We've been seeing each other for a while, but at our age you don't want too much of a splash."

"And when will the big day be?" Mrs. Lacey asked.

"Oh, we've decided to get married in Rome. It will be quiet."

"Rosella, she is marrying that nice man whose pub Larry goes to. The Farrells have always been very decent people. You know, I go back very far, Nancy, there aren't many like me left, but I even remember his grandmother."

When she was offered tea, Nancy declined and took her leave. She went slowly along Court Street. Normally, when she had to walk through the town, she tried to avoid people who wanted to stop and talk. But this time she sought people out. She even made a visit to Dunnes Stores. And to everyone she met she showed the engagement ring and told them that herself and Jim had wanted to keep things under wraps until now, but they would be getting married in Rome in April. They had the date fixed and the arrangements made.

II

Rosella was waiting for Eilis in the hallway. She put a finger to her lips as soon as Eilis approached and indicated that her mother should follow her as quietly as possible upstairs.

"It was just something I said in passing," Rosella whispered when they were in the bedroom. "Granny was saying how lonely she would be when we left, and I replied by suggesting that she come with us. It was just a remark."

"And what happened?"

"You see, this is what she has been planning all along. She already has her passport, her visa. All she needed was to buy a ticket. She made me show her my ticket and she made me come with her to Aidan O'Leary's travel agency to get her a seat on the same flight as me and Larry."

"For how long is she planning to stay?"

"That's the problem. She told the woman in the travel agency that it didn't matter what return date she put on the ticket. But, for the moment, it says on the ticket that she is staying for a month."

"Who is going to look after her?"

"I didn't know what to say."

Mrs. Lacey was in the hallway shouting to them.

"Eilis, are you there?"

Eilis and Rosella went downstairs and followed her into the kitchen.

"Now," Mrs. Lacey said, "I'd hoped we'd all be able to fly back together so I went into your room, Eily, to see could I find your ticket. And you are down to fly the week after next and not next week with us. So I took the liberty of showing your ticket to the nice lady in the travel agency and she made a phone call and then told us that she would be able to change your ticket for a small fee."

"This is a surprise," Eilis said.

"Well, in your letters, you were always inviting me."

"But you never said you would like to come."

"You even said I had a standing invitation. And I'd like to see where you live and where Rosella and Larry live. It sounds like a very nice place."

When Eilis went into her room and checked her suitcase, she found that the envelope with the photograph was missing. She waited until she heard Rosella going upstairs and then she returned to the kitchen.

"You know," she said to her mother, "I'm not sure this is the best time for a visit."

"What? I have my ticket booked."

"Yes, but maybe we should see about changing it."

"Am I not welcome, then?"

"Rosella won't be there, she is going to university. Larry will be at school all day and then he'll either be out with his friends or doing his homework. I have a job and, because I've been away, I'll be working full-time when I get back."

"I'm sure I'll find some way of getting through the day."

"It's not a town. There are no shops nearby."

"Rosella has told me all about it."

"I would prefer if you came later. Let us all get settled in first. And there are other problems."

From her large apron pocket her mother took out the envelope.

"I know all about the problems," she said.

"Did you take that from my suitcase?"

"I was searching for your ticket and I saw that it was addressed to Rosella. Don't worry. I haven't shown it to her. But I did read the letter."

"You shouldn't have opened it!"

"I might say the same to you. Do you open all our letters?"

"Of course I don't!"

"And I won't tell Rosella that you intercepted her letter. I think it would be useful to have me with you when you go back to America. It will be something else to think about."

"I've warned you that you'll be on your own in the house for most of the day."

"How do you think I live here?"

When Rosella came back to the kitchen, Mrs. Lacey said, "Oh, another thing happened. Just as we got home from the travel agency, who came here, only Nancy Sheridan? You should have seen her, she was sporting an engagement ring. It looked too small for her finger. I don't know how she got it on."

"Nancy Sheridan is engaged?" Eilis asked. "But she was here for your birthday and she didn't mention anything."

"It was announced only today, she said."

"Who is she engaged to?"

"To Jim Farrell. It has been going on for some time."

"No, seriously," Eilis said. "Who is she engaged to?"

"That was her news. You should have seen her. She was out of breath with excitement. And she is engaged to Jim Farrell."

"Jim Farrell of the pub?"

"That's exactly who she's engaged to. We both congratulated her, didn't we, Rosella?"

Rosella nodded in agreement.

Eilis waited until Rosella left the kitchen and followed her into the hallway.

"My mother must have got this wrong," she said.

"No, she hasn't."

"Tell me again."

"Mrs. Sheridan is engaged to the man who owns the pub, Jim Farrell."

Eilis left the house quietly and walked along John Street towards the phone box. She stood outside while two teenage girls were involved in a long conversation with someone, giggling and laughing and interrupting each other.

If they could just hang up and let her make her call, she could, in a few minutes, walk back home reassured that Jim was not engaged to anyone, least of all Nancy Sheridan.

The idea was preposterous. She would feel silly even asking Jim about it. Nonetheless, she wished she could talk to him now. She felt an urge to knock on the glass of the phone box to ask the girls to hurry up. Even though they had noticed her waiting, they showed no signs of finishing.

What was strange, she thought, was how easy it was for Jim to consider uprooting. His parents were dead; his siblings had left the town. He mentioned no close friends or associates except Shane, who worked for him. Eilis knew how the owner of a bar might stand apart, his friendliness as much a function of his job as his ability to keep his distance. He could, as he told her, just walk away, rent out the bar, find a suitcase and be in America the next day. Or, if he decided, it could happen in a month, or six months, or a year. It was peculiar, then, that he was pressing her as though much depended on her making up her mind now that he could come to America.

Eventually, when one of the girls let out a scream of laughter, Eilis rapped on the glass. For a second, they looked embarrassed, cowed, but then they shrieked again as one girl tried to grab the receiver from the other to let their friend know that they would call back later.

By now, Eilis knew Jim's number by heart. When she dialed it there was no reply. She let the phone ring and ring. Since the two girls were waiting outside for her to finish, she was unsure what to do until she noticed the phone book on a ledge. The number of the pub, she found, was listed. When she dialed, the man who answered was not Jim.

"The boss is upstairs," he said. "Do you have the number of the house?"

"I do," she said.

She rummaged in her purse to find another coin so she could phone the house again. As she placed it in the slot, one of the girls rapped on the glass before they moved away, as though frightened, and then returned.

Eilis let the phone ring until it rang out.

She walked back to find her mother alone in the kitchen.

"Does Rosella know," her mother asked, "that you were once engaged to Jim Farrell?"

"I wasn't engaged to him!"

"Well, the whole town thought you were."

"I saw him all those years ago when I was home. But I am sure Rosella doesn't know that and doesn't need to."

"Well, I certainly won't tell her."

"I am grateful for that."

"Nancy wanted us to know that she called in specially to tell you the news. She wasn't just passing. And I wondered if you're upset that Jim is engaged. I mean, surely you've got over him after all the years!"

"Of course I have got over him!"

"If you had married him, things would have been very different."

"I suppose."

"It was funny listening to Nancy. Of course, I knew all about her and Jim."

"What did you know?"

"Sarah Kirby told me. I meet her in the shops. She's very friendly. She knows the woman who lives in a flat over McCarthy's bread shop and that's directly opposite Jim Farrell's. And one night late when she went to do a widdle she could see across into Jim Farrell's living room from her landing. And Jim had company, female company. He seemed to be enjoying himself. And who appeared soon afterwards into the street, only Nancy Sheridan? And Sarah's friend saw her rearranging her clothes, making herself decent before she set out for home."

"And you've known this all along?"

"I have."

"And why did you not tell me?"

"I made a decision early in life not to be a gossip. And it has always stood to me."

"Telling me would hardly be gossip," Eilis said.

"You know, I told Nancy I was happy for her," her mother went on, ignoring what Eilis had just said. "What else could I say? But I have my doubts."

"About what?"

"When I go to my reward, I will expect your father to be waiting for me in heaven. How else would I live if I didn't have that to look forward to? And on his deathbed that's what we talked about and it gave us both great comfort. Imagine then if I went and got married to a second fellow! What would happen then? What would I say to your father? And that makes me wonder what Nancy will say to George Sheridan when the time comes. But I said nothing. I told her how delighted I was, even though I didn't mean it."

Since her mother was so determined to keep things to herself, Eilis wondered if she knew she had been seeing Jim. Someone could have spotted them in Dublin, or observed them at the wedding. And then passed on the information to someone who would, in turn, have told her mother. It was unlikely, she thought, but she could not be sure.

Later, Eilis went back to the phone box, which was empty this time. Once more, she called the pub to be told that she should try the house upstairs. But there was still no answer from that number. Again, she let it ring and ring. When she was halfway home, she turned and went back and tried for the last time but there was no reply. She decided then that she should go and find Jim, whether he was in the house or the pub.

III

Jim parked in the Abbey Square and made sure not to pass through the Market Square. He did not want to meet Nancy by accident. He would, he thought, have a bath and a change of clothes and get something to eat before phoning Nancy and arranging to meet her.

The following morning, he resolved, he would go to the bank as soon as it opened and withdraw what money he might need. He would leave Shane to look after his car, but ask him first to drive him to the station to catch the lunchtime train to Dublin.

Shane, when he found him in the bar, agreed to stay for another half an hour and then come back, as usual, at four.

"Can you tell Colette I'd like to see her?" Jim asked.

"Today?"

"Definitely today. As soon as she can."

Shane glanced up at him. Jim could see that he was about to ask if anything was wrong and then thought better of it.

He would ask Colette if she and Shane wanted to take over the pub.

He went up to the top floor of the house, to the room at the back where he threw things that were no longer needed. There were some old suitcases here; he was sure of that. But when he found them, they looked too shabby. The biggest was frayed at the edges. Another had a broken lock. He selected one whose locks worked even though it was discolored. Once in Dublin, he could replace it.

He phoned the Mont Clare Hotel, near Westland Row in Dublin, where his parents had often stayed, and reserved a room for three nights, although he presumed he would be there for longer. He would leave a note for Eilis saying that was where he might be found. Maybe he could accompany Eilis and Rosella and Larry to the airport in Dublin and see them off.

While the children might be puzzled at his presence, it would be a good way of signaling to them that he and Eilis had become close.

But he would not suggest this in his note to Eilis. He would say it to her only when they spoke by telephone.

It might be better, he thought, to leave the note for Eilis when it was dark, after he had spoken to Nancy.

He ate something, had a quick bath and changed his clothes. As he was preparing to go downstairs, the phone rang. He did not want to risk answering it in case it was Nancy. Once he had seen Colette, he would call and arrange to meet Nancy early in the evening. He would tell her it was something urgent, something vitally important, but he knew that when he came face-to-face with her, he would have no idea how to begin.

He listened as the phone rang out before ringing again a minute later.

Downstairs, Shane told him that a woman had called the bar just now wanting to speak to him.

"Was it Nancy Sheridan?"

"No, it definitely wasn't. Nancy was here this morning looking for you. No, it was someone else."

"What did Nancy want?"

"I don't know. I told her you were out and would soon be back."

The pub was completely empty when Shane had gone. Usually, no matter what, there would be a few customers.

Jim sat on a stool and looked around him. As soon as he was old enough, his father would let him come into the pub, and Frank Fortune, the barman who worked for his father, would keep bottle caps for him. He would take them upstairs in a box, spread them out on the floor in his bedroom and play with them. He could line them up as soldiers and have mock battles between them or make them into hurling teams. And always there was a faint smell of beer from them and that, too, became part of their attraction.

He could easily, he thought, spend the rest of his life here, serving drinks, keeping business steady, and then going back upstairs once closing time came. Going to live in the countryside with Nancy would have been a big change. Sleeping beside her at night; waking in the morning beside her. But every day he would have returned to this familiar place.

He would have had to make no effort. If someone came in now, he would know exactly how to greet them. Even if he didn't know them, he would be able to make a quick and accurate judgment about them. But once he got on the train tomorrow, his judgment would be of little use to him. Away from the security of the pub his own easy confidence would not matter.

And that would just be Dublin. How would he explain himself in America? In Enniscorthy, his name, the same name as his father's, was written on the outside of his building. In America, he would just be a man who had followed a woman across the Atlantic, a man who didn't even know the names of American beers and whiskeys, who would be unsure how to deal with a difficult customer and uncertain how to work an American cash register.

He would learn. He would find a job but it mightn't be in a bar. It would be strange to have a job that finished at five or six. He and Eilis would spend all their evenings together.

Soon, it occurred to him, he would miss this pub and the rooms upstairs. He thought of a winter night in rented accommodation and nothing ahead. He would think of Shane and Andy, remember that each group who gathered knew where to sit, the new customers in the back, the old-timers close to the front door.

His leaving would be just another change. The group of men who once assembled at the bar on a Saturday in the early evening to discuss the week's events had dispersed. One of them died, another became housebound, the others gradually stopped coming. They were, for a few years, he believed, as well informed as any commentators on television. Often, when he came across an article in one of the newspapers, he thought of showing it to them only to realize that the group no longer existed.

It was even possible that, with Rosella and Larry grown up and living their own lives, he and Eilis might drift back to Enniscorthy, take over the business once more. But that, he knew, was just dreaming. He would probably never serve a drink in this bar again. Maybe he had done that for long enough.

When Shane returned, Colette was with him.

"Can I take you upstairs, missus?" he asked.

She nodded, her expression oddly grave, almost unfriendly.

Usually, when Colette came upstairs, she offered to make him tea and teased him about his untidiness. This time, she went straight to the farthest window and looked out into the street.

"So why didn't you tell us?" she asked.

"Tell what?"

"Tell what Nancy's been telling everyone for the past hour. I met her on Slaney Street, where she was showing everyone her ring, and we met her just now again when we were walking down Weafer Street."

Jim was about to ask her what she was talking about, but he realized he should be careful.

"Nancy is great," he said.

"She was all flushed and excited when I saw her first, but just now she seems exhausted."

"She works too hard."

"She says you've been going out for some time. I can't get Shane to tell me whether he knew or not."

"Shane keeps things to himself."

It struck Jim that he really should go and find Nancy.

"Nancy says that you're planning to build a bungalow out the country."

"Oh aye, if she says it, it's true."

"You seem very matter-of-fact for a man who's just got engaged."

"There'll be plenty of time for that."

"For what?"

"Oh, you know. Everything."

"Is that why you wanted to see me? To tell me about the engagement?"

"Yes, I wanted to tell you."

Shane appeared in the doorway.

"Nancy Sheridan is downstairs looking for you. I didn't say you were here."

"No, no," Jim said. "Tell her to come up."

"I'll be going, so," Colette said. "Congratulations! And everyone will want to know if you're having a big wedding. What will I tell them?"

"Tell them to ask Nancy."

Jim moved quickly to the window and stood where Colette had been standing.

Nancy barely nodded at Colette as she met her in the doorway. She waited until Colette was out of earshot.

"I've been looking for you all morning. There was a terrible crisis. I had to make a very quick decision."

She gazed directly at him. Even though there was a quaver in her voice she seemed in full control until she looked away again. And then he saw how nervous she was. She closed her eyes and sighed.

"I don't know who to blame. But I bumped into a woman who had all the news about us looking at the site. And then I had a call from Lily Devereux and she knew all about it."

Jim had never heard Nancy telling lies before. When he looked down, he noticed the ring on her left hand. It must be, he thought, the ring that George had given her, or one that she had bought or borrowed just now.

He remembered that when she asked him why he had spent a night in Dublin, he had tried to be vague and not go into too much detail. He had told no direct lies. Nancy, on the other hand, was giving him all the details.

"And then I discovered that the whole square knew. When I met Mrs. Roderick Wallace walking her dog, she smiled at me and said she'd been hearing great things about me. And then I met a nurse from the County Home and she had all the news from Mags O'Connor. And I asked Gerard if he had told anyone, but he swore he hadn't. And then I couldn't find you. So I thought I would put on this ring and be absolutely straight with anyone who asked. I phoned Laura and then I phoned Miriam. I was so afraid that they would hear from someone else. That was a big worry."

As she finished, there was, Jim saw, an appeal in her voice and a sort of desperation in how she looked at him. She could not have known that he planned to leave in the morning, because no one knew that. But she must somehow have found out about Eilis. That was the only explanation.

And it seemed to him, because she had not bothered to invent a credible reason for announcing their engagement today, that she wanted him to know that.

When she sat down in an armchair, she seemed tired. He wondered if this might be the moment to spell out to her what he wanted to do. He could tell her about Eilis and inform her that he planned to go to America to be with her. And not only that: he was leaving Enniscorthy the next day, so it might not make sense for her to continue wearing her engagement ring.

And then when she lifted her head and locked eyes with him, something else occurred to him. The reason she had put on the engagement ring was not to impress the town. That could wait. The engagement ring was for Eilis Lacey to hear about.

And Eilis might already know. If she didn't, someone would soon tell her. Eilis, of course, would not believe it. How could she believe it? And what would he say to her if she asked him if it was true?

Nancy stood up.

"You look as though you've caught the sun," she said.

He nodded.

"Well, I'm glad the announcement is made," she went on. "Maybe we can have a proper celebration later?"

"That would be good," Jim said. "I'll phone you."

"Why don't we arrange it now?"

"Sure."

"I'll ask Gerard to close the shop himself. And maybe you can ask Shane to do the same? What about midnight? And you must have a bottle of champagne languishing in the store?"

"I'm sure I do."

She made her way towards the door and then turned and walked back as far as the armchair. For a moment, he thought she was going to sit down again, but instead she took him in directly, evenly, fearlessly. She beckoned him to come and embrace her. He moved slowly across the room and put his arms around her. Soon afterwards, he accompanied her down the stairs. At the front door, they held each other again. When he reached to touch her hand, he felt the engagement ring. She smiled.

"I'll see you later."

When she had left, he was struck by what she had done. She had spoken in a tone that he could neither resist nor argue with. She could easily have confronted him directly about Eilis, but that would have opened the way for him to tell her he was leaving.

As the phone rang, he was sure it was Eilis. There was still a possibility that she did not know. For a few seconds, he was tempted

COLM TÓIBÍN

to answer it. But no, he would need to see her in person. He would even call in to her mother's house if he had to.

A while later, when the phone rang one more time, he was in the bathroom. He stood listening to its echoing sound.

He sat in one of the armchairs in the living room wondering what he should do.

Fifteen minutes later, he heard a knock on the front door and went downstairs. When he opened the door, Eilis slipped in without speaking. In the living room she sat first in the same armchair where Nancy had been, but then she changed to a less comfortable chair. Jim went back to the window.

"You've not been answering the phone," she said.

"I wanted to see you face-to-face."

"That's no reason not to answer the phone."

"It's good that you called in, anyway."

"I am here because Nancy Sheridan appeared on our doorstep brandishing an engagement ring that she says you bought for her."

"She came to your house? At what time?"

"I wasn't there. I stayed in Cush after you left to clean up. Have you been engaged to Nancy all along?"

"I can explain what happened."

"Can you explain how you are engaged to a woman who was once my best friend?"

"It's not as simple as that. The truth is that I love you and I want to be with you."

"And you told Nancy that?"

"Told her what?"

"That you'd asked me if you could follow me back to Long Island."

"I didn't tell her anything."

"How did she know, then? It was hardly a coincidence that it's the same day as we were on the strand in Cush."

Eilis stood up and looked across the room at him.

"You didn't tell her," she said. "I didn't tell her. So who did tell her? No one else knows. Unless you've told someone. Have you told anyone?"

"Of course I haven't."

"Yes, it's not like you to tell anyone anything. Have you seen Nancy today?"

"I saw her just now. She came here."

"Did you give her the ring?"

"No."

"Is today the first day she has been wearing it?"

"Yes."

"You learned about it when you came back from Cush?"

"Yes, Colette who's married to Shane told me."

"Did Nancy mention me by name when she came today?"

"No."

"But you agree with me that it is too much of a coincidence that she chose today to put on the ring and she chose our house to visit. She wasn't just passing. She told my mother that she had come specially to let me know."

"Yes, it's too much of a coincidence."

"How long have you been together?"

"A while."

"And why didn't you get engaged before?"

"She wanted to wait until after Miriam's wedding."

"So now would be about the time for the announcement? And that's why you wanted me to make a decision. Before any announcement."

"Yes."

"And eventually she guessed. Isn't that what happened? You must have done something or said something that gave her a clue."

"I'm sure I didn't."

"In any case, she guessed."

Jim nodded.

He noticed how calm Eilis had become. While some of her earlier questioning had an edge of anger, she now sounded almost gentle and curious, and intrigued by what Nancy had done. He realized that one wrongly judged answer could cause her to stand up and leave. A long silence could do that too, he thought. But he also knew that he should not try to change the subject.

He wanted to let her know that everything he had said this morning was still true. He wanted to follow her to America. But if he said that, she could ask him to tell her what he had promised Nancy. Did that still hold? Was that still true? No matter what he said, Eilis could remind him that he was engaged to another woman.

Eilis sat down again. It was possible, he saw, that she had already, in her own mind, dismissed any idea that they might still be a couple. All she was doing now was piecing together what had happened.

If he wanted to speak, he believed, he would get only one chance. She still said nothing, but gave no sign that she was preparing to leave.

"There's one question I want to ask you," he began.

She looked up.

"Just one?"

"If the phone rang in your garage on Long Island one morning, or one day, and it was me and I was in New York, or was even closer, and I had come to see you, what would you do?"

Eilis appeared puzzled, as though she hadn't heard him properly. But he knew not to repeat the question; instead, he should give her time to take it in. He kept his eyes on her and let the silence linger. She didn't move at all. He wondered if she was thinking about something else or if she was working out how to reply.

He began to count the seconds as they went by, until he got to a hundred and then two hundred. He could feel that his own face was burned from the midday sun at Cush. But Eilis's color had not changed. She was pale. She looked around the room and then directly at him. He sensed that his question still hung in the air and then it became obvious that she wasn't going to answer it.

The light was beginning to wane when she finally stood up. He wondered if there would be a moment now in this room or in the hallway below when he could embrace her, maybe even kiss her. She kept him at a distance, however. He followed her but she was behaving as though he wasn't there.

When she had gone, he decided that he would go down to the bar. He did not want to sit alone all evening. He smiled ruefully at the thought that if he went for a walk around the town he would meet people who would congratulate him on his engagement and he would hardly know how to respond.

He was not prepared for what happened when he went into the bar. Led by Andy, a loud roar of congratulations went up. All the fellows who had been at the match in Bellefield were gathered at a number of tables. They stood now, yelping, raising their fists in the air.

"Jimmy is the champion," they shouted.

When Jim saw Shane, Shane raised his arms to indicate there was nothing he could do to stop this. Gerard and Larry and Martin were among the group who made towards him, and they set about raising him on their shoulders.

"Jimmy Farrell, sportsman of the year," Andy shouted.

"Jimmy for the cup," Gerard roared.

Jim was resting precariously on Larry's shoulder while Martin held his leg.

"Free drinks! Drinks on the house!" someone shouted. "Jimmy's engaged!"

Jim searched desperately for Shane and, when he got his attention, intimated to him that he should intervene, come over and rescue him. Shane told the group to let Jim down.

"Leave the man alone."

Behind the bar, Jim hardly knew what to do. He kept away from the group who had lifted him into the air and he avoided Andy too. For a second he was tempted to tell Andy to go home, but he restrained himself. All the time, Shane stayed close to him, saying nothing.

And Jim, irritated by Shane's close attention, and worried that Gerard and his friends were planning some further celebration, decided to go to the store and find a bottle of champagne. He would hide it under his jacket and disappear back upstairs.

He sat in the living room as it grew dark. The end of August always made him sad. How strange this year, he thought, that he didn't have any time for that! But there would be time. Ten o'clock came and then eleven.

He went down and stood in the hallway without turning on the light. He knew what he wanted to do. He wanted to slip out into the street where he would hope to encounter no one. And then he would walk slowly, keeping in the shadows, towards Eilis's house. He would ask to see her, even though it was late. He imagined her coming to the door, her mother calling from the back of the house or from an upstairs room, asking who was it, who was it at this time of night? Jim would not come in, he would stand in the doorway and, in a whisper, he would repeat the question he had asked Eilis earlier. But when he tried to imagine her response, he saw no one at all. The front door of her house was open, but the hallway was empty, and there was just her mother's voice repeating, "Who is it? Who is it at this time of night?"

Jim stood in his own hallway trying to see Eilis, trying to hear what she might say. He leaned against the wall and closed his eyes. Maybe tomorrow he would have some idea what to do. But for now he would wait here, do nothing. He would listen to his own breathing and be ready to answer the door when Nancy came at midnight. That is what he would do.